Summer at Conwenna Cove

Summer at Conwenna Cove

DARCIE BOLEYN

CANELO

First published in the United Kingdom in 2017 by Canelo

This edition published in the United Kingdom in 2019 by

Canelo Digital Publishing Limited
57 Shepherds Lane
Beaconsfield, Bucks HP9 2DU
United Kingdom

A CIP catalogue record for this book is available from the British Library.

Print ISBN 978 1 78863 416 8
Ebook ISBN 978 1 91142 060 6

This book is a work of fiction. Names, characters, businesses, organizations,
places and events are either the product of the author's imagination or are
used fictitiously. Any resemblance to actual persons, living or dead, events
or locales is entirely coincidental.

Look for more great books at www.canelo.co

Printed and bound in Great Britain by Clays Ltd, Elcograf S.p.A.

For Freya, our gorgeous greyhound girl, who brings such love and joy, and for the real Gabe, may your days over the rainbow bridge be happy ones.

Prologue

I know the answer to this, I honestly do.

Eve rolled her shoulders to try to ease some of the tension that had settled there throughout the course of the day like slowly solidifying concrete. Perhaps she'd slept awkwardly last night, but then didn't she sleep badly every night? She bit her lip as a sudden blinding flash ricocheted across her vision, accompanied by an icy pain that shot through her skull.

'So what do you think, Mrs Carpenter?'

'Hmmm?'

Eve inhaled slowly, hoping to clear her head, but echoes of discomfort remained. She didn't have time for this, especially not during the highly important half-termly governors' meeting. There was so much to get through.

'Mrs Carpenter, I asked if we really *should* be considering taking on new staff in the next academic year. I mean, it's already May and the timetable is almost complete. Is it fair to make such drastic changes *now*?' It was the condescending tone of Bill Dempsey, a portly fifty-something local businessman who sat on the school's finance committee.

'Well…' Eve rubbed the bridge of her nose to try to disperse the throbbing that was making her eyes water. She lowered her hand and reached for her glass of water.

She was probably dehydrated. In fact she was, without a doubt. She hadn't drunk enough as she'd been rushing round since five that morning – *as usual*! Her trembling hand knocked against the glass and she watched as it fell in slow motion, emptying its contents all over the papers she'd placed in front of her just half an hour ago. Over her work: her precious document outlining how employing a new alternative learning needs teacher would be *the* way to raise standards.

'Fu... lip!' escaped her lips as she quickly replaced the expletive she would have released had she been elsewhere and in different company.

Horatio Jones, the parent governor to her right, leapt to his feet as the water dripped off the edge of the table and plopped onto the plush beige carpet.

'Eve, are you all right?' he asked, brushing off the front of his trousers.

She tore her gaze from him and met the curious stares of the other governors and her senior leadership team. Her deputy head, Amanda Green, was looking at her with concern, but when she met the eyes of her assistant head, Donovan Connelly, she found pure glee. She'd cocked up and he was enjoying every moment of it, like a hyena watching a wounded antelope trying to right itself.

But before she could begin to feel indignant, another flash of agony stabbed her brain like a scalding poker and she gasped.

'Eve?' She felt a hand on her shoulder and tried to turn, but even moving her head a fraction made the pain worse and caused more blurry lines to fracture her field of vision. 'Eve, shall I call an ambulance?' It was Amanda.

'No... don't think so. Be okay... in a minute.'

She blinked and rubbed her eyes, but the room seemed to have been immersed in water and the edges of her vision shimmered as if someone had licked a finger and smudged them, then sprinkled them with glitter. Eve liked glitter; she liked sparkly things.

But not like this.

She squinted but it made no difference.

Something was *seriously* wrong.

She hoped for a moment that it was actually one of those weird dreams that she had to endure some nights, where any moment she'd find herself totally naked in whole-school assembly. Except for the pasties – what was it with those small flesh-coloured circles and their appearance in her dreams? As if they provided sufficient coverage when everything else was on display! But ever since she'd worn a pair to prom with a strapless dress and the left one had popped out and landed on the dance floor, then got stuck to a sixth-former's heel, it seemed that she'd never have a nightmare about full humiliating nudity sans pasties again.

She covered her eyes, hoping that a brief reprieve would make it all better. She could hear people breathing, shuffling and clearing their throats, evidently uncomfortable.

I can't afford to be ill. I'm too busy, have too much to do.

'We need to get her to the hospital. Pass me my bag, Donovan! *Now!*' Amanda took control, coming to her rescue, and Eve sent out a silent thank you for the no-nonsense, practical approach of her deputy.

But as that thought slipped away, the last thing she remembered before she was consumed by darkness was throwing up all over her new – and very expensive – navy and white brogues with the kitten heel, and hearing a barely disguised murmur of joy from Donovan as she slumped in her chair, coffee-tainted drool trickling down her chin.

Chapter 1

Eve sat in the passenger seat of Amanda's car and allowed Amanda to fasten her seat belt. As they drove out of the hospital car park, she stared through the windscreen at the dark sky.

What a day it had been.

The gentle motion of the vehicle was soothing and she fought her exhaustion.

'Sleep if you want to, Eve. I'll wake you when we get to your house.'

Eve offered a brief nod of thanks then closed her eyes.

She thought through what had happened over the past few hours. The doctor at the hospital had told her she'd had a migraine accompanied by some sort of stress-related attack. She'd perched on the raised bed covered with crêpey blue paper that creaked and tore whenever she moved – reminding her of when the younger children attempted somewhat unsuccessfully to sneak out farts in lessons – and tried to absorb what he was saying. As a teenager, she'd suffered from migraines, crippling ones that lasted for hours, but she'd seemed to grow out of them at some point. Once her exam anxiety had passed, if she remembered correctly. Now, however, she'd suffered one after all these years, and it must have been a bad one as she'd thrown up then blacked out. The doctor suspected that as she'd felt the symptoms of the migraine coming on, she'd suffered an anxiety attack, which had ultimately made the whole experience even worse.

Stress and exhaustion were the likely triggers, and when Amanda – who had evidently taken Eve to the hospital, although her memory of the drive there was rather hazy – had filled the doctor in on the hours Eve had been working, and about the painful events that had occurred over recent months, he'd expressed his surprise that she hadn't been ill before now. The doctor, who appeared to be in his mid-thirties like Eve, and who looked as exhausted as she felt, had then told her that the short blackout she'd suffered had likely been due to low blood sugar or to hyperventilating, which she might have succumbed to in her panic. He'd recommended that she go home and rest because there was no telling when a migraine could make a return. It might never happen again, but it could be back within hours.

Rest?

It was something Eve rarely did. Sitting still or lying in bed were not her favourite pastimes. Keeping busy, that was what she was all about. Keep busy... no time to dwell on things.

Amanda pulled up in front of Eve's house and cut the engine.

'We're here,' she said as she gently nudged Eve's arm.

Eve opened her eyes. She hadn't slept, but closing her eyes for a while had helped with the headache that reminded her of a hangover.

'I'll come in with you and get you settled then head home. Unless you want me to stay?'

'No, no!' Eve waved a hand at her. 'I'll be fine. I just need to get into bed and to sleep. It'll all be better in the morning.'

They got out of the car and walked up to the front door.

'I'll be okay from here, I promise.'

'Call me in the morning?'

'Of course. And thank you.'

They hugged briefly, then Eve unlocked the door.

'You need to take better care of yourself, Eve. You'll burn out if you're not careful.' Amanda frowned at her. 'I was really worried.'

'I'll try. I will...'

Amanda nodded then returned to her car and Eve closed the door behind her.

She knew Amanda was right, but she had no idea where to start.

-

Eve opened an eye and peered around.

It was light. She was in her own bed. At home.

She opened the other eye then sighed and stretched tentatively.

Phew! No pain.

But... did that really happen... at work?

She cringed.

Yes, it did.

Lying in her own bed, the synthetic peach-blossom-fragranced duvet pulled up to her chin, Eve's heart hammered. This wasn't right. This wasn't her. She didn't slow down; she didn't surrender to frailty. She needed to get up, get showered and get dressed.

A buzzing from her bedside cabinet grabbed her attention. Probably someone from work asking what time she'd be in.

I can't do it…

She gripped the duvet with trembling hands and ground her teeth together.

Her mobile buzzed again, an unwelcome reminder of the outside world, as someone left a message.

I just can't…

The pounding of her heart increased. She could hear the blood whooshing through her ears and her whole body shook. Was she about to suffer a heart attack? Was this it… the end? Would she die alone without even a cat to gnaw at her fingers as rigor mortis set in?

Pull yourself together!

She focused on slowing her breathing, on taking deep breaths in and out to the count of ten, until her heart had slowed and she was able to control her limbs again. She needed to get up and make a cup of tea and to eat something, *then* she'd be able to think clearly.

She pushed the duvet aside and wriggled to the edge of the bed. The king-size bed she'd bought just two years ago with Darryl, when she'd still been able to convince herself that everything was okay between them, that there was hope of a life and a future together. A future that included Saturday-morning snuggles with her own little family. But now, the bed seemed ridiculously oversized for one and she often felt lost in it, more like the pea than the princess from the fairy tale.

Her bedroom was a tip. If people at work, hell, if the pupils could see how their smartly turned-out, ambitious and dynamic head teacher actually lived, they'd be shocked. Horrified even. She'd let things go after Darryl left; *before* Darryl left, if she was honest. But she just didn't have time to clean, to replace light bulbs and put clothes away. When something needed washing, she flung it into the overflowing basket on the landing then went out and bought more. She could afford to, after all. She earned a good wage and she had no dependants.

She hunched over.

No dependants.

That, along with months of anguish, was what had triggered her attack.

She'd been busy as usual, rushing around school, picking up bits of litter the caretaker had missed and peering into classrooms to check that all was well. She'd missed lunch, granted, and hadn't eaten since she'd forced down a piece of toast at breakfast. Apart from the mouldy bits, that was, and she'd picked them out as she swallowed black coffee, because, of course, there'd been no milk in the fridge.

So the doctor had been right in suggesting that she hadn't eaten enough yesterday. But that wasn't what had upset her. It had been something far more painful that had sent her into the whirling pit of agony. She hugged herself as she recalled the moment when Sandra Winters, the chair of governors, had waddled into the meeting. She'd been huge, smiling, glowing and beautiful.

Full of life.

Literally.

Eve rubbed her own belly, so empty it was concave. But she just had no appetite. She got to her feet and padded over to the full-length mirror. Before her stood a scrawny woman with short blonde hair streaked with grey. It was cut in what her hairdresser referred to as a pixie style, but right now it just looked a mess. Her eyes were dark hollows, their former emerald green now dull as moss; her cheeks were gaunt and her shoulder blades razor sharp. She pulled her vest top down a bit and it flattened

9

her chest even more. Where had her breasts gone? Just a year ago, they'd been swollen and blue-veined as her body changed with its new condition.

But that had been then.

Her eyes stung and she blinked hard.

No point dwelling on what *had* been. *What* might *have been if you'd just stopped...*

She eyed her reflection again, determined to properly assess what stood in front of her. Extending from her grey knickers – *good job I wasn't given a full body examination yesterday at the hospital* – were two slightly fuzzy spindly legs with knobbly knees.

Not a good look for a woman four years past thirty.

She had to admit it, she was worn out, a shadow of the ambitious, dynamic young woman she had once been. She'd always been driven, it was true, driven by the need to succeed in her career. But while she'd been focused on that, everything else in her life had taken a back seat, and look at where she was now.

–

'You just need a break, Eve,' Amanda said as she stirred two sugars into a mug of tea.

'But I can hardly run off, can I? It's only May!' Eve thumped her mug on the table and gazed around her glossy high-tech kitchen. It had everything a family could want, from its bountiful work surfaces to its shiny (unused) gadgets, to its enormous silver double-door American fridge. Of course, she couldn't see the surfaces, as they were currently littered with half-empty takeaway cartons, bottles with various amounts of wine in and, strangely, a pair of pink knickers that hung from a cupboard handle.

How did they get there? However, if you ignored the mess, it was a perfect kitchen for a family; yet it had no family.

Eve had no family.

Apart from her parents, that was, who ran a hairdressing salon in Italy, and she rarely saw them. They were busy with their own lives and she didn't like to bother them unless it was absolutely necessary, having always felt like a burden. Then, of course, there was Aunt Mary who lived in Cornwall, but Eve hadn't seen her in years. Mary sent Christmas and birthday cards, and still placed a twenty-pound note inside them, even though Eve had long since told her not to worry now that she was all grown up. Every six months or so, under the shadow of guilt, Eve would contact her aunt. Admittedly, most of the time she just send a deceptively cheerful text message − it was much easier than having an actual conversation. And that had been the pattern of things.

The room surged as she realized that she hadn't spoken to Mary in months, not wanting to have to talk to her about... well, about everything. In fact she'd ignored the increasingly frequent calls from her aunt, and deleted her voice messages without listening to them. It was easy to push people away when you were busy, when you had a job to do, but when you slowed down, even just for a day or so, it was amazing how guilt caught up with you.

Shame crawled all over Eve like stinging ants and she shivered.

'Eve, I think you need to re-evaluate your life.' Amanda spoke softly, the trained counsellor in her kicking in. 'You're only thirty-four and you've just suffered a pretty violent migraine because of stress and exhaustion. And as the doctor said, it was probably a full-blown anxiety attack. It's hardly surprising, as you live your life at a hundred miles an hour.'

Eve nodded. She couldn't deny it. Everything she did was at speed – work, love, sex, IVF, work, miscarriage, work, sleep, work. She'd been speeding along the career motorway for so long now, never slowing down to gaze at the fields and houses, never stopping to take a break, that she didn't know how else to be.

'You're pretty busy too,' Eve said as she gazed as Amanda. Her friend and colleague was a pretty forty-four-year-old with a well-maintained ginger bob, dressed in a smart black suit with minimal jewellery. She looked the part of deputy head teacher and she was damned good at her job too.

'Yes, but I have… *balance.*'

Eve nodded; Amanda was right. She had a loving husband, two teenage children, a golden Labrador and a spacious semi-detached home in a nice area. Amanda's husband was a successful author, so he worked from home and Amanda was able to go out to work knowing that dinner would be on the table when she got back and that the dog would be walked. Unless her husband was working to a deadline, that was, and even then he was still highly supportive of his wife's career.

What did Eve come home to?

'My house is a pigsty.'

Amanda looked around the kitchen and nodded. 'It's a bit on the messy side.'

'I can't just abandon everything, can I?' Eve asked the question, even though she knew that she couldn't go on as she had been; that she couldn't, right now, consider setting a foot back in school. Not yet, anyway.

She gasped at the realization. It was momentous: terrifying.

'What is it?' Amanda asked, her face etched with concern.

'I can't go back.' Eve chewed at her bottom lip.

'Where?'

'To work.'

'Well, no, I don't think you should this week.'

'Not after what happened. I threw up all over myself... in front of the governors!'

'Uh... yes, you did. But you were very unwell, Eve.'

'Yes!' Eve laughed, a strange, hollow sound in her untidy kitchen. 'So I was.' She stood up, and as she did so, the cord at the waist of her baggy jogging bottoms snapped and they fell to the floor.

She looked down, then at Amanda, and they both started to giggle, although Eve recognized her own laughter as bordering on hysteria.

She shook her head as she tugged the trousers back up her legs, trying to ignore the fact that her friend had probably just had a clear view of the out-of-control bikini line that was sprouting from of the sides of her knickers like some sort of wild crotch beard. 'I found these on the floor this morning. They're not even mine... They must be Darryl's, which is really embarrassing as it shows how long it's been since I cleaned or tidied. But Amanda... I do know that I can't go back... at the moment. I need a break. I think I have done for a while.'

'Oh honey, you're so *good* at what you do. You mustn't despair. This is just a blip because you need a break. Once you've recharged, it'll all seem different. You've done amazing things in your time at the school. I mean, just look at the last school inspection report. *Outstanding!* How many head teachers can stick that on their CV?'

'I know. But I've given my life to it, Amanda. Taking a break is a scary concept.' Her throat ached and she had to swallow hard to force out her next words. 'I have nothing except for my job.'

'You have this house.' Amanda chewed her bottom lip.

'Yes, and look at it. A family home in need of a family. I drift in and out of here like some kind of ghoul, leaving more and more mess in my wake. There are *three* bathrooms here, for God's sake! And a downstairs loo! What do I need four toilets for? I can't even keep one clean.'

'You're right about that. I went into the downstairs one and there was a surprise party going on.' A smile played across Amanda's lips and Eve registered that her friend was trying to lighten the mood.

'A what?'

'You hadn't flushed.'

Eve's cheeks burned. 'Sorry about that. But do you see what I mean? I'm so busy I don't even have time to flush a poo.'

Amanda nodded. 'Why not take a few weeks off, see how you feel? Get a doctor's note and focus on resting.'

'I can't rest here.'

'Too many memories?' The kindness in Amanda's eyes made Eve's chest tighten.

'Way too many. I can't stand thinking about what might have been.'

'Have you…'

'Heard from Darryl?'

'Yeah.'

'Not since the last solicitor's letter. He's filed for divorce and I don't blame him. I mean… it hurts. Still. But I didn't treat him right; I ignored his suffering and just threw myself back into work. He couldn't do the same. He asked me to slow down, to go away somewhere just the two of us to try to heal, but I couldn't do it. I know he still blames me for losing the… the…' Eve's throat ached and she rubbed it hard, as if she could dislodge the vice-like pain that gripped her when she allowed herself to think about what she'd lost. What *they'd* lost. Because Darryl had been broken by it too. Even more broken than she'd been, because she hadn't allowed herself to dwell.

'Yesterday… was it seeing Sandra?'

'I think so. Not that I begrudge her that wonderful happy glow or anything!' Eve held up a hand then realized it was shaking so lowered it and pressed it into her lap.

'Of course not.'

'But… I hadn't seen her for a while because she'd been on bed rest, and then seeing her so full and fat and with so much to look forward to just brought home how much I was missing.'

'So why don't you try to get away for a bit? Perhaps to the coast? We can sort things out at work to cover for you.'

'You can't, though, can you? I'm a head teacher. I can't just go off on holiday in term time.'

'You suffered a terrible loss and didn't allow yourself to grieve. These are extenuating circumstances, Eve. I'll deal with any fallout.'

'Maybe.'

'You could visit your parents in Italy?' Amanda's tone was hesitant, her eyes wary.

'That's not going to help.' Eve shivered. 'I couldn't bear trying to explain it all to them. I only gave them the briefest outline of events. Not that they'd care anyway.'

'Could you just have a quick sunshine break then? Grab a last-minute deal to Spain or Crete, perhaps?'

The idea of getting on a plane filled Eve with a sudden cold dread. Travelling to a foreign country alone seemed way too big a deal to manage in her fragile state. She drummed her fingertips on her thighs and took slow, deep breaths.

An idea began to form.

'I do have my aunt... who lives in Cornwall.'

'Is that your father's sister?'

'Yes. His twin sister actually.' Eve had been selective with how much she'd told Amanda about her family, in spite of their friendship. After all, what kind of woman didn't make time for her father's sister, the woman she was so close to as a child? But now there didn't seem to be any point in withholding the information. 'I haven't seen her in a while but she was always lovely. With my parents working so much, I spent a few summers – okay, *all* my childhood summers – in her Cornish cottage and it was heavenly. My mother never liked her; they had a clash of personalities, I think. The last time I saw her was about... Oh my! It must be when I graduated from my teaching course. She came because my parents were... otherwise engaged.'

She glanced at Amanda, trying to ascertain if her friend was judging her, but all she saw was kindness. 'I can't believe I haven't made the effort to see her since then, but I've been so...' She was about to use her regular excuse. *Too busy... Just like Mum and Dad always were.* Too busy to see family. Too busy to make love to her husband. Too busy to learn how to cook. Too busy to take bed rest when the doctor advised her to slow down after she started spotting. *Too busy... too busy... too busy.*

'You need to go, Eve. I think Cornwall sounds like a very good plan.'

'It's so beautiful there, Amanda. You can't imagine how beautiful until you see it: the colourful cottages, the bustling harbour, the cobbled streets, the pretty little cove and the copious amounts of greenery everywhere. It's such a vibrant place to be. And the air... Well it just smells amazing!' Her heart lifted as she recalled the fresh salty air that she'd filled her lungs with as a child, as she remembered how soft the powdery white sand of the cove felt between her toes and as she thought of how it would be to walk along the harbour eating freshly cooked fish and chips then indulging in an ice cream from the local parlour.

'I'm going to ring her right now.' A shiver of delight ran down her spine and her belly flipped. 'Before I change my mind. Then I need to ring Sandra to inform her and book an appointment with my GP. Part of me is screaming out that this is wrong, that I'm being weak, that it's career suicide. But the other part is cheering me on, insisting that this is the right thing to do. The *only* thing to do if I want to get better.'

'You only have one life, Eve.'

'Just the one. Yes, it's time to re-evaluate. I do just need some time, don't I? I will be okay again?'

'Of course you will, honey. Now get organized!' Amanda leaned over and hugged her. 'This is what you need to do. Work can wait. The school isn't going anywhere.'

As Eve allowed her friend to comfort her, she bit her cheek hard to stop the tears from falling. She was torn. For as much as she wanted to believe that she had to sort herself out, to grab life with both hands and live again, she wasn't a hundred per cent sure that this *was* the right thing to do. She'd always known what she wanted, always known where she was headed, always been confident that her decisions were the right ones. That was what had made her so successful at what she did.

But now, when it came to her life, the world outside of education, she was suddenly at sea. She had sacrificed so much that she didn't know what she wanted any more, or who she was, or *how* to live.

Perhaps a change of scenery would help, a short break away from the city, catching up with a woman she'd once enjoyed spending time with. A woman who had been so kind and caring throughout her childhood and who – Eve admitted it to herself now – she had neglected. Perhaps this was one of the things that was niggling at her. After all, she had been remiss in her treatment of Aunt Mary, pushing her away just as she'd pushed Darryl away. If she was able to make things up to her aunt and to spend some time in the idyllic little town, she might be able to make some decisions about her future.

But first she had an uncomfortable realization that she was going to have to try to come to terms with her past.

Chapter 2

Eve had zoned out for much of the three-hour drive from Bristol to the small historic fishing village of Conwenna Cove. She'd driven on autopilot, a strange numbness settling over her like a warm blanket. She wouldn't fight it, not yet. It was better to arrive safely and settle in before she attempted to even begin to deal with what was happening to her.

It would be good to stay somewhere she didn't know many people, somewhere she could be almost anonymous, somewhere she could try to evaluate exactly what had happened in her life and to decide where she went from this point on.

When she had finally plucked up the courage to telephone Aunt Mary, she'd tried her aunt's mobile number first but it went straight to voicemail several times. Eve guessed it could be because the signal in Conwenna wasn't particularly strong or consistent. So she'd tried the landline instead and been thrown into a panic when a man had answered, suddenly filled with the fear that Mary had moved, or even died, during their period of non-contact, although her aunt's texts would not – of course – have come from the afterlife. The man's voice had been deep and gruff and she'd been unable to ascertain his age as he'd said so little, though he hadn't had the Cornish accent she knew so well. However, when she'd told him her name, she'd heard his sharp inhalation of breath, then suffered in the ten-second silence that followed. Eve had felt judged in that silence, though she couldn't tell if it was paranoia due to her fractious state or if there had been something icy in his tone when he'd finally replied, 'Did you say *Eve*?'

'Yes. I'm Mary's niece.'

'I see.' He drew out the S and it reminded Eve of a snake hissing.

'Can I speak to her, please?'

Another silence.

'Hello?' Eve feared that he was about to break bad news.

'Hold on.'

'Thanks.' She bit her tongue to prevent herself from asking, *Who are you and what are you doing in my aunt's home?*

She heard him placing the receiver on a table, the one next to the cottage's front door presumably, and she pictured the old-fashioned telephone her aunt used to have with the curly wire. The receiver used to have a peanut coating as Mary often answered the phone whilst chewing on her favourite snack. Did she still eat peanuts? Did she still have the old phone? It was quite possible, seeing as how the man on the other end had left the receiver where it was and not carried it with him, as he would have done had it been a free handset.

I should know these things.

'Hello?' A woman's voice came on the line, sounding frail and wary.

'Aunt Mary?' Eve asked.

'Who is this?' The voice wobbled.

'Aunt Mary, is that you?'

'Hello? Phyllis?'

'No, it's Eve. Who are you?' Had Mary developed some form of early-onset dementia?

'Now come on, Irene.' In the background, another voice, this time with warm tones and familiar cadences. 'Let me have the phone and you can go drink your tea.'

'But there's someone on the line. I think it's Phyllis.'

'No, I don't think so, Irene. Phyllis calls every other day and she rang yesterday. I think this call is for me.'

'No!'

'Yes, it is.' So patient and calm. 'Now hand me the phone or your tea will get cold.'

'No!'

'There's cake, too.'

'Oh... I like cake.'

'I know you do. It's lemon drizzle.'

'My favourite.'

Eve heard shuffling as someone moved away.

'Hello?'

'Aunt Mary?'

'Goodness, is that *you*, Eve? When Jack said your name, I thought he must've misheard.'

'Yes.' On hearing the delight in her beloved aunt's voice, Eve had been overwhelmed by emotion, suddenly unable to vocalize all the things she'd prepared to say by way of explanation. 'Um... it's been a while, I know.'

'I've been wondering if... *when* you'd call, dear. Are you okay?'

Eve nodded, then shook her head, trying to swallow the lump that cut off her voice.

'Goodness, we haven't spoken since... Oh, I don't know when. Did you get my cards?'

'Yes. Thank you,' Eve squeaked.

'And the flowers after... I'm so sorry about what happened, Eve. Such a dreadful loss. I wanted to come to you, but there was so much going on here and no one to take care of the animals, and you were so insistent about going straight back to work...'

'I know.' Eve's throat ached. 'I was... I *am* okay.'

'Such a strong, independent young woman you are. You've always been the same.' Mary's voice carried a wistful tone that suggested she admired Eve's strength but also doubted it would last indefinitely. 'How are things now with Darryl?'

'Not good.' Understatement of the century.

'Oh sweetheart. I had a feeling... though your texts didn't really say much. I guess it was what they didn't say that alerted me. Eve, I do wish I'd been able to come to see you.'

'I could have come to you, Aunt Mary, but it was just so busy here.' She cleared her throat, aware that she was making the same old excuse. 'As for Darryl... He's, um, he's been gone a while.'

'How awful! I'm so sorry, sweetheart.'

'I'm all right, though. I'm managing.' Eve tried to force brightness into her tone, but instead her voice had a slightly manic edge to it.

'And how's work?'

She sighed.

'Not so good either? I know how much you love your job.'

'I do. I did... But...' Eve swallowed hard then opened her mouth, but nothing came out.

'Is it time for a visit? I'm certain that some good sea air and home cooking would do you good.' It was as if her aunt was psychic. How could she know what Eve needed?

'Please!' she croaked.

'Come as soon as you're ready, dear.'

They had stayed on the line for another hour as Mary filled her in on how she was taking care of Irene, the elderly mother of a friend, so that Phyllis could have a well-earned break, and how she'd been busy with her vegetable garden and her cats and dogs, as well as helping out at the old farm with the greyhound sanctuary.

When Eve finally hung up, she'd been drained yet cautiously optimistic. It had been too long since she'd spoken to her aunt and she regretted not doing so sooner, just as she admitted to herself that she'd been trying to avoid the lovely warm woman because she'd feared having to dredge up all the emotions she'd been suppressing for so long. She also realized that she hadn't found out about the mysterious Jack who'd answered the telephone. Knowing her aunt, it was probably just the milkman or a delivery man. Never having had children of her own, Mary had always had a thing for waifs and strays, taking anything from three-legged cats to the widowed vicar under her warm, compassionate wing.

And now, thought Eve, here she was, on her way back to her second childhood home.

As she neared the end of her journey, she held her breath. Her belly filled with a thousand butterflies and she tensed as she drove over the brow of the hill, and there before her was Conwenna Cove.

The sea stretched out along the horizon for as far as she could see, sparkling in the warm May sunshine. She wound down the window and breathed deeply of the fresh air, filling her lungs greedily. Boats bobbed on the blue expanse and she saw a windsurfer carried quickly across the water's surface. Seagulls soared above, swooping now and then to the harbour below, and as she descended the hill, she devoured the picture-perfect image of the village with its pastel cottages, its never-ending greenery and its familiar landmarks from the shiny red roof of the RNLI boathouse to the peaks of the cliffs that surrounded the cove.

She was overwhelmed suddenly by a deep sense of homesickness. Not for Bristol, or Conwenna Cove, or even her parents, but for Aunt Mary. She couldn't wait to be reunited with the woman she'd been apart from for so long, or to try to make up for her own appalling neglect and for the precious lost time.

–

Jack Adams wiped a hand across his brow. The afternoon was warm and the physical labour was making him sweat. He was no stranger to manual work, but it was important that he got this right. Mary Harris had been so good to him since his arrival in the Cornish village six months ago and he liked helping her in return. Right now, he was sawing wood to make up three new raised beds for her back garden. Mary loved to grow her own fruit and veg and she was gradually teaching him about what to plant and when, as well as about the medicinal properties of certain plants. The old Jack, the man he was before his injury, would probably have been dismissive of such knowledge, regarding it as unimportant and irrelevant, but he knew now how precious life was and how even the smallest things that mattered to people were to be respected. A lot about him had changed over the years.

He picked up the saw again and started the rhythmic movement along the pencil line he'd drawn. Soon the wood gave beneath the metal blade and he lifted the plank and blew off the loose sawdust to inspect his handiwork.

'There you are!'

He turned to find Mary smiling as she walked up the garden. When she reached him, she proffered a small circular tray and he took a glass of cloudy home-made lemonade.

'Thank you.' He swallowed the refreshing citrus drink in two gulps. The ice cubes clinked together as he returned the glass to the tray.

'It's looking good. You've been busy this morning.' Mary placed the tray on the ground then settled her hands on her hips as she surveyed the woodpile. She reminded him of an ageing Tinker Bell, tiny yet tenacious. Something about her just sparkled and he wouldn't have been surprised to see a pair of gossamer wings fluttering on her back. 'How long do you think it will take to get the beds finished?'

'Not long. Two to three days as long as the weather stays fine.'

'Fantastic. Perhaps you can collect some more manure from the farm. The composters are full too, so help yourself when you're ready.'

Jack nodded.

'The seedlings will be in early next week at the grocer's.'

Jack smiled. The small greengrocer stocked everything from fruit and veg to eggs to plants. It was a family-run business and a warm, friendly place to shop.

Mary looked at her watch. 'I do hope Eve won't be long. I'm quite worried about her driving all that way after what she's been through, yet she insisted that she didn't want to take the train. Said she couldn't cope with being around lots of other people right now.'

Jack fought the urge to shake his head. He'd learnt about Mary's niece gradually over the six months of his stay, as Mary had told him various things about Eve, and he wasn't particularly impressed. What kind of woman was so wrapped up in her job that she failed to visit her aunt? Not just failed to visit but rarely telephoned her, choosing instead to send the odd brief text message. From what he'd seen of Mary, she was kind and caring, selfless in fact, and he knew that if she hadn't had so many commitments she'd have gone to visit Eve in Bristol. Although, if he was honest, he'd pieced together things that Mary had said, and gathered that she didn't know if she'd be welcome there. It was as if she worried that she wasn't good enough for her niece with the high-profile teaching career. So although Mary professed to be too busy and too needed in Conwenna, Jack believed that Eve's apparent stuck-up attitude probably had more to do with her reluctance than she was letting on. It grated on him even more because, being the lone child of a single mother who'd passed away when he was eighteen, he didn't have anyone. He'd have loved an aunt like Mary, a family of his own.

'You will join us for lunch, won't you, Jack?'

He paused, then dusted off his old jeans, keen to buy himself some time.

'I can't, sorry. I've uh… got to head up to the farm. I promised Neil I'd help out with that broken fence on the manège. It needs fixing asap or there'll be greyhounds running off everywhere.' He grinned at the image of dogs escaping from the woodchip-covered space that had been built to exercise them safely. Once those dogs had the chance to run, they were like the wind.

'Well I'll put some aside for you then,' Mary said. 'It's vegetable soup and my special cheese bread.'

Jack's mouth watered. Mary knew he had a weakness for her cheese bread, her soup, her lasagne, her cakes… just about everything she ever made. 'That would be great, thanks.'

Mary tilted her head and Jack paused. She'd heard something. Sure enough, he could make out the sound of tyres crunching over the gravel road that led to the cottages. His stomach lurched at the joy in her expression; he was concerned about her, fearful that she might get hurt.

Eve Carpenter had better not cause any pain to the kindly woman who'd taken him in and treated him as if he were a member of her family, or she'd have him to deal with.

He was already annoyed with her and she hadn't even arrived yet.

Chapter 3

Eve smiled as she slowly manoeuvred her car along the winding gravel road that led to her aunt's home. It was surrounded by a variety of trees that gave the feeling of being hidden away from the rest of the world. It could be in the middle of nowhere rather than just above a Cornish village. The trees created a sense of timelessness and of privacy, as did the dappled light that squeezed through the branches to the ground below, highlighting some areas and plunging others into shade.

She still had the window open and she savoured the air that rushed into the car. It was cool and fragrant, carrying the earthy scents of flora and fauna and the delicate scent of the hundreds of thousands of bluebells that carpeted the ground as far as she could see. Some were dark blue, young and fresh, while others were paler, as if faded with age.

Finally she drove into a clearing and pulled up in front of the two pretty cottages that Mary owned. Her heart squeezed. Here she was, at her aunt's home, years since her last visit, but it still looked exactly as she remembered it. The sturdy whitewashed building that made up Bluebell Cottages dated back three hundred years. Once a single long cottage, it had been divided into two when a previous owner had blocked up the doors that joined one half to the other. The small-paned windows were set back in the thick stone walls, their woodwork painted forget-me-not blue to match the latticed frames that arched over the blue front doors. The green foliage that climbed around the doorways was already showing some fuchsia rosebuds and promising beautifully scented flowers in the coming months. It added to the picture-perfect image and Eve was overwhelmed with an unfamiliar emotion as she gazed at the cottages.

Then she realized what it was.

Happiness.

Or at least the hope of happiness.

The hope that there might be something more to life than the turmoil and doubt that she'd been experiencing; that there was life beyond loss, and life beyond her complete involvement in her career. She'd never thought that she would consider her dedication to her career a flaw, but over recent months she'd been aware of doubts creeping in, even though she'd tried so hard to suppress them.

She opened the car door and stepped out, then walked to the start of the small footpath that led down to the edge of the property and offered a fabulous view of the village below. Her aunt had told her she'd had the path cleared years ago because although she liked the privacy of the trees, she also wanted to be able to enjoy the view of Conwenna Cove. Eve could see why, as she gazed at the pretty fishing village that spread out below, with its higgledy-piggledy pastel cottages and the busy harbour where a variety of boats were anchored, their small windows glinting in the afternoon sun.

She sucked in the fresh salty air as she watched the white breakers out at sea and felt an overwhelming urge to get out there to swim. It was a positive move coming here;

she would be able to spend some time in Conwenna Cove and have a chance to work through her feelings, daunting as that prospect was.

'What better place to heal, dear?'

Eve jumped and turned to find her aunt smiling at her from the doorway of the closer cottage. She was wiping her hands on a lilac apron that was tied around her waist. Eve's vision blurred as she walked into Aunt Mary's ready embrace. She had to lean over slightly to place her chin on Mary's shoulder, but then her aunt was only five foot tall, making even Eve's five foot four seem statuesque. Growing up, Eve had never thought of Mary as small, recalling her as a presence to fill any room, but as she'd got older, she'd realized that Mary's personality was so big, so warm, friendly and confident, that it made up for what she lacked in actual height.

'You know, Eve, they say Conwenna Cove has mystical healing properties. People have been coming here for centuries to rest, relax and recuperate. I'm not sure that I believe the magic bit but I certainly believe that resting in a beautiful location near the ocean can help you to recover from an ordeal. And goodness me, don't you need it; you're a bag of bones.'

She held Eve at arm's length and shook her head. 'When did it get so bad you forgot to eat?'

Eve swallowed hard and tried to find the right words but she was at a loss, suddenly feeling like a child in need of comfort and security and as if she might burst into tears at any moment.

'Come on then! Let's get your things inside and I'll make us a nice cup of tea. Seems like we've a lot to catch up on. I'll pop the kettle on while you get sorted.'

As Aunt Mary walked away, Eve knew that she'd given her the chance to compose herself and she was grateful. She opened the boot and pulled out her suitcase and holdall. She placed them next to the driver's-side door and reached in for her oversized handbag – her very expensive designer handbag that she'd bought on a whim just weeks ago. As she slipped her arm through the handles, she felt how empty it was. *A metaphor for my life.* She looked the part but inside she was empty: no love, no fulfilment and no one to cuddle up with at night. The fashionable bag had seemed at home in Bristol, but outside her aunt's quaint cottage, surrounded by trees and birdsong, where if you listened carefully the sound of the waves was just audible, it seemed completely incongruous.

A bit like Eve herself.

She turned quickly to grab her suitcase and holdall, keen to get inside before her thoughts became too maudlin, and stumbled into a large body. She bounced off the hard chest and slammed against her car door before finding her balance.

'Ouch!'

Was that a snigger?

She looked up to find a tall, broad man in front of her, evaluating her with intense dark eyes. She did a quick appraisal in return and estimated him to be about six foot tall and around seventeen stone. He was *huge*.

'Sorry about that. I thought you'd heard me. Mary sent me out to help.' He paused for a moment but Eve was struck dumb after bumping into the wall of muscle. The man shook his head as if he'd just encountered a complete idiot, then walked off with her luggage and into Mary's house.

Eve rubbed her forehead and wondered if she'd have a bruise at the point of impact, then suppressed a flicker of annoyance, though she wasn't sure if it was with herself or the stranger, as she traipsed after him into the cottage. She didn't recognize him, didn't know who he was to Mary, and had no right to make an instant judgement about him based on a ten-second encounter. But she couldn't help recalling the mirth in his eyes, and wondering why he'd limped slightly, as if favouring some old injury.

–

Eve entered the cool hallway of the cottage and paused as her eyes adjusted to the darkness. She could smell lavender, lemon and clean washing. The scents of a home that was lived in. She took in the small table with the old telephone, just as she'd imagined it, and brushed her fingertips over the curly beige phone wire.

A memory surfaced, clear as day, of using the phone when she was about ten to call her parents. It was summer; she'd been wearing denim shorts and a frilly green vest top with strawberry ice cream splodges down the front. Her upper lip was salty from swimming in the sea and she was filled with childish excitement at the freedom she had when staying with her aunt. There were no set times for breakfast and dinner, no early bedtimes when she'd lie staring at the ceiling, listening to her parents entertaining in the room below, wishing sleep would claim her and help her forget about her loneliness.

When staying with Aunt Mary, she'd phoned her parents once a week as a courtesy, but every time she spoke to them they'd seemed uninterested, and she'd known even then that they didn't miss her. They were glad to get her out of their hair so they could live their lives unhindered by worrying over babysitters or school runs. As Eve had spoken to her mother, she'd wound her fingers in the curly wire, round and round, until she'd been unable to free them. When the call had ended, she'd had to call for Mary, and her aunt had hurried to her side then laughed at the mess Eve was in.

Eve shook her head. Scents always conjured memories and she wondered how many more she'd experience here. Even though the one about being caught up in the wire wasn't pleasant, what came afterwards was. Her aunt had packed them a picnic basket and they'd taken the three rescue dogs she'd had then along the path to the edge of the property, past the cottage that served as a vet's surgery and down the steep, winding cliff path to the small private cove. They'd both stripped down to their costumes and raced into the water, splashing, laughing and screeching as the dogs raced around them. When they finally tired, they'd wrapped up in sandy blankets and enjoyed freshly baked bread, local creamy Cheddar and crunchy apples grown in Mary's garden. They had been good days, the ones spent with Mary; Eve realized that they'd probably been the best days of her otherwise lonely childhood.

A noise from the rear of the house shook her from her reverie and she walked through the cosy lounge with its oak beams that had dried lavender and herb bouquets hanging from them, and its eclectic range of furniture – two of the sofas were taken up by cats and dogs who barely stirred as she passed them – into the open-plan kitchen-diner where Mary was standing at the Aga stirring a bubbling pot.

She placed her bag on a chair then approached her aunt. 'That smells so good.'

'Vegetable soup, dear, and there's cheese bread too.'

Eve's stomach growled in response and she laughed. 'It must be the sea air.'

Mary nodded. 'It'll do you good to get your appetite back.'

'I hope so. I didn't mean to become... this thin.'

'It's not healthy. It might be fashionable but you've no reserves left to fight things off or to deal with what life brings. But I can understand, Eve. I've been there myself.'

'You have?' Eve eyed her aunt carefully, taking in her salt-and-pepper bobbed hair that she had worn tucked behind her ears for as long as Eve could remember. Of course, the last time she had seen Mary, her hair had been light brown, streaked with just a little grey, but that had been a long time ago.

Mary turned her hazel eyes to meet Eve's. They twinkled in her pretty tanned face, surrounded by tiny white lines where the sun hadn't penetrated. 'I might be a bit on the curvy side now, but things change after the menopause, you know.' She shook her head. 'Of course you don't know, you've years ahead of you before that happens. But let me tell you, Eve, I have gained a few pounds since it all started.' She laughed. 'Saved me a fortune in female products, though!'

Eve nodded slowly, slightly embarrassed by her aunt's openness.

'Anyway, I digress... When I was younger, a long time ago, I went through a difficult phase in my life and I lost a lot of weight. Stress and grief are bad for the mind and the body.'

Eve wanted to ask her aunt about what she'd been through but held back because she suspected that Mary would tell her more when she was ready. If she wanted to share, that was.

'The dogs in the lounge are very chilled, aren't they? Neither of them got up to check me out.'

Mary chuckled. 'They're both quite old. Harry is about nine. He was found wandering the lanes. He's been here three years now and he's so lazy! It's as if once he found his couch, he swore never to move. The other one is Clio. She's eleven and has been a bit poorly recently, so she rarely stirs except for food or a comfort trip to the garden, although I do try to get them out for a gentle walk at least once a day. I brought her down from the rescue sanctuary at the farm last year. Her owner was old and frail and had to go into a care home. It was very sad and it took her a while to adjust.'

'Lucky for Clio that you were here. Don't the cats bother the dogs, though? I thought all ex-racing dogs chased cats.'

Mary shook her head. 'They've allowed the dogs to settle in. I won't deny that at first there was some hissing and scratching, but they came to a mutual understanding. Basically, the cats are in charge.'

Eve nodded. 'Aunt Mary... Who's the man that brought my bags in?'

As if on cue, she heard heavy footsteps thumping down the wooden stairs and into the hallway. A shadow fell across the kitchen floor, breaking up the warming sunbeams that streamed in through one of the large kitchen windows. Eve shivered.

'This is Jack Adams,' Mary said. 'He lives next door. He's my tenant.'

Eve looked at the large man and fought the urge to recoil under the intensity of his gaze. What was it with his eyes? She felt as if he could see deep into her mind and her heart and examine all the bad things she'd ever done. She pulled herself up to her full height, held out her hand and adopted her formal head-teacher voice. 'Pleased to meet you, Jack. Properly, I mean. After bumping into you outside. I…' She cleared her throat. 'Was it you I spoke to on the phone?'

He scowled at her, his dark brows meeting above chocolate-brown eyes. Those eyes could have been so soft and gentle if only he didn't appear to be so hostile towards her.

Eve waited, her hand outstretched, for what felt like hours, but it was in fact only seconds before he enveloped it in one of his. As their palms met she felt the calluses on his skin, and as his fingers wrapped around hers she was aware of the brute strength of his grip. He held her hand for a moment and her heart rate increased as an unexpected warmth spread through her, then he suddenly dropped it and she was left confused, and a bit embarrassed, although she wasn't sure why.

'Eve, could you set the table, please?' Mary asked. 'Jack, I know you said you had things to do, but will you stay and have a quick bite to eat?'

'I have to get up to the farm,' he replied quickly. Eve watched as he leant over and kissed Mary on the cheek. 'But I'll be home around five.'

'I'll keep it warm for you, dear.'

'You're an angel!' He straightened up then strode out of the kitchen without giving Eve another glance. She was at once hurt and offended, as if this strange man with his bad manners should have shown her more courtesy. But then she didn't know him and he didn't know her. He was, apparently, her aunt's tenant, though what Eve had

experienced of him so far left a lot to be desired. *Yet...*
She had caught the softening in his expression when he
looked at Mary and heard how his voice changed as he
spoke to her.

He couldn't be all bad if he showed her aunt such
respect and affection, now could he?

Chapter 4

As Jack walked through the lanes to the farm, he thought about Eve Carpenter. He tried not to, but for some reason the petite blonde kept forcing her way into his mind. That was the problem with women like her; they just got under your skin and before you knew it, you were trusting them and letting them make you vulnerable.

Eve was a lot like Mary physically. She wasn't much taller than his landlady and she had the same small features. *But those eyes!* They were so big and green, like emeralds if he was being poetic. Her hair was cropped short, which gave her an elfin appearance and made her seem vulnerable. He wanted to be annoyed with her – after all, she'd neglected Mary for a long time – but there was something about her that also made him feel a bit... funny.

He shook his head and climbed over a stile into the field that bordered the farm. He'd probably just been too long without sex and the first attractive female that stepped into his path – or bounced off his chest – had turned his head. That was what it was. Yet when he'd taken her hand in his and seen the spark in her gaze, Jack had known that there was more to Eve than her facade would suggest. She looked every bit the manicured career woman, from her designer skinny jeans and blouse to her giant handbag and expensive haircut, but she was so thin, so jumpy, so... fragile. Jack knew he had a soft spot for wounded animals, and he sensed that Eve was wounded, so he'd have to ensure that he kept his wits about him and didn't fall for her charms. He'd dealt with a broken heart once and he had no intention of going through all that nonsense again.

–

Eve sipped her tea slowly and watched her aunt over the rim of the mug. Mary was tending to Irene, her ageing guest, and Eve was in awe of how patient and kind she was being.

'Come on then, Irene, drink your tea before it gets cold.'

'Yes. But I do like lemon drizzle cake with my tea.'

'I know, dear, but you've just had your lunch and you don't want to eat too much, do you?' Mary smiled at Irene but the older woman stared back blankly.

'Just a small slice?'

'Oh, go on then, but we'll have to take a gentle stroll around the garden afterwards.'

Irene laughed and clapped her hands. 'A stroll would be lovely.'

Mary cut a home-made cake then handed Irene a slice on a small china plate and looked at Eve. 'Would you like some?'

Eve was about to decline but then recalled what Mary had said to her earlier about her weight loss. 'Please.' She accepted the proffered plate. As soon as she popped a piece of cake into her mouth, it watered at the delicious combination of sweet and sour. The sugar in the drizzle contrasted perfectly with the tartness of the lemon juice and the perfect lightness of the sponge. 'This is SO good!'

Mary nodded. 'I'm glad you like it. It's very easy to make.'

'I've never been any good at baking,' Eve said, finishing her slice of cake.

'That's not strictly true, Eve.'

'Phyllis can't bake for love nor money,' Irene chipped in.

'Who's Phyllis?' Eve asked.

'My daughter, of course,' Irene replied, shaking her head. 'Can't you remember anything?'

Eve raised her mug and hid a smile. Irene was a sweet old lady. Mary had briefly explained to Eve that she was suffering from the onset of dementia, which meant that she had periods of lucidity followed by episodes of confusion. Her memory was not the best, so her reprimand aimed at Eve was rather ironic.

'Could I have some cake, Mary?' Irene asked, holding out her plate.

'Irene, you just had a piece.'

'Did I?' She fluttered her short white eyelashes, then gave a small laugh. 'So I did. Worth a try, though, eh?'

Eve and Mary laughed as Irene got up from the table. 'Shall I do the dishes?'

'No, it's okay. I'll do them,' Eve said.

'Well I shall return to my room to take a nap, then.'

Irene had been napping when Eve arrived but Mary had told her that her elderly guest tired easily and that she often catnapped during the day.

'That was a delicious lunch, Aunt Mary.'

'I'm glad you enjoyed it and I'm hoping to feed you up while you're here.'

'Sounds good to me.' Eve took the plates to the sink and stared out into the garden. It was lusciously green, with plants and trees in every pot and patch of earth that she could see. Some were flowering, some had buds on and some were shoots just emerging from the earth. She knew her aunt had always had green fingers but didn't remember her having this many things growing in her garden.

As Eve filled the sink with soapy water, Mary appeared at her side with a tea towel. 'You know, I've had a lot of help out there from Jack.'

Eve started at his name. 'Really? He doesn't look like a gardener.' *Then what does he look like?* She shrugged the voice away.

'He wasn't. Until he came here.'

'You taught him?' Eve immersed a plate into the water and rubbed at it with the small washing-up brush.

'Some things. But others he just knew instinctively. He's very good with plants and animals. He might be a big lad but he has a heart of gold, that one.'

'I don't think he likes me.' Eve bit her lip. How had that escaped? Where was her filter?

Mary placed a hand on her shoulder. 'What makes you say that?'

'He's been quite...' *Rude? Abrupt? Mean?* But had he been any of those things?

'Oh I know he can come across as a bit reserved, aloof even, but he's been through some difficult things in his life. He was a marine and he served in Afghanistan.'

'Goodness!' That would explain his size and physique, then.

'He's quite fit, isn't he?'

Heat rushed into Eve's cheeks. 'Aunt Mary!'

'Oh, just because I'm getting on, I can't appreciate a good-looking man when I see one? Come on, Eve.' She nudged Eve with her hip. 'He's a lovely young man and he's settled well in Conwenna. He's not put all his demons behind him yet, but time will help with that.'

'And your home cooking?'

'Yes, Eve. Good food always helps the soul to heal. You can't get better if you have no reserves. You need your physical strength alongside your emotional strength. One doesn't work without the other.'

Eve swilled out the mugs then placed them on the draining board. She yawned and stretched her arms, suddenly exhausted. 'I think the journey must have taken it out of me.'

'I think the past few years have taken it out of you. Why don't you take a nap then we can walk the dogs before dinner?'

'I never nap in the day, Aunt Mary.'

'Well perhaps it's time to start. Now go to your room and get some rest. I'll wake you in an hour or so if you're not up.'

Eve gave her aunt a hug then went up the creaky narrow staircase and into the cosy low-ceilinged room she'd always stayed in as child. Jack had put her bags at the bottom of the bed beside an old pine trunk and she placed her oversized handbag next to them.

Then, kicking off her shoes and climbing up on the double bed with its purple and blue patchwork quilt, she lay down, and fell instantly asleep.

–

Eve slowly surfaced to consciousness like a diver rising from the seabed, then stretched out and gazed around. The bedroom was warm with late-afternoon sunlight and she guessed that it must be gone four. She couldn't remember the last time she'd slept so deeply. She sat up and went to the window then flung it open and breathed deeply of the air. It bore the scents of earth and salt, of fertility and life.

Her room overlooked the back garden with its vegetable patches, its fruit trees and a variety of herbs in raised beds. It was wonderfully green. There were a few more raised beds in the process of being built and she recalled her aunt telling her that Jack was making them. According to Mary, Jack was quite handy to have around. Darryl hadn't been like that; he'd had no manual skills at all, and while Eve hadn't minded – not being particularly practical herself – she could see how such skills would come in useful.

A noise caught her attention and she leaned a bit further out of the window to peer into the garden of the cottage next door. Jack came around the corner carrying a large package wrapped in brown paper. He stumbled as he climbed the two grass-covered steps that led to a generously sized wooden shed because he clearly couldn't see over the package. Eve gasped, worrying that he'd hurt himself, and he turned instantly at the noise and stared right at her. She lifted a hand to wave but he scowled, so she thought better of it and backed away from the window.

What on earth was he up to? The package he'd been carrying looked like a board of some type and she wondered what it could be. Perhaps he was making something in the shed, or perhaps it was a new TV. It was big enough to be one of those forty-plus-inch screens. But why would he be taking it out there?

Eve shrugged. It didn't really matter; what did matter was that Jack had caught her watching him and now he probably thought she was spying on him. Or worse, that she fancied him and couldn't help gazing at him from her bedroom window. She cringed. *Great start, Eve! Now Mr Grumpy thinks you've got the hots for him.*

She decided to unpack as a way of distracting herself. She hung her dresses in the large old-fashioned wardrobe that actually had a key in the lock, and her T-shirts and jeans in the drawers of the pretty old dresser with a round mirror on top. The edges of the mirror were darker where the protective coating had obviously worn away and exposed the silver nitrate to the air – something she'd learnt in a science lesson she'd observed once. But she thought it gave the mirror character, just like the scratches on the wooden floorboards and the slight fading on some of the squares of the patchwork quilt where the sun had shone through the window on them.

Eve paused, waiting for the pang of regret or guilt to come because she wasn't at work; for the desire to be back there in school to sear through her heart and soul, as it would've done in the past. But nothing happened. It must be numbness caused by the shock of her anxiety attack, migraine and exhaustion. No doubt it would soon seep back in.

She slid her suitcase and empty holdall under the bed, then checked her appearance in the mirror. Her hair was sticking up on one side where she'd slept on it and there was a crease down her left cheek. So not only had she looked like a peeping Tom but a scruffy one too. She rubbed at her cheek then ran her hands through her hair, but it stubbornly sprang back into place. Well, it would have to do. Aunt Mary had told her she'd wake her in an hour, but she was sure she'd slept for longer, probably more like two hours. She'd better go downstairs and help with dinner. She might even learn something while she was here, which would be a good thing as her culinary skills certainly needed improvement.

–

'Hello, Eve, how did you sleep?' Mary asked as she walked into the kitchen.

'Very well, thank you. Too well, in fact. You should have called me.'

Mary peered at her over the top of small rectangular glasses. 'Do you know, I completely forgot!' She gave a wink that suggested that she'd not forgotten at all but had in fact left Eve sleeping because she thought she needed it. 'I've been pottering around in the garden, then I came in here and Irene was making a bit of a fuss.'

Irene shook her head. 'Don't exaggerate, Mary.'

'You were, Irene, don't fib.' The two women giggled like teenagers.

'What happened?' Eve asked as she took a seat at the table.

'One of those damned cats brought a mouse in and dropped it in my lap!' Irene said, her white eyebrows shooting up to her hairline. 'If there's one thing I can't abide, it's vermin!' She fluttered her hands around her face and laughed some more.

'Yes, it caused quite a bit of excitement,' Mary said, 'especially when we had to try to catch it.'

'And did you?' Eve asked, lifting her feet from the floor just in case.

Mary nodded. 'Yes, of course. And I took it up to the end of the garden and released it, so don't worry. We get a lot of mice and the like coming down from the fields. The cats are well fed, so they don't chase them for food, but occasionally they like to toy with them.'

Eve looked at the table, which was covered in flour and small bowls of freshly chopped herbs. 'What're you making?'

Mary dusted her hands with flour then began kneading a ball of dough. 'Garlic and rosemary focaccia bread.'

'Yum!' Eve licked her lips.

'Want to take over?'

'I couldn't. I can't even warm beans in the microwave without making a mess.'

'It's easier than you think,' Mary said, working a handful of chopped rosemary into the dough.

'Some of you career women miss out on so much,' Irene cut in. 'You just don't have the time to do things from scratch because you're so busy. My granddaughter's the same. She lives in London.'

'That's not strictly true. Some women do manage to do it all,' Eve replied, thinking of Amanda, who was keen to climb the career ladder yet also managed to fit in baking sessions with her children at the weekends and during holidays. Amanda also made a delicious curry, which Eve had enjoyed on several occasions when they'd had a girls' night in. Although now she thought about it, she couldn't recall the last time they'd done that. It might even have been before the twins... before her life started to crumble.

'Eve!' Mary's voice broke into her thoughts. 'Are you okay? You just blanched.'

'She doesn't look well at all,' Irene added. 'Was it all the talk of mice?'

'I'm... I'm all right. I just have a bit of a headache. Not used to napping in the afternoon.'

'Well forget about the cooking for now. Why don't you take the dogs for a stroll? It'll do them good to have a gentle walk and give you the opportunity to take a look around, perhaps work up an appetite before dinner.'

'I thought you said they weren't keen on moving from the sofa?' Eve said.

'They're not, but if a walk's on offer, they can usually be persuaded. Just take it slowly and if they get tired, come straight back.'

Eve went to put her trainers on and grabbed a zip-up hoodie from her cupboard, then skipped down the stairs. She was keen to get out in the lovely afternoon and have a look around the old village to see if anything had changed.

As she reached the bottom step, she heard a deep voice coming from the kitchen and she had to fight the urge to run straight back up the stairs. It was Jack. Would he tell Aunt Mary that she had been staring at him from her bedroom window? That could be really embarrassing and she already felt like an idiot.

She walked through to the kitchen but found Jack in her way, blocking the doorway. His shoulders almost touched the frame on either side, and his grey T-shirt stretched across his bulging biceps. Eve cleared her throat, not wanting to have to touch him in case she suddenly caressed him instead.

Jack turned and glared down at her. 'Oh, it's you. Finished gazing at the view now, have you?'

'What?' Eve decided to feign innocence but a blush stole up her chest and neck then flared in her cheeks. Her body was betraying her even as her mind screamed at it to remain calm. This was just a man after all, and she was accustomed to having a position of authority over many men in school; to being completely normal and in control of herself whenever she was around men. But taken out of her usual environment and placed in close proximity to a large and, she had to admit it, rather hunky male – although he was a bit rude – she seemed to be losing her ability to remain cool.

'How's the view close up?' Jack whispered as he leaned towards her.

Eve took a step backwards and ran a hand through her hair. 'I was just admiring the garden.'

Jack nodded but his eyes glinted. 'Of course you were.'

Was he teasing?

'Off you go then!' Mary said as she approached them and handed Jack two leads.

Eve stared at Mary. 'I thought I was walking the dogs.'

'Well, as I'm busy, I asked Jack to go with you. He can show you around and help you get your bearings.'

Eve opened her mouth to make an excuse, any excuse, but nothing came. Her mind went completely blank.

'Come on, Harry, Clio!' Jack called as he walked through to the lounge. '*Walkies!*'

Eve watched as the dogs stretched and yawned then slid off the sofas and wagged their long tails before dancing around the room as if they'd both lost ten years.

Jack attached the leads to their collars and walked them outside. Eve followed, playing with the zip on her hoodie. She felt like a teenager being forced on a date with the son of her mother's friend. Which had happened once. Eve's mother had been such a control freak that she'd decided it would be a good idea to matchmake. The boy had been equally as reticent as Eve, though, and the evening had been a complete disaster, never to be repeated.

Jack handed Eve one of the leads and set off down the driveway and onto the gravel road, leaving Eve almost running to keep up. She turned to wave goodbye and found Mary and Irene standing outside the cottage, their heads together with big grins on their faces. They looked like they were conspiring and Eve just hoped her suspicions about their intentions weren't right. There was no way that anything could ever happen between her and Jack Adams. No way at all.

Chapter 5

Jack walked briskly until he realized that his pace was putting too much strain on Eve, Harry and Clio, so he slowed down and made an effort to keep his paces shorter. Even with his injury, he could still move quickly; it was only when he went slower that it became more pronounced. He hated that he had the limp but thought he'd got off lightly compared to some. The doctors had been able to save his leg; many of his fellow marines and other soldiers hadn't been that lucky.

Eve panted at his side.

'You're not very fit, are you?' Jack asked.

'I'm not used to speed-walking, no.'

'Isn't that the one where their bums wiggle madly as they walk?' Jack asked, then did an impression, swinging his hips wildly from side to side so that Harry stared at him curiously.

Eve laughed. 'Yes, that's the one.'

'I couldn't keep that up. My leg wouldn't stand for it,' Jack said, then bit his lip. He didn't want to have to explain all that right now. Eve would probably only stay for a few days and he had no intention of sharing his private history with her. Opening up to a woman was dangerous.

But Eve didn't ask. She was gazing at the scenery, her face open and vulnerable.

'The bluebells are beautiful, aren't they?' he asked, his voice coming out gruffer than he'd intended. He cleared his throat.

'It's gorgeous here and it's always been the same. When I drove through here earlier, I remembered all the summers I spent here as a child and the times I used to walk along this road just to enjoy the bluebells. They're so delicate and pretty.'

'Like a carpet of blue, right?'

'That's what I thought earlier.'

He smiled. She didn't seem like a hard-hearted cow, but perhaps she was good at hiding her coldness.

They walked the rest of the way to the main road in silence, listening to the birdsong and the crunching of their feet upon the gravel. Jack wondered if Eve was thinking about the last time she was here and if she had any regrets about not coming back sooner. But he didn't know her well enough to ask and there was no point getting to know her anyway. She'd soon leave, and if she was in fact a self-obsessed career woman, he was better off not wasting his time learning more about her.

When they walked out onto the main road, Eve froze. She stared straight ahead, her attention fixed on the horizon. Between the trees, framed by the leaves and branches, was a perfect view of the horizon. The sky was amber now, with red-gold streaks, and the water glowed as if lit from below. Jack looked from the view to Eve and he had to drag his eyes away from her face in case she caught him staring at her; the serenity he saw there made something inside him shift, and it scared him.

'It's so beautiful.'

'I love it. I couldn't imagine being anywhere else now.'

'How long have you been here?'

'About six months.'

'Don't you have family?'

'No.'

'Me neither. Well, except for my parents, but they live out on Lake Garda and I rarely see them.'

'Like Mary,' he huffed.

Eve stopped suddenly. He expected her to snap at him, almost wanted her to. An argument with her would give him the opportunity to raise the issues he had with her for neglecting Mary. But instead her eyes glistened as she met his gaze. 'I've been remiss in my treatment of my aunt. I know that. I should have contacted her more often. It's just… things have been difficult. *Life* has been difficult.' Her voice cracked on the final word and Jack reached out instinctively and touched her arm.

'I'm sorry. I didn't mean to upset you. I didn't know. Mary never told me much about you. All I do know is that you have a very kind aunt there who clearly loves you very much.'

Eve stared at her shoes and Jack watched, that thing inside him shifting again, as a tear ran down her cheek. She wiped it away with the back of her hand and sniffed.

'I really am sorry, Eve. I tend to be a bit… harsh some-times. I know that. My counsellor told me it's a defence mechanism.'

She met his gaze again, and as he stared into the watery emerald depths of her eyes, his heart gave a flip and he found himself wanting to pull her into his arms. He shuf-fled his feet, confused by his reaction to this woman he barely knew. It had been quite some time since Jack had been attracted to someone. But Eve Carpenter was pretty, prettier than he'd realized when he'd first seen her, and when she was sad like this – even though he was conscious that it was totally against his better judgement – he had a strange urge to offer her comfort and try to ease her pain.

'Counsellor?' she asked as she pulled a tissue from her pocket and dabbed at her eyes, then wiped her nose.

'Long story. Perhaps I'll tell you about it some time.' *But probably not.*

'Okay.' She attempted a smile.

'How about I take you into the village and buy you an ice cream from Scoops and Sprinkles?'

'What about dinner?'

'I won't tell Mary if you don't.' He winked, then proffered his arm.

Eve slid her hand into the crook of his elbow and a warm tingling spread through his belly.

'Ice cream it is, then.'

As they walked down to the town's main street, along narrow cobbled streets lined with colourful cottages adorned with hanging baskets and window boxes, Jack couldn't help wondering at his erratic behaviour around Eve. He'd been reluctant to get to know her at all, and had decided when she arrived that he'd keep his distance, but he already sensed that there was something in her that mirrored his own vulnerability. The vulnerability that a real man like him didn't admit to easily, although in counselling he'd had to acknowledge it in order to start healing.

He didn't know exactly what had hurt Eve, but something had, and it made him want to offer her a shoulder to lean on. Dangerous ground, especially as he doubted that she was going to hang around, but while she was here, he could at least get to know her a bit better. He knew it was a huge turnaround from his earlier thoughts, but he couldn't help himself.

And after all, he reassured himself, there was nothing wrong in being friends with his landlady's niece, was there?

–

Inside the ice cream parlour, Eve took the large waffle cone from Jack and laughed. 'How on earth am I going to eat all this?'

'You'll manage. You have to; it's a Conwenna tradition.'

Jack thanked Alice, the owner's daughter, who smiled shyly at him from behind the counter, then followed Eve out of the shop. Scoops and Sprinkles was on the main street of the village that led down to the harbour. It had a pink and white front with colourful cartoon images of frozen delights painted on the window. Behind the glass, some of the most popular flavours were on display. When Jack had asked Eve what she wanted, she'd been spoilt for choice. She'd stuck to chocolate and vanilla, but she hoped that next time she'd be brave enough to choose something more daring.

Next time?

She hoped there would be a next time with Jack, because since she'd broken down in the lane, he'd altered towards her. It was as if he'd had a preconception of who she was and how she'd behave towards him, and since he'd seen her sadness, he'd softened.

She liked the softer, kinder version of Jack. She just hoped he'd stick around.

He led her towards the harbour, then gestured at a bench. They sat down and he took Clio's lead from Eve, then looped it over his broad forearm with Harry's. The dogs stared out at the water, their long tails wagging as they watched the seagulls diving into the water and swooping to pick at scraps that had fallen from bins or blown away from tourists' picnics.

'So what's it like living and working in a busy city?' he asked Eve, between licks of rum and raisin.

Eve swallowed her mouthful of chocolate ice cream before trying to reply. 'It's busy.'

'Very different to here?'

'Have you ever lived in a city?'

Jack nodded. 'When I was younger, with my mother.'

'You said you didn't have any family.'

'I don't.'

'Oh.' Her heart pounded. She'd said the wrong thing and worried he'd turn cold again.

Jack popped the last of his cone into his mouth and Eve waited for him to swallow, hoping that she hadn't offended him. 'My mother was the only family I ever had. I never knew my father; he was a married police officer and a lot older than my mother. When she got pregnant with me, he didn't want to know as he already had a grown-up family. So she moved away and kept on moving. She never fell in love again; she just wouldn't allow herself to care about anyone.' He paused and rubbed the back of his neck. 'She died when I was eighteen. I never tried to find my father. I don't know if it's strange, but I never had a desire to. He didn't want me from the start so why would he want to know me now?'

'Oh Jack, I'm sorry.'

He shook his head. 'Don't be. It was a long time ago. Eighteen years, to be precise.'

'So you're thirty-six?'

'I know…' He placed a finger on his chin and tilted his head. 'I don't look a day over twenty-five.'

'Well… I'd have said forty but…' Eve gasped as Jack squeezed her waist and tickled her. 'Hey! Cut that out!'

He pulled away suddenly. 'Sorry.' His cheeks flushed. 'That was too much, right?'

'It's okay.' Heat rose in her own cheeks. She hadn't been tickled in what felt like a lifetime, and just then, Jack's instinctive reaction had made her feel… almost carefree. 'I'm just really ticklish.'

'Thank you.'

'For what?'

'Giving me future ammunition.'

'No! No tickling, it's a weakness of mine.' She shook her head then looked at the cone in her hand. 'I'm never going to get through this.'

Jack leaned forward and took a bite. Then another. The cone was half the size.

'Uh… thanks.'

Eve nibbled at what remained, then decided to surrender. 'Do you want the rest?'

'Sure.' He polished off her ice cream then threw the serviette in a bin next to the bench.

'So what happened to your mother? I mean, if you want to tell me. You don't have to. I know you know that and I'm not being nosy…' Eve watched Jack carefully, uncertain if he'd want to talk about it.

'Breast cancer.'

'That's awful.'

'It was. But she wasn't ill for long. It was one of those cases where she was diagnosed and gone within weeks. She was small… like you. There wasn't much of her to fight it. In a way, I'm glad.'

'What'd you mean?'

'Well if she'd been bigger and stronger, the battle might have taken longer and she'd have suffered more. As it was, I was young. A bit selfish, I guess. Her being so ill didn't seem real because I still believed in my own immortality. Within a few weeks of her dying, I signed up.'

'You were a marine, right? Aunt Mary told me.'

'Commando.'

'So you would have been embroiled in Afghanistan?' Eve probed gently.

Jack nodded. 'Shall we walk these two? Burn off some of the ice cream?'

'Of course.'

They took the path along the harbour, and Eve noticed a few businesses that hadn't been there when she was younger, including a sweetshop called Sugar and Spice, a fifties diner called Zoe's, and an art gallery, A Pretty Picture, where Jack paused in front of the window. Eve gently rubbed Clio's long neck as she gazed at the paintings on display. There were a few portraits of fishermen and of the harbour and some of local scenery.

'Shall we take a look inside?' Jack asked.

'What about the dogs?'

'Most shops around here are dog friendly. It doesn't pay to be hostile towards man's best friend when you rely on tourist income, as a lot of holidaymakers bring their pets along.'

Jack opened the shop door and Eve followed him inside. It was cool and dark and smelt of furniture polish and mints. Jack nodded at a man behind the counter then beckoned Eve to his side.

They stood before a range of landscapes and Jack pointed out familiar landmarks. One featured Conwenna Cove from the perspective of a fisherman looking up at the village from his boat, and Eve could see the chimneys and upper part of the roof of Mary's cottages. 'I really like that one.'

'It's clever, isn't it?' Jack replied. 'If you look carefully, you can see the shadow of the boat in the water and the dappled effect caused by the cloud cover.'

Eve peered closer, suddenly aware of her ignorance about art.

'How do you know so much about it?' she asked.

Jack shrugged. 'I dabble.'

He walked across the shop, so Eve followed him. 'What'd you mean, you dabble?'

He shook his head and she saw a muscle in his jaw twitching. She wasn't sure if it was mirth or agitation causing it, so when he spoke again, she let out a quiet sigh of relief.

'This one here is by a local artist.'

Eve gazed at the portrait of a muscular greyhound standing in a field. Its fur was so shiny it appeared silver. The creature had bright amber eyes that emanated intelligence and sensitivity.

'It's so beautiful. Greyhounds are such elegant creatures.'

Jack grinned and his cheeks flushed ever so slightly. 'And this one?'

This time, two greyhounds stood outside a stable. One was completely black except for a white patch on his chest; the other one was black and white and its markings reminded Eve of those on a cow. The dogs' mouths were open and they looked as if they were grinning. To the left of the stable, just behind a wooden fence, was a parked car with two people inside.

'Adoption day.' Jack pointed at the car. 'Two lucky dogs about to be taken to their forever home. Or *fur*ever home, as it's fondly known.'

'Do you know the artist?' Eve asked.

'Something like that.'

'I've never been able to draw or paint. It's definitely a gift.'

'We all have our talents. I bet there are lots of things you're good at?' Jack tilted his head.

Eve chewed her lip. 'I can't draw. I can't cook. I can't sew or knit. I was quite good at maths and science when I was younger and I was very good at English. I was also a good teacher.'

'Do you still teach?'

'I'm a head teacher now.' *Now? Am I still?*

'I know, Mary told me. But some heads still spend time in the classroom, don't they?'

'They do. I didn't, though. I mean, I don't. I'm too busy running the place.'

'Do you think it's better to be removed from the classroom then? Once you're in leadership?'

'I don't know. I'm not sure there's a perfect way of doing it. I did enjoy teaching but being a manager took over, I guess.'

'Will you go back to it?'

Eve's heart started to pound and she gripped Clio's lead tighter. She'd only just arrived in Conwenna that afternoon but already she felt as if she'd been away from Bristol for days. Would she return to her job, to the long hours, the insomnia and the loneliness of an empty house? 'I...'

A dart of pain pierced her skull and she slapped her hand against it.

'Eve?' Jack grabbed her arm. 'Eve, what's wrong?'

The pressure. The exhaustion.

'Outside,' she croaked.

'Of course!'

She let him lead her back into the fresh air, then held onto him as another pain followed the path of the first one.

'Let's sit you down.' Jack lowered her onto a bench and she gripped his hand as her heart thundered behind her ribs and she felt as if it would burst from her chest. Hot tears ran down her cheeks and she trembled violently as she struggled to catch her breath. She was vaguely aware of Jack telling her to calm down, that it would be all right, that this would pass.

When she finally managed to breathe slowly and open her eyes, she found that she was resting her head upon Jack's shoulder as he gently smoothed her hair. She knew she should move but she was afraid that the pounding in her chest would return, so she stayed still, frozen in time, with her face against Jack's T-shirt, listening to his strong, steady heartbeat until she felt reassured that her own had fully returned to normal.

'Eve? Do you need to see a doctor?'

She slowly lifted her head. 'I don't think so.'

'Are you sure?'

'It's just tension. An… anxiety attack.'

'Is this why you left Bristol?'

'Yes.' She met his concerned gaze. 'Stress and… and migraines. Nothing more serious. Apparently.'

'Stress can take a dreadful toll upon the body and mind.' He nodded.

'So I've learned recently.'

'So it's better for you to avoid talking about work then?'

'For a bit, it would seem.' She tried to smile but her palms were clammy and she felt cold to her bones. The aftermath of these attacks was as strange as when they began. They took hold of her quickly but left slowly, almost like treacle seeping out of a jar. And even when her heartbeat had returned to normal, she still felt the remains of the panic hovering around, clinging to her like an old hangover, ready to spiral if she didn't do her best to keep it at bay.

'Well if that's the case, we'll talk about everything except for that thing you usually do when you're, you know, somewhere else other than here.' He smiled. He was very handsome when he smiled, and so gentle for such a large man. If he'd carried on stroking her hair, she suspected she could have fallen asleep in his arms. Eve couldn't recall the last time someone had relaxed her so quickly or so tenderly. She'd only just met Jack Adams but she already felt safe with him. Was that wrong? Was it her anxious state that was making her feel this way?

But as she sat back on the bench and watched Jack rubbing Harry's soft ears, the dog gazing at him with complete trust and adoration, Eve became convinced that Jack was a good man. The type of man she might have been able to build a life with, had her circumstances been different. As it was, she wasn't actively searching for a relationship; her life was such a mess, and it wouldn't be fair to bring anyone else into it right now.

In fact, it wouldn't be fair to bring anyone into her life ever again, especially when she thought about exactly what she'd done wrong.

Chapter 6

Jack and Eve walked around the harbour once more before returning to Mary's. They took it slowly, Jack insisting that Eve hold his arm just in case she felt unsteady again, and she was grateful for the support.

When they arrived back at the cottage, Jack handed the dogs' leads to her.

'Aren't you coming in?'

'I'll be over in about ten minutes. I just need to have a quick wash.'

'Oh, okay. See you soon.'

Eve pushed open the door, unclipped the dogs' leads, then smiled as they both trotted through to the kitchen with Eve right behind them.

'Hello, Eve! Did you have a nice walk?' Aunt Mary rubbed Clio and Harry's heads. Their long tails waved back and forth as they expressed their happiness at being home with their owner.

'I did, thank you. It was lovely to see the village again.'

'And these two didn't get too tired?'

'They seemed okay, but to be honest we did stop a few times, so they had time to recuperate along the way.'

'Oh good!' Mary patted the dogs once more, then they turned and headed into the lounge and, Eve suspected, the comfort of the sofas. 'Dinner's almost ready.'

'I'm starving,' Eve said, surprising herself after the amount of ice cream she'd consumed. 'Jack said he won't be long. He's just gone to wash.'

Mary nodded then crouched in front of the Aga and removed a heavy rectangular dish. Eve's mouth watered as the aromas of garlic and tomatoes reached her nostrils. 'Is that lasagne?'

'It is.'

'It smells delicious.'

'There's wine open if you'd like to pour a glass.'

Eve took a seat at the circular pine table and lifted the bottle of red wine. She read the label: *Australian Shiraz. 2014. Rich berry fruit flavours and spicy undertones.*

'Pour me one too, please,' Irene said as she entered the kitchen.

Eve glanced at Mary but her aunt nodded, so she filled three of the glasses from the place settings on the table. She considered pouring some for Jack, but thought it best to wait until he arrived.

'Can I do anything to help?' she asked, feeling bad that she was sitting while her aunt was so busy.

'No, dear, it's all under control. Anyway, tomorrow's Sunday so you can help with the roast.'

'Really? You'd trust me with that?' Eve took a big gulp of her Shiraz to hide her surprise.

'It's not as difficult as you might think.' Mary chuckled as she placed the lasagne dish in the middle of the table with a basket of garlic bread.

'Evening!' Jack said as he strode into the kitchen. Eve almost gasped at how jaw-droppingly gorgeous he was. He'd changed into a clean pale blue T-shirt that clung to his arms and shoulders and showed off the golden hue of his skin. His faded jeans accentuated his muscular thighs and slim hips. In the fading light, his eyes and hair seemed darker than ever, and as he caught her eye, he flashed her a grin that made her cheeks flame.

'Would you like some wine?' Eve asked.

Jack held up a bottle. 'I brought one just in case. Thought it would be nice to celebrate your arrival. I know it means a lot to Mary.'

Eve poured him a glass then handed it to him and he took the seat next to her. His scent washed over her, fresh as spring rain and alpine air. Eve fought the urge to shuffle closer to him and sniff his T-shirt. Instead, she leaned forward and checked the alcohol percentage of the wine; it must be the wine because something was having a strange effect upon her. She felt giddy. Tingly. And not in a bad way, which was nice after experiencing so many unpleasant physical symptoms recently. In addition, the sensation was one she hadn't felt in some time. She'd been closed down for so long, suppressing all emotion and sensation, as if they came hand in hand, but one afternoon in Conwenna Cove, combined with a nap, a walk in the fresh air and half a glass of wine, had awoken something in her that she couldn't explain. It reminded her of the holiday feeling she'd experienced in the past; the sweet exhilaration of knowing that two or more weeks of relaxing, eating and freedom stretched ahead.

But she knew this was just a temporary relief, as she wasn't sure how long she planned to stay in Conwenna. She'd just set out knowing that she needed to heal and recuperate, guessing that she'd take a few days, or maybe even a week. She hoped she'd know when she was ready to return to work. She hoped she *would* feel ready to return.

Right now, however, as she watched Jack turn on the lamps in her aunt's kitchen, then light two candles and bring them to the table, Eve didn't want to think about what she'd be doing in a week's time, or even two. Right now, she just wanted to live in the moment, and to enjoy the evening.

–

Jack tucked into Mary's delicious lasagne and watched as Eve began to relax. When she'd arrived earlier that day, she'd been tight as a coiled spring, but through the course of the afternoon, she'd unwound. Not fully. There was still tension there; in her shoulders, in her jaw, in her eyes. But it was slowly seeping away.

He had been extremely worried when Eve had experienced some kind of stress attack in the village. He'd seen similar things in his fellow marines in the rehabilitation centre where he'd gone to recover after his injury, but they had been marines and soldiers, people who'd experienced the terrors and stresses of Afghanistan. Eve was the head teacher of a secondary school. Surely her experiences were different, less severe? He knew, though, from his group therapy sessions, that anxiety affected people in different ways and that people had varying levels of tolerance. Mary had always spoken of her niece and her career with great pride, but she had once confessed to Jack that she feared Eve might well burn out. Eve had recovered quite quickly this afternoon, though, and seemed to be relaxing now, so he hoped she'd feel a lot better soon.

He was surprised at how quickly his feelings towards her had changed and it made him wary, yet he was also glad that he'd softened towards her. It would have been difficult having her here for however long she planned to stay if she had been the hard, cold woman he'd imagined. But she wasn't; he was sure of it.

But what would happen when she did feel better? Would she head back to Bristol and not be seen again for years? It was possible; after all, you heard about it all the time. How those intent on following a career path often put their job first and neglected their loved ones in the process. What was the phrase he'd heard a woman use on a TV chat show that Irene had been watching? That was it: she'd said that her sister would sell her granny to get ahead. At the time it had made him laugh, but really, it wasn't funny at all.

Jack hated to think of Mary being abandoned again. Hell, he hated to think of Eve going back to whatever it was that had made her so unwell. He shouldn't care so much; perhaps he shouldn't get involved at all. He hardly knew the woman but he realized that he wanted to get to know her and that made him uneasy. And also a bit excited.

'Jack?'

'Hmmm?' He looked up.

'I was just telling Eve that the village fair is on the thirtieth of this month.'

'Yes, of course.'

'It's quite an event. I think you two would enjoy it.'

'That's over three weeks away, though, isn't it?' Eve asked. Jack watched the colour draining from her cheeks.

'Yes, dear. It's always so much fun.'

'I don't know if I'll be here then. I mean, it's the start of half-term and I'll need to go back...'

Jack swept a piece of garlic bread around his plate, clearing up the tomato sauce, then popped it into his mouth and crunched it. But it stuck in his throat and he had to take a big slug of wine to wash it down.

'Well, you take as long as you need, Eve.' Mary's eyes were filled with concern. 'You shouldn't rush back, sweetheart.'

Eve chewed her lip and Jack wanted to reach out and take her hand, to convince her that what Mary was saying was right. He'd seen how unwell she was, how the stress had got to her; she should take her time and recover fully. A relapse was possible otherwise, wasn't it? But he didn't feel that it was his place to chip in, so he remained silent.

'Can I have more wine, please?' Irene held out her glass.

Jack lifted the bottle and shrugged at Mary, who mouthed, *Just a little.* Irene enjoyed a glass of wine but he knew that getting her drunk would not lead to a restful sleep for anyone. The previous weekend, he'd come back from a late-night stroll to find Mary and Irene in the back garden, Irene dressed in a bright pink nightie and green wellies as she dug through the flower bed. Mary had been calmly telling her to leave the gardening until it was light, but Irene had stubbornly insisted that the flower bed needing weeding immediately. Jack had managed to convince her to go back inside by telling her there was cake in the kitchen. When he'd asked what had happened, Mary told him she'd taken a quick shower while Irene was napping, but when she'd come back downstairs, Irene had already been up and had almost polished off a bottle of cooking sherry. So Irene plus excessive amounts of alcohol led to night-time gardening, and Jack didn't fancy a repeat performance of that. He knew Mary wouldn't be keen either.

When everyone had finished eating, Jack helped Eve to clear the table. She'd gone quiet since Mary's comments about her staying on and he was concerned.

'Are you okay, Eve?' he asked quietly as he ran hot water into the sink.

'What?' She raised her green eyes to meet his. 'Oh yes, I'm fine.' She handed him a plate.

'It's just that when Mary asked about the May fair, you seemed troubled.'

'I'm fine. Thank you.'

'Well if you want a sounding board, I'm a good listener.'

Eve smiled and nodded. 'Thank you. I appreciate it.'

The fact that she didn't divulge any more confirmed that she wasn't keen to talk about it. He couldn't help feeling a bit hurt. But what had he expected? That because he'd held her earlier when she'd been shaking, she'd open up to him completely? And anyway, would he even want her to? The last thing he wanted was to have a woman rely on him.

They did the dishes in silence, as Irene chattered on about her days on the stage and how she was looking forward to her cruise with Frank Sinatra. No one tried to correct her about the late crooner; it seemed unfair when she was evidently enjoying herself so much.

Jack had found a sense of peace in Conwenna Cove. The pain he'd suffered after leaving the marines and finding out that the woman he'd loved wasn't who he thought she was had faded and eventually been replaced by acceptance. And sometimes, on rare occasions, by hope. He didn't expect to feel happiness, but when he did, it was relished. These days, happiness came in the form of a sunny day, seeing a dog rehomed, or a delicious dinner cooked by Mary. He didn't expect to find love again either, knowing as he did that it could tear a man's heart in two and grind him down like nothing else. He had been able to replace the dreams he'd once had with substitutions. And that had sufficed: by expecting less, he was less likely to be hurt or let down. But now, as he listened to Irene, he realized he had also been afraid to expect too much. Irene – who had once danced and laughed and loved – still had hopes for the future. Despite her advanced years and sporadic memory loss, she had dreams she wanted to come true. Whatever your age, it was good to have aspirations, to have hope. And for some reason he couldn't explain, it was suddenly very important to him that the petite blonde woman next to him knew that too.

Chapter 7

Eve stretched out in bed like a satisfied cat. She was so comfortable. The mattress cradled her body and the pillows were like fluffy clouds beneath her head. She knew it was morning because there was light peeping around the edges of the curtains, but she had no idea what time it was.

And the thought made her smile.

Usually, she'd wake around four thirty then try to stay in bed until five, maybe even five thirty, but she'd spend most of that tossing and turning, thinking about the day ahead and what she'd need to do. Today was different. She'd slept deeply and couldn't recall dreaming. Since she'd suffered her loss, her dreams had been vivid, disturbing jumbles that had haunted her throughout the day unless she kept busy, yet last night she'd escaped the usual horrors. Perhaps it was being in a different location. Perhaps it was because she'd relaxed in good company the previous evening. Perhaps it was the red wine…

Whatever the reason, Eve was grateful.

She stretched again and wiggled her toes, savouring the sensation of just lying down; being peaceful. The duck-down duvet was soft and airy and it made her feel as safe and warm as she had when she'd stayed with her aunt as a child. She could lie here and imagine that she was a child again, safe from all worries and harm, and that later on in the day Mary would take her to the beach, where they would build sandcastles, eat sandwiches and paddle in the sea. It was a wonderful warm feeling to lose herself in that childish place, even if just for a few minutes. Perhaps Mary was right about Conwenna Cove and being around family who cared; it could help her to heal.

Then Jack's face popped into her mind. Handsome, caring Jack. Or so he'd seemed yesterday. She'd helped him with the dishes after dinner then had a cup of tea with Mary and Irene. Jack had excused himself, stating that he had a few things to sort out before bed. He'd kissed Mary's cheek and Irene's hand, then paused next to Eve as if wanting to say or do more. But he hadn't. Eve wasn't surprised, because she hardly knew him, but she also knew that if he'd tried to kiss her cheek, she'd have let him.

She flushed as she remembered what she'd seen just before she climbed into bed. She'd brushed her teeth then realized she was thirsty, so crept downstairs to get a glass of water. As she'd been running the tap, she'd heard a noise next door, so she opened the back door and crept out into the garden. There was a short fence between the cottage gardens with a trellis on top. It offered some privacy, but as the roses climbing the trellis weren't yet in bloom, Eve was able to see through it and had caught sight of Jack walking up the garden carrying a bottle of water and a black case, wearing nothing except for the jeans he'd had on earlier.

She had wanted to look away but found herself unable to do so. The night had been clear and her view of him unhindered. When he'd reached his shed, he'd turned and placed the water on the ground, and his muscular chest and arms had been exposed in all their glory; every part of his honed torso shown to perfection in the silvery moonlight. He'd unlocked the shed with a large key he retrieved from his pocket, then turned back to pick up his water. At that moment, something had poked Eve in the bum and she'd screeched. When she turned, Clio was right behind her, wagging her tail as if she'd just stumbled upon a great game.

Eve had quickly turned to check if Jack had heard her, but he'd disappeared from view. She'd rubbed Clio's head then ushered her inside and locked the door, hoping that Jack hadn't realized that she'd been watching him.

Again.

She sat up in bed and rubbed her eyes, the calm she'd felt on waking now seeping away. What *was* Jack doing out there at all hours and without a shirt on? He had a perfectly good cottage, so why was he spending time in a wooden shed? Were there some illegal plants growing out there that he had to tend to at night when no one else was around, or did he have a weird hobby that had to go on behind locked doors? She really hoped not, because it wouldn't be good for her aunt to have an unsavoury tenant. However, it could be perfectly innocent. Perhaps he had his own gym out there and he'd gone to work out. That would certainly explain his ripped physique. She decided to try to find out what he was up to when she had the chance. It would help put her mind at rest when she did leave Conwenna Cove.

She swung her legs over the edge of the bed, then stood and slipped her dressing gown on. She located her slippers then made her way to the bathroom. When she plodded down the stairs, she listened carefully, trying to work out how many people were in the kitchen. She could hear Mary, Irene and a man.

But it wasn't Jack.

'Morning, Aunt Mary!'

'Ah, hello, Sleeping Beauty.' Mary crossed the kitchen and hugged Eve. Irene raised a mug in greeting from her place at the table. 'Edward, this is my niece. Eve, this is Edward Millar from the village.'

'Pleased to meet you.' The white-haired man held out a hand and Eve shook it firmly. 'I've heard a lot about you, Eve. Mary talks about you all the time.'

'Hi,' Eve replied, trying to remember if her aunt had mentioned this man before.

'Edward's a local fisherman. He came bearing gifts,' Mary said as she pointed to a white paper parcel next to the sink. 'Nothing like freshly caught megrim sole.'

Eve nodded, though she'd never heard of the fish before. Any fish she ate these days either came in bread-crumbs from the supermarket or was served in a restaurant smothered in a fancy sauce.

'There's tea in the pot.' Mary pointed at the table.

Eve took the chair next to Irene and filled a mug.

'Well I guess I'd better be going,' Edward said.

'Nonsense, stay for breakfast.' Mary shook her head and nudged him as she approached the sink. A broad grin broke out on his weathered face and Eve froze, her mug of tea halfway between the table and her lips. Was there something going on between Mary and the fisherman?

'I'd better not. You've company today. But I'll see you soon?'

'Yes, of course.' Mary nodded. 'Let me show you that shrub I was talking about.' She ushered him out through the back door.

'If the wind blows, you'll get stuck like that,' Irene whispered, breaking into Eve's thoughts.

Eve closed her mouth. 'Oh! Yes... I was just...'

'They're getting along very well, you mark my words,' Irene said, then tapped the side of her nose, leaving a toast crumb there. 'Be a wedding there soon, I shouldn't wonder.'

'Really?' Eve tried not to stare at the crumb, wondering if she should tell Irene about it.

Irene nodded, then jumped out of her chair and began frantically swiping at her skirt. 'That *damned* cat!'

Eve leaned forward to look under the table and found one of her aunt's cats staring up at her. It lifted a paw and licked it, then began cleaning its face as if it had no idea what it had done wrong.

Irene screamed and got up onto her chair.

'What is it? What's wrong, Irene?' Eve tried not to stare at Irene's ankles, where flesh-coloured pop socks sagged above her brown moccasin slippers.

'There!' Irene pointed wildly at the floor. 'And there!' The chair wobbled precariously and Eve didn't know whether to try to hold on to Irene or look for the source of her terror.

She jumped as something skittered across her own slipper and she saw a small creature disappear into the living room. 'What was that?'

'It's bloody Tulip!' Irene shouted as she wobbled, her arms flailing as she tried to maintain her balance. 'She keeps dropping mice on my lap. Thinks it's funny, the little minx.'

Eve grabbed Irene's hand to steady her, and as their fingers met, she had to bite her lip to stifle a giggle. Poor Irene and naughty, naughty Tulip. The cat probably thought it was being kind by giving Irene presents.

'Come on, Irene, let's get you down.'

Eve helped the older woman into her seat. She'd only been up for half an hour and already the day was showing signs of offering plenty to distract her and help keep her mind off her own problems.

And what about Aunt Mary? It seemed like she had a rather important distraction of her own.

–

Jack stepped out of the shower and wrapped a towel around his middle. He'd been awake since dawn but had stayed in bed until eight to see if he could drop off again. It hadn't worked, so he'd got up and gone for a run instead. Sometimes he had to force himself to run because the discomfort in his leg could be almost unbearable, but when his mind was so busy and conflicted, bodily pain was a welcome relief. Besides, he knew he had to keep pushing himself physically and mentally or he'd go under, and he wasn't about to allow that to happen again. Exercise was good for him, whether it caused him discomfort or not.

Then there was his other form of self-medication.

Last night, he'd been compelled to go straight out to the shed after he'd returned from Mary's. Something was burning in him and he had to deal with it immediately. It was Eve's fault; he just couldn't get her out of his head. He wanted to go back out there now to continue what he'd started, but it would have to wait. Mary had invited him around for lunch and he wanted to finish the raised beds so she could plant her seedlings.

He grabbed another towel off the rail and dried his head and neck, enjoying the rough sensation of the line-dried material against his scalp.

What was that?

He thought he'd heard a noise downstairs.

And again?

He dropped the extra towel and opened the bathroom door slowly, then crept onto the landing, avoiding the creaky boards. Someone was in his cottage. Chances were that it was just Mary; she often popped round to leave him cakes or to drop off ironing that she'd sneakily taken from his pile of clothes. He could do his own ironing perfectly well but Mary seemed to like taking care of him and he quite liked being taken care of. But he always did as much as he could to show her how grateful he was, whether it was running errands or helping her out in the garden.

Mary had helped him to get his part-time position at the dog rescue sanctuary. He'd been in need of something to do to fill his days, to feel useful again, and she had suggested that he volunteer up at the farm for a while. A few weeks there had led to an offer of employment, and though it didn't pay much, combined with his pension from the marines it covered his small outgoings and gave him a purpose. Being around the dogs was therapeutic, and he knew that they'd helped him to move on and deal with some of his issues. People he'd encountered during his time at the sanctuary often said that the hounds helped them as much as they helped the hounds, and he had to agree. Counselling following his injury had been beneficial, but day-to-day life could still be difficult after what he'd been through. Animals were great healers, especially the hounds with their gentle, funny natures and their simple needs. Just this week, a new hound had arrived at the farm, a big black beauty they'd named Gabe. He was an ex-racer, straight from the track, but despite his size, he was one of the gentlest dogs Jack had ever come across. And he'd already won a special place in Jack's heart.

Something rattled in the kitchen, so Jack hurried down the stairs. It was unlikely to be an intruder, but Mary usually called out a greeting and he hadn't heard one. It could be one of her cats, of course, or even a fox. Sometimes they were drawn down from the fields by the smell of food. He really didn't fancy finding one going through his bin, though, because the clean-up operation afterwards was never pleasant.

He pushed the kitchen door wide and braced himself, fists ready, legs apart.

'Oh!' Eve gasped when she saw him.

'Oh!' Jack scowled, shock and confusion rushing through him, carried on adrenalin. 'What on earth are you doing?'

'My aunt asked me to find a large saucepan that she thinks is here from when you made mulled wine at Christmas apparently... and... uh...' Her eyes flickered up and down Jack's body and he pushed his shoulders back instinctively, suddenly conscious of the fact that he was still dripping from the shower and clad in just a towel.

'Did you find it?'

'No, I...' Her cheeks turned bright pink under his gaze and he strode across the kitchen towards her. She turned her head slightly as if to avert her gaze. 'Jack!'

'What?' He reached around her and opened a cupboard.

'It's your... uh... your thing.' She covered her eyes and gestured in his direction.

'My *thing*?' What on earth was she talking about? 'Here you are.' He held the large saucepan out and Eve took it blindly.

'There!' She peered from between her fingers and pointed towards his front. He looked down, and sure enough, his manhood was on display where his towel had gaped open.

'Shit!' He opened the towel and pulled the ends forwards to better wrap it around himself, but Eve gasped again and he realized that she had uncovered her eyes and just got a full-frontal flash. He froze with his hands in the air, towel midway to being wrapped back in place – the reality of what was happening too ridiculous to actually be happening – and heard a giggle.

'Well I never!' It was Mary, standing at his back door, watching him with a hand on her chest.

He quickly covered himself and met the laughing eyes of his landlady.

'I had hoped that you two would get on, but I didn't expect you to become *this* friendly so quickly.' Mary took the saucepan from Eve. 'I think I'd better leave you to it. Dinner's at one!'

'Mary! It's not how it looks,' Jack said, aware that it looked really bad.

'Oh I'm sure it's not, dear. Nothing ever is. Have fun!' Mary left the kitchen still laughing and Jack stood in the middle of the room, the water from his shower drying rapidly on his skin.

'I'd better go.' Eve shuffled past him, head down, cheeks glowing, and went to the door. 'Sorry about that.'

'Which bit? Sneaking into my house or seeing my *thing*?' A smile played on Jack's lips at how awkward the situation was. He'd never been shy about his body; living with other marines 24/7 didn't leave you a lot of time to worry about who saw your crown jewels, but this was different. He'd just flashed two women he really didn't want to offend. 'You could have let me know you were in here, Eve. Might have spared us both a rather... embarrassing moment.'

'I heard water running and I didn't want to disturb you. I could hardly come upstairs when you were showering, could I? Besides, Aunt Mary told me to just let myself in and find the saucepan. She thought she knew where it would be, but I don't know my way around your kitchen so I couldn't find it.'

Jack shrugged. 'I guess not. But I bet you weren't expecting that little show, were you?'

'Oh I wouldn't call it little!' Eve quipped, her green eyes flashing, then she dashed out the back door before Jack had a chance to reply.

Chapter 8

Eve carefully lifted the deep tray out of the oven and placed it on top of the Aga, then used a large spoon to baste the roast potatoes. The oil in the pan sizzled as she turned the potatoes to ensure they were evenly browned. She was about to put them back in the oven when Aunt Mary placed a hand on her arm.

'Not yet!'

'No?'

Mary shook her head. 'Seasoning.'

'But we seasoned them before they went into the oven.'

'And now we'll do it again,' Mary said. 'Extra flavour.'

Eve watched as Mary ground peppercorns over the potatoes then sprinkled them generously with sea salt. 'There you are. Give the tray a shake before you pop it back in.'

Eve did as she was instructed then closed the oven door. 'What's next?'

'The chicken is ready so I'll let it rest for a while before carving. You can lay the table and drain the peas.'

'Five settings?' Eve asked.

'No, dear. Just four.'

'Oh.' Eve chewed her lip. 'I thought maybe Edward would join us for dinner.'

Mary paused, a large wooden spoon in her hand. As she met Eve's eyes, butter dripped off the spoon and into a bowl of carrots. 'And why would you think that, Eve?'

Eve shrugged. 'Oooh... I don't know. Just something Irene said.'

Mary shook her head. 'Don't believe everything Irene says.'

'I heard that!' Irene plodded into the kitchen. 'I might be going senile but I'm not deaf.'

'Sorry, Irene,' Mary said as she sprinkled parsley over the carrots. 'I just meant that Eve shouldn't always take what people round here say to heart. There's a lot of joking goes on.'

Irene nodded sagely. 'It's true. But Edward's got a soft spot for you, Mary. You can't deny it.'

Mary brought the bowl of carrots to the table then took a knife from the block on the oak dresser and started to carve the chicken. Eve watched her, wondering if she'd say more, but after a few minutes had passed, she guessed that the conversation about Edward was over. For now...

'You want me to do that, Mary?' Jack strode into the kitchen and held out his hands.

'Thanks, Jack.' Mary gave him the fork and carving knife then gestured at the oven. 'Roasties should be done now, Eve.'

'Okay.' Eve tore her eyes from Jack's broad shoulders and crouched in front of the oven to remove the potatoes. As she lifted the heavy tray, the oil rushed to one end and lapped over the side, spilling onto her wrist. 'Ouch!' She dropped the tray onto the unit and inspected her arm.

'What is it?' Jack was at her side. 'Let me see.' He took her hand firmly and led her to the sink, then turned on the cold tap. 'Put it under the flow.'

Eve winced as icy water splashed over her throbbing flesh where a red patch was already beginning to bloom. The shape reminded her of a poppy.

'Oh dear!' Mary peered over her shoulder, her face etched with concern. 'That must be stinging.'

'It should be fine. Just a splash of oil but we caught it in time. Might be a bit red and sore, but no major burns,' Jack said, his eyes glued to Eve's wrist. She went to pull her arm back but he stopped her, holding her elbow in place so that the water continued to run over her. 'Not yet.'

'Okay.' Eve held her breath. Jack was so close that their thighs were touching, and his fingers were cool on her skin. He was so calm and in control in the way he'd immediately brought her to the sink. He knew what to do and he did it in the blink of an eye. Instinctively.

Eve released the breath then inhaled again, and as she did so, her nostrils were filled with Jack's rousing male scent. It was uplifting, with notes of citrus and fresh rain combined with something deeper underneath, a scent that stirred her in places she'd long since believed numb. Butterflies leapt into life in her stomach and heat coursed through her body.

'That should do it.' Jack gently released her elbow then handed her a clean towel. 'If it starts stinging again, let me know and we'll get it back under the water.'

Eve nodded. 'Thank you.'

'No problem.' Jack held her gaze for a moment too long with his chocolate-brown eyes that made her feel like melting into his arms, then returned to the chicken.

'I told you I'm no good at this domestic stuff,' Eve said to Mary.

'Nonsense, dear. You just need some practice. And perhaps fewer distractions.' Mary glanced at Jack then winked at Eve.

Dinner was delicious and Eve had to discreetly undo the top button of her jeans afterwards. She'd even accepted a bowl of ice cream and Swiss roll, but now she was regretting eating it all as her belly was fit to burst.

'After all that, I need a nap,' Irene said.

'I don't blame you,' Mary replied. 'You youngsters all right to do the dishes? I'll settle Irene, then I need to pop down to the village.'

'What, to take that extra dinner you put out to Edward?' Irene chuckled.

Mary shook her head, but as she followed Irene from the room, Eve saw that she was smiling.

'You want to wash or dry?' Jack asked.

'Wash.' Eve pulled on rubber gloves and winced as the material touched her burn.

'How's your wrist?'

'It's okay. A bit sensitive, but thanks to your quick thinking it's much better than it would have been.' She filled the sink with fresh water and squirted in some washing-up liquid.

'So, Eve. Uh… is there no one waiting back in Bristol for you?'

'What, apart from the sixteen hundred pupils on roll?' She shuddered at the thought.

'No. I meant… you know…'

'A man?'

He nodded as he took a glass from her and dried it with a tea towel.

'No.'

'Oh. I thought there might have been.'

'There was… I *was* married. I mean, I am married, legally, but not for much longer.'

'What happened?'

Eve stared through the kitchen window at the pretty garden. A tiny bird hopped along the luscious grass then up onto the wooden edge of one of the raised beds, where it glanced around rapidly, checking for predators and competition before raiding the soil for worms.

'It's okay if you don't want to talk about it. I didn't mean to pry. I'm just surprised that there's no Mr Carpenter.'

'Well there is… but we're separated. Have been for a while.'

'My marriage ended too.'

'Sorry.'

'It's not your fault.'

'How long were you married?' The question slipped out before Eve could stop it. But what was the etiquette when discussing ex-spouses with your aunt's tenant, the man who had already – on two separate occasions – come to her rescue.

Jack took a deep breath then let it out slowly. 'Just over two years. She thought it would be glamorous being married to a marine. Instead she found out it was lonely when I was away so often and for such long periods of time, and even more distressing when her husband was injured in the line of duty.' Eve watched his face carefully. Tension made his lips pale as he pressed them together and she felt she should share too, now that he was opening up.

'Darryl and I split up last December.'

'Quite recently, then?'

Eve nodded. 'We weren't really happy for some time though.'

'Sadly that's the way it can go.'

'It was just before Christmas.'

'Ouch!'

'The worst time of year…'

'To be alone.'

Eve handed him the final plate, then emptied the sink. During their conversation she hadn't even noticed that she'd washed everything. She peeled the rubber gloves off and draped them over the cupboard door directly beneath the sink.

'Do you miss her? Your wife?'

'Ex-wife now. She asked for a divorce after she told me she was in love with someone else.'

'Oh no.' Eve laid a hand on his arm.

He took her hand and turned it over, then ran a finger over the red mark on her wrist where the fat had splashed. A shiver ran up Eve's spine and goose bumps rose on her arms. What was it with this man? The slightest touch from him could cause the most dramatic reaction in her.

'He was her childhood sweetheart, the man she'd always loved. I was just a diversion; someone to make her feel better when they split up. But we married quickly because I was on leave and I thought she was gorgeous and funny and I never knew if I'd come back from Afghanistan. We lost so many out there and I just wanted a chance at happiness. For Jodie, it was a mistake and I believe she knew it the moment we stepped out of the registry office. Maybe even before that.'

Eve gazed into his eyes and saw residual pain there but also integrity and warmth. He was guarded, his initial reaction to her had shown her that, but she could tell that he had a lot to offer. How sad then that he should have been hurt.

'Jodie was younger than me. Ten years younger. It would never have worked and I was a fool to think it could. Not because of the age difference but because we were too different and because she'd always been in love with another man. In answer to your question about missing her... I miss what I thought we could have had. But not actually her, I guess. She was the perfect woman but it was all surface, an act she put on for me like she put on her blonde hair extensions, fake tan and make-up.' He stopped stroking Eve's wrist but kept hold of her. 'Do you miss Darryl?'

Eve considered the question. In the past she would have replied yes, out of some sense of loyalty to what she'd had with her husband and what they'd lost, but now she didn't know. 'I'm not really sure. I mean, I miss having someone around. My house is so big and empty. I miss planning a future with someone and having a light on after work when I get home in the evenings. The darkness, you know, it can be so lonely at times. But I wonder now if that's all Darryl actually was for me.' She gasped, alarmed at her realization. Poor Darryl! He hadn't deserved that. Did she treat him like a doormat then, walk all over him whenever it was convenient? 'Oh my goodness, that makes me sound like such a bitch. What must you think of me?'

Jack smiled, then raised her hand to his lips and kissed the palm gently, folding her fingers around it as if to keep the kiss there. 'Eve, I don't think you're bad at all for admitting that. Life is tough and some of us marry for the wrong reasons. Some of us marry for the right reasons but find as time goes on that they're no longer right any more. From what you've just told me, it seems like your relationship changed over time. That's not your fault and it wasn't Darryl's fault. It's just life.'

Eve nodded, then turned back to the sink and wiped around the edge with a cloth. Jack was right in some ways, relationships did change, but she hadn't told him the full story about why things between her and Darryl didn't work out. If she had, he would certainly have thought that she was in the wrong. What kind of woman did what she had done? What kind of mother did what she had? What kind of wife had that made her? Darryl had every right to leave her and that was a fact that Eve would have to live with for the rest of her life.

–

Jack closed the front door behind him and took a deep breath. It was cool and fresh, a perfect Monday morning that promised a beautiful day ahead. He zipped up his grey hoodie against the morning chill then walked away from the house.

'Wait up!'

He turned at the unexpected voice.

'Jack…' Eve panted as she caught up with him. 'Is it okay if I come to the farm with you?'

'Uh… yes, if you like but shouldn't you be resting? I thought that was the whole point of coming here.'

'It is, yes, but resting and *resting* are two different things.'

He tilted his head to the side and stared at her pretty face. She looked better than she had when she arrived on Saturday but she still had dark shadows under her eyes and it would take a while to put some weight on her. 'Are they?'

'Yes. Resting for me means not being at work, not thinking about work and yet being active. With lots of coffee breaks.'

'I see.' He didn't but he wanted to humour her.

'Usually I'm up at five and in work as soon as I can be. This is the first Monday in ages when I won't be at school. I could sit here all day, but if I do, I'm worried I'll just think about what I *should* be doing. So if you let me come with you, it will keep my mind off it. Surely that's a good thing?' She nudged him with her shoulder and he gazed down at her. She was so petite and slender. He could easily lift her with one hand and the thought made something inside him stir.

'Well, okay then. But you have to promise me that if you get tired, or if you start to feel at all... anxious, you'll let me know immediately.'

'I promise.'

'It's not easy up at the farm. There's a lot of dog sh— poo!'

Eve grinned. 'I can handle dog sh— poo. I've been dealing with sweaty, germ-ridden people for as long as I can remember... and that's just the teachers!'

Jack laughed. 'Come on then.'

As they walked through the lanes, Jack admired the scenery as he always did. He'd never tire of the natural beauty that began just outside his front door and spread for as far as the eye could see.

'These hedges are so pretty. I don't think I've seen so many different flowers together in ages.'

'I've been trying to learn the names, to be honest.'

'So you could impress the ladies?'

He chuckled. 'Not exactly, but I'll try it now, shall I?' He stopped walking and pointed at the hedge in front of them. 'There you have a bare stone wall base, most likely erected by a local farmer to show where his land begins. They also serve the purpose of keeping his animals in.'

'It's like a nature documentary.'

Jack cleared his throat. 'If you look closely, you can see the lichens and moss that grow on the stone. This one has a particularly thick covering here.'

'Oh yes. I see that. So what's the name of that flower?' Eve pointed at a cluster of small yellow flowers that were shaped like tiny slippers.

'That would be the common bird's-foot trefoil.'

'Impressive!'

'Thank you.'

'Let's try another.'

'I can see you must be an exacting head teacher.' He winced. 'Sorry. Didn't mean to mention the thing we're not supposed to discuss.'

'It's okay. Don't worry about it.'

Keen to change the subject, Jack fingered the soft white petals surrounding a bright yellow centre. 'This is an oxeye daisy. Not to be confused with a common daisy.'

Eve smiled. 'Is there such a thing as a common daisy?'

He shrugged. 'I'm not sure about that, but it sounds good, right?'

She nodded. 'What about that blue one?'

'Ah… now that's a sheep's-bit. You sometimes find them at the edges of hedgerows but often you'll come across a carpet of them in a field.'

'I like their fluffy round heads.'

They came to a stile in the hedge. 'If we cut across the fields here, it'll save time.' He climbed over, then held out a hand for Eve. She jumped down and they made their way across a small field. When they reached the end, they crossed another stile.

'Oh, that's just perfect!' Eve clapped her hands as she gazed down into the valley.

'That is Foxglove Farm, so named because—'

She held up a hand. 'Don't tell me! It's because of an abundance of foxgloves.'

'How ever did you guess?'

They descended through the grass of the next field and it swished against their ankles. Jack was worried Eve might trip because she kept gazing around her, although he could understand why she wanted to take it all in.

'So this is where they make the ice cream, right?'

'It is. Didn't you ever come here as a child?'

Eve shook her head. 'The greyhound sanctuary wasn't here then and you could buy the ice cream in town so I had no reason to visit. But it's beautiful.' She glanced nervously at him. 'Do the cows graze in here?'

'Sometimes, but you don't need to be afraid of them.'

'They're so big, though, aren't they? And solid.' She wrinkled her nose.

'You don't have a cow phobia?'

'No. I just wouldn't want to be up close to one. It might kick me or something.'

'Only if you startle it or annoy it. Most of the time they're pretty sedate and happy just to graze.'

'I'll take your word for it.'

At the end of the field, Jack opened a gate then stood back. 'After you.'

'Thank you.'

He closed the gate and latched it behind them. When he turned back to the track, Eve was already walking up to the farm. The morning sunlight made her short hair shine like gold. She'd dressed appropriately in jeans, trainers and a black jumper that was sheer enough for him to see that she wore a fitted T-shirt underneath. As she turned to him to beckon him forward, he could see her curves in profile. Seeing her like that, as she stood with the wind in her hair and roses in her cheeks, stirred him deep down. But he had to stay strong around her. Eve Carpenter had been through a lot recently and so had he, in the past. Sure, she was beautiful, funny and endearing – in her way – but that was where this had to end. There would be no getting closer to her this morning, or any morning for that matter.

'The scenery here is just breathtaking!' Eve said as he reached her side. 'It makes me sad yet happy. Do you ever get that?'

Jack followed her gaze across the fields, where the green and the yellow and the grey stone walls just stretched on and on. The view always comforted him because it made him feel that his own existence wasn't that important. He would only be here on earth for a short while, just like every other human, but that didn't matter. What mattered were moments like these where he could enjoy the view alongside another person; someone who understood. 'Yes. I know what you mean. In the grander scheme of things, we're pretty insignificant.'

'So whatever happens in my life, whether I'm a success in my chosen career or not… it doesn't really matter, does it?'

'Not as long as you're okay with it.' She was reaching for comfort, he knew it. She wanted him to reassure her, to tell her that being away from work didn't matter, so he did. 'You're doing the right thing, Eve. Don't worry about it now. It will all be okay.'

She met his eyes and he was rendered speechless by how hers glowed, their green so luminous it was shocking. His heart pounded so hard he could barely swallow.

'I think you're right – it will be okay. Being here makes me hope it will.'

'Do you know what you'll do if you don't go back?'

She worried her bottom lip then released a heavy sigh. 'I'm not sure, but I'm hoping the answer will come to me.'

'I'm sure it will.'

She nodded. 'If I go back... if I don't go back...' She didn't finish what she was about to say because a horn beeped behind them, making them both jump, and a vehicle pulled up alongside them.

'Jack!' It was Neil Burton, the farm owner.

'Hey, Neil!'

'Get in, both!'

Jack opened the Land Rover's front passenger door and gestured to Eve, but she shook her head and opened the back door, so he climbed in next to Neil.

'Neil, this is Eve, Mary's niece.'

'Nice to meet you, Eve.' Neil gave a quick sideways nod.

'You too.'

'So you're staying in Conwenna for a while, are you?'

'That's right, yes.'

'Good, good! So we'll be seeing more of you, then? Always the need for an extra pair of hands at the sanctuary, you know, or mucking out the cowsheds.' He chuckled and his jowls wobbled under his salt-and-pepper beard. He looked exactly like Jack had always imagined a farmer would, with his messy hair sticking out from under a flat cap and his green knitted jumper with elbow pads straining over his ample belly.

Jack turned in his seat and saw Eve smile at Neil in the rear-view mirror. He wondered if she realized that Neil was teasing.

Foxglove Farm consisted of a series of buildings. There was the original old farmhouse with an extension that had been added about twenty years ago; the two barns where Neil's animals were housed; then further back beyond the house, set in its own space, the converted stable block and yard that made up the greyhound rescue sanctuary. To the left of the farm, in one of the large fields that Neil used for crops for personal use, were two cottages that he rented out to tourists.

The farm was a mix and match of old and new and Neil and his employees were often seen repairing things because the funding for the rescue centre wasn't always consistent. Neil explained to Eve as he drove towards the buildings that he had inherited the farm from his father and his grandfather before him. Years ago it had thrived on supplying the local community with fruit and vegetables, but due to fluctuating prices of produce and the politics surrounding farming these days, he had decided to focus on the dairy farming side of the business and the resulting ice cream, which was made in an annexe at the back of the farmhouse by his wife and two long-term employees. The rest of his earnings came from renting the cottages, hiring out a field for the annual village fair, and the pony treks that one of his three sons ran.

Jack knew things were sometimes tight, but he'd rarely heard Neil complain. In his late fifties, he was old-fashioned like that: he maintained a stiff upper lip and just got on with things and made the best of it. But what Jack admired the most about him was his love of dogs and how he'd set up the rescue sanctuary three years earlier. He'd told Jack that when he died, he wanted to know that he'd made a difference, even if it was small, and Jack could understand that.

Neil pulled up in front of the farmhouse and cut the engine, then swung open the door and stepped down. Jack did the same then went round to help Eve out.

'So this is Foxglove Farm.'

Eve looked around. 'It's very pretty, isn't it?'

'It can be noisy with the dogs but the rental cottages are far enough away that they're not disturbed by the noise.'

'What about Neil and his family?'

Neil walked around the vehicle. 'We're used to it. Don't notice the racket any more when they start up.'

'And you work here regularly, Jack?'

'I do a few hours here and there, helping out with the dogs and some general maintenance. Whatever Neil needs, really.'

'Couldn't manage without him now,' Neil said, placing a heavy hand on Jack's shoulder. 'There's a new dog coming in for assessment this morning, Jack, if you could check her out.'

'Of course. Eve's going to shadow me for the day if that's okay?'

'More the merrier! Like I said, an extra pair of hands is always helpful.' Neil tweaked his flat cap at them. 'I'll see you later. Things to do, people to see and all that.' He walked across the yard and disappeared into one of the barns.

'So that's what I'm doing, is it? Shadowing?'

'If you like.' Jack saw the mischief in her eyes.

'Kind of like a secondment.'

'Perhaps we'd better discuss a wage for you then?'

'Oh no! Please don't do that. I wouldn't dream of it. I don't need paying.'

'I wasn't thinking about paying you in cash. I had a few other ideas in mind.'

Eve's cheeks turned pink and he realized why. 'I didn't mean that like it sounded. I meant that I'd take you out for dinner or something. Nothing... uh... untoward.'

'I didn't think that for a second, Jack. I guess it can't pay a lot anyway, though. With it being a charity.'

Jack smiled. 'Not really, but I'd probably do it for free.'

'But how do you manage?' Eve bit her lip. 'Sorry. That's none of my business.'

'It's fine. Nothing wrong with being curious. I have a modest pension from my time in service and a few other tricks up my sleeve. I get along all right. As would you.'

'I hope so. I don't mind the prospect of losing the money so much as the security of knowing who I am. Teaching has been where I've felt safe.'

'Perhaps now you'll find security in other ways. But enough chit-chat, underling, time to get you to work. I intend to take full advantage of this free labour for as long as possible.' He dusted his hands off dramatically.

Eve laughed and her face lit up. Jack's heart lifted at how mirth made her appear healthier and more relaxed. He realized that he wanted to see her smile more, to see the positive effects it had upon her, and he vowed to do what he could to make her stay enjoyable, because if Conwenna Cove had the same effect upon her as it'd had on him, then that would be good for Eve and good for Mary.

–

Jack and Eve crossed the yard that was sandwiched between the farmhouse and the smaller barn and headed for the stable block. She could already hear barking. From the front, it looked like a normal stable with its eight dark wooden doors and overhanging roof. When they reached it, Jack directed her around the back of the building and it was then that she noticed the kennel runs. They were like large cages, designed to give the dogs access to air, a short run and a toilet trip. At the far end of each run was what appeared to be a large dog flap set in the back wall of the stable block.

As Eve and Jack rounded the corner, they were greeted by a chorus of barks and howls as they were spotted by the dogs. Jack jogged up to the wire of the first pen and Eve jumped as a large fawn dog leapt against the wire.

'Hey there, boy, calm down,' Jack soothed as he rubbed the dog's muzzle through the fence.

Eve stood next to him and watched. 'That is a *big* dog!'

He nodded. 'Some of the male greyhounds are fairly large. But this fella, named Rolo, is a big softy, so you've nothing to fear.'

Eve slowly lifted her hand but the dog pulled back its paws then bounced against the wire again, making it rattle and causing her to gasp. She instinctively pulled her hand back and tucked it under her arm.

'It's okay, Rolo. Eve's new but she'll soon get used to you.'

The dog whined in response then licked Jack's fingers before bouncing around again.

They moved on to the next pen but Eve found her gaze dragged back to Rolo. 'How long has he been here?'

'About six weeks, I think.'

'Will he find a home?'

'Hopefully. We have a fairly high success rate, but some dogs take longer than others to find the right home. It depends on a variety of factors, such as what condition they're in when they arrive, how they are with people – especially children – and also how they are with other domestic animals like cats and small dogs. Rolo there is a handsome boy but if he's not good with cats or smaller dog breeds then that would obviously put some potential families off. In more fortunate cases, we find that the dogs can be trusted around smaller animals, but it doesn't always work. And sadly, some of them have been so badly treated before they make it here that...'

Eve scanned his face. 'They have to stay in the sanctuary?'

He nodded but didn't reply. Eve could tell from the bobbing of his Adam's apple that he found the subject emotional.

'That must be very sad. But at least they do have the sanctuary. That's a really positive thing.'

She placed a hand on the fence in front of her and peered through. She could see the dog flap moving slightly at the end of the run but nothing emerged. 'Who's in there?'

'That's our newest male arrival.'

'Is he shy?'

'Kind of...'

'What's his name?'

'Gabe.'

'Will he come out?'

'Probably. His curiosity usually gets the better of him.'

As Eve watched the flap open a fraction more, she sensed that the dog wanted to come out but needed some encouragement.

'Shall I call him?'

'You can try.'

'Gabe! Hey, boy... Come on out and say hello.' She waited and the flap lifted as if the dog was about to emerge.

'Come on, Gabe!' Jack called. The other dogs burst into a fresh round of barks and howls and Eve fought the urge to cover her ears.

'Gabe!' she tried again. 'Come on, sweetheart.'

As she watched the flap lift right up, her heart thundered. What would he look like? What condition would he be in? Would he be friendly or terrified?

She held her breath as a dark shape emerged slowly from the kennel. He padded along the concrete of the run then approached the fence slowly, cautiously, almost crawling towards them. Eve bit her lip then glanced at Jack. He was staring at the dog, his jaw tight, his fingers curled around the wire.

'Come on, Gabe.' Jack's voice was soft and low. He lowered into a crouch and Eve copied him.

Gabe finally reached them but kept his head down, his long neck stretching back to large shoulders. His black fur shone, outlining the powerful muscles that lay beneath. Eve's throat ached; such a large creature shouldn't be so afraid.

'Oh Jack!' She covered her mouth with a trembling hand.

Jack reached out and wrapped an arm around her shoulder. 'He was abused by the dog trainer who had him. Sadly it's the same story for lots of greyhounds. They're used to race, to make money, then cast off when they get injured or too old. Some of the puppies are culled before they even get to a racetrack because the trainers and breeders know they won't make good racers.'

'That's so awful.'

He sighed. 'I'm not saying that all greyhound trainers abuse their dogs, because they don't. There are some positive stories but the sport itself, in my mind, needs better regulation. In fact I'd go so far as to say it needs to be banned. But that's my opinion and there are those who would argue with me over it. I just get so sad when we see dogs that are afraid of people, when they come here bony and covered in sores where they've scratched flea bites, or their feet have been burned by standing in puddles of urine. It makes me so mad. And, of course, some dogs aren't raced at all.'

'What else are they used for?' Eve dreaded the answer.

'Hunting. Baiting.' He frowned. 'Two months ago we had a six-year-old female here named Cassie. Her face and front legs had multiple scars from where she'd been bitten by foxes and other smaller animals. Some people...' He shook his head.

Eve watched as a muscle in his jaw twitched. He was tense, his body rigid. He was angry that dogs had been hurt, angry that other dogs would continue to be hurt, and frustrated by the whole situation. Jack had a big heart and clearly struggled with what he saw as injustice.

Eve quickly wiped away a tear before it escaped and trickled down her cheek.

'But he'll be okay now, won't you, Gabe?' The dog lifted his head a fraction but his long tail stayed between his back legs. Large brown eyes stared at Jack then at Eve, the eyebrows above them rising in turn, as if he was trying to work out who could be trusted. His confusion pierced Eve's heart.

Suddenly she felt as if she would explode with sorrow.

'Jack, I can't stand it!' She stood up and the dog leapt backwards.

'Careful, Eve. Take it slowly.'

'Oh my goodness. I'm so sorry, Gabe.'

She stepped forward and pushed her fingers through the wire, but the dog lowered its head right down again and slunk away until it reached the back wall of the kennel, then turned and disappeared through the flap.

'I'm so, so sorry! I didn't mean to scare him.' Tears burst from her eyes and she sobbed as Jack caught hold of her and pulled her against his chest.

'Hey, it's okay,' he murmured into her hair. 'It's pretty emotional the first time you visit. I was the same.'

'What?' Eve croaked, her voice muffled by his hoodie.

'When I first came here, I didn't cry at the time, but later on, when I went home and sat there alone thinking about what I'd seen, it did break me.'

'You cried?' Eve asked, leaning back so she could see his face.

He nodded. 'Not like you, of course... all messy and snotty.'

She sniffed.

'But it did get to me more than I'd imagined it could.'

'But what... about...' Eve's voice caught as fresh sobs racked her frame. She was devastated that she'd frightened the gentle giant of a dog.

'Gabe will be okay. He's still settling in and within a few weeks you'll see a difference. I promise.'

Eve buried her face against Jack's chest again so he couldn't look into her eyes and read her thoughts. She realized that she wanted to see Gabe's transformation, that she'd love to see him grow in confidence and learn to trust people again. That she wanted to be one of the people he learned to trust. But a few weeks? Would she even be here then? She pushed the thought away, aware that it was too much to consider right now. She had things to sort through in her head, matters to put to rest before she'd be able to return to Bristol. She'd only intended taking a few days, a week at the most, but already she was doubting her original decision, reassessing its wisdom. Perhaps she needed longer than a few days to get better. Perhaps a few weeks would be more sensible. But how could she ring Amanda and break that news? It made her want to stay right where she was that minute, in the arms of a man she already felt so safe with. A man she'd let in, to her past and her present; someone who'd got closer to her in three days than any other human being had for a long time.

Whatever happened, she wanted to be around Jack and close to the sea for a while longer. When she was stronger, then she would deal with her long-term plans. But right now, Eve was going to overthrow the habit of what felt like a lifetime and live in the moment.

Chapter 9

'Come on then, Eve!'

'What?' Eve stared up at her aunt from her position on the sofa. She was worn out after a day up at the farm and just wanted to put her feet up and relax for a while. It wasn't just the physical aspect of the labour that had been hard but the deeper emotional impact of being around the dogs and hearing about what they'd experienced. All the dogs that she had met had been friendly, exuberant and even funny. Except for Gabe. And whenever Eve had thought about him, she'd filled up all over again.

She hadn't seen Gabe before she'd left but she had looked for him as they'd passed around the back of the stables. He must've been hiding inside, though. She had asked Jack again about the big black greyhound but he'd told her to come back to the farm with him later in the week and try again to win the dog's confidence. Persistence and patience were key, he said. Eve knew that while she was good at being persistent, patience was not her strongest quality, but if that was what she needed, then that was what she'd learn.

'We have some baking to do.'

'We do?'

Aunt Mary nodded and held out a hand. 'I know you're tired, but Irene is leaving tomorrow and I want to make her some cakes to take with her.'

Eve got to her feet and followed her aunt into the kitchen. 'You know I can't—'

'Bake?' Aunt Mary interjected. 'So you've said. But you'll learn.'

Eve went to the sink and washed her hands for what felt like the thousandth time that day, then put on the apron her aunt handed her and waited for instructions.

Aunt Mary handed her a portable scales and a bag of self-raising flour. 'Weigh out eight ounces, please.'

Eve stared at the flour.

'Go on, dear. It won't bite, you know.'

'Okay then!' Eve opened the bag of flour and coughed as it puffed up into her face.

'Careful, Eve, don't rush. Baking is an art, you know.'

'Art isn't one of my strengths either.'

'Well, with a nice white floury face like that, you could always head to the circus and be a clown instead.' Mary chuckled at her own joke and Eve grabbed a tea towel and wiped her face.

'You know, Eve, you didn't always rush things.'

'What?'

'When you were younger and you used to stay here with me, you were far more relaxed.'

'I was?'

'Oh yes. I mean, I know your parents were... uh... strict. And when you used to come here even as a very young child it would take you a few days, sometimes a week, to unwind, but it did happen and it was beautiful to see.'

Eve listened carefully, absorbing the information hungrily. So she hadn't always been so driven, so career-focused and uptight? She knew she'd enjoyed the summers here as a child, but now that Aunt Mary had mentioned it, she did seem to recall a time when she hadn't walked around with her shoulders taut with tension and when she'd been able to switch off her mind to do other things. *Like baking.* Yes, they had baked together when she'd stayed here, and if she remembered correctly, she'd enjoyed it.

'Life has been hard on you, dear. Sadly it is for everyone in some way or other, but we ride the highs and lows as we would a stormy sea and we must make sure we grab hold of the good times and savour them. Like today. For me, this is a good time, being here with my wonderful niece.'

Eve blinked hard. Her vision had blurred. She'd been pushing herself for so long that the idea of a time when she'd been happy just being, just existing, even if it was just the summers, seemed too wonderful. What if she could find that side of herself again and be the woman – or girl, even – who didn't have to pursue a career just to feel that she was worth something, just to feel some form of security.

Wouldn't that be just incredible?

Her aunt rubbed her shoulder then gave her a quick hug. 'It's okay, Eve. This is a difficult time for you but I promise it will pass. Everything does.'

Eve nodded. The words of comfort meant so much to her. It helped to be told that although she was in a whirling pit of indecision and confusion right now, she would come out the other side. What the other side looked like, she had no idea, but it was there, waiting for her to take the necessary steps to heal.

Aunt Mary released her then placed an upright cheese grater, a small plate and a large mixing bowl on the table, along with a box of eggs, a block of butter, two lemons and a bag of caster sugar. She cut a chunk off the butter. 'It needs to be room temperature for the chemistry to be right,' she explained as she dropped it into the bowl. She opened the bag of sugar then tipped a generous amount into the bowl with the butter.

'How much did you put in?' Eve asked, her throat finally loose enough for her to speak.

'About four ounces.'

'How'd you know you got it right? You didn't weigh it.'

Mary tapped the side of her nose. 'I've been doing this a long time, Eve. I'm kind of good at estimating.'

'Okay... What's next?'

'Zest one of the lemons over the small plate using the cheesegrater.'

Eve did as her aunt told her, being careful not to catch her fingers on the sharp metal.

'Now you cream the butter and sugar together until they're light and fluffy.'

'Cream?'

'Basically beat them together,' Aunt Mary replied.

Eve looked down at her thin arms. She'd removed her jumper when she got back from the farm and now just wore her black T-shirt.

'Yes, Eve. Give it some welly.' Aunt Mary smiled, then handed Eve a wooden spoon.

Five minutes later, Eve's right arm was aching and she had sweat on her brow but the mixture in the bowl was fluffy and her aunt nodded her approval.

'Now you beat four eggs in a separate bowl and gradually add them to the butter mixture. But mind they don't curdle.'

Eve tapped an egg against the smaller bowl that Mary had placed on the table and allowed the contents to slide out. 'Dammit!'

'What's wrong?'

'I got shell in there too.'

'Here...' Mary handed her a piece of kitchen roll. 'Use the corner of this to fish it out. No point wasting a whole egg.'

It took Eve about ten minutes to break all the eggs, because every time she broke another one, she lost a bit of shell. She shuddered as she imagined Irene biting into her favourite lemon drizzle cake only to crunch on a piece of eggshell. That would not be pleasant at all. Once she'd beaten them, she began to add them slowly to the butter and sugar. The mixture became bright yellow as the yolks blended into it and it slipped easily around the bowl.

'Add some flour if it's starting to curdle.'

Eve emptied some of the flour from the bowl of the scales into a sieve then shook it over the mixture.

'That's the way. I can see you're concentrating hard there, Eve, because your tongue is sticking out the corner of your mouth.'

'It is not!'

'Is so.' Mary winked at her and Eve stuck her tongue out further at her aunt, then giggled.

'Stop it now, I'm trying to concentrate.'

As she gradually added the rest of the flour, she was aware how good it felt to be doing something constructive. Something creative. And how good it was to be here with her aunt.

'Let me check it now.' Aunt Mary held out her hand for the wooden spoon. She tilted the bowl sideways and expertly spooned the mixture around. 'That's perfect, Eve. You just need to add the lemon zest then get it in the oven.'

Eve tipped the small plate of yellow zest over the bowl and brushed it into the mixture, then gave the whole thing another stir.

'It will take around forty-five minutes to cook,' Aunt Mary said as she placed a loaf tin lined with baking paper in front of Eve and helped her to pour the cake batter into it.

After Eve had slid the tin carefully into the oven, her aunt beamed at her. 'See! Not so hard after all.'

'No. That wasn't bad,' Eve said, as a surge of pride warmed her right through. 'Kind of like a workout too.' She rubbed her right bicep.

'Yes, baking can help keep bingo wings at bay!' Aunt Mary laughed and shook her own arms. 'Time for a nice cup of tea.'

Eve nodded. 'That would be lovely.'

When Eve removed the cake from the oven almost fifty minutes later, she placed the tin on the wire rack on the kitchen worktop and sighed. It smelt incredible. And she'd made it herself. With Aunt Mary's careful guidance, of course, but it was a start.

'What do I do now?'

'Prick it all over with a fork, then, as it's cooling, mix two tablespoons of caster sugar with the juice of both lemons and pour it over the top. It will create a crunchy drizzle once the cake has cooled.'

'I wish we'd made two of them now.' Eve licked her lips.

'Well, let Irene take this one and you can make another one later.'

'Good plan.'

Eve followed her aunt's instructions and soon the cake was covered in the sour-sweet drizzle.

'Well done, Eve! I told you you could do this.'

'With your help.'

'You're better than you think you are, dear. You just lack confidence. It's got lost in that job of yours. You can enjoy life too, you know. And you will.'

'I hope so.'

'This is just the start.'

Eve smiled at her aunt. She really hoped that what she said was right.

'I'm going to pop down into the village for a while. I'll take Irene with me so she can stretch her legs. If you want to try again, there are plenty of ingredients in there to use.' Mary gestured at the cupboards.

'I might just do that,' Eve replied.

As Aunt Mary left the kitchen, Eve wondered if she was going to see Edward again. It was none of her business, but she just hoped her aunt was happy, because she deserved to be. And Edward had seemed like a nice man. Perhaps he would feature in Mary's future plans.

She turned her attention back to the cupboards.

Her stomach flipped.

Could she do this? Could she bake unattended?

Why not?

What was the worst that could happen?

–

Two hours later, Eve slumped at the kitchen table with her head in her hands. Her back and arms ached and two of her fingers had plasters on. She was exhausted and beyond disappointed.

'My oh my! What happened here?'

She raised her head to find Jack standing in the doorway gazing at the mess.

'It looks like a dragon just came and breathed fire on everything.'

Eve buried her face in her arms again. 'I know,' she mumbled.

'Pardon?' Jack approached her.

She lifted her head. 'I said I know.'

'But what *did* happen? I mean, since dragons don't exist. At least not to my knowledge.'

'It's not funny!' Eve snapped, her cheeks burning. She must look like such an idiot. Every surface was covered in pots, pans and tins, each one filled with some form of burnt offering.

In front of her on the table was a cake-batter-splodged cookery book by a well-known celebrity baker that Eve had found on Mary's kitchen shelf. She'd decided to try to stretch herself and rather than making another lemon drizzle cake, which would have been the sensible thing to do, of course, had attempted some much more complicated delights. Only they didn't look anything like delights when she'd removed them from the oven.

'I tried to run before I could walk.'

Jack sat opposite her and placed his large hand over one of hers. 'There's nothing wrong with a bit of ambition.'

Eve stared into his laughing brown eyes. She knew he was being kind but she was irritated with herself. 'I should just stick to what I *am* good at.'

'And what's that?' he asked, his expression neutral, his head tilted.

'Oh… I don't know… My job!' Eve gulped. 'Oh my job!' She collapsed onto her hands again and tried to squeeze away the tears that stung her eyes. She bit her lip hard, but try as she might, she couldn't escape her despair, and she started to shake.

The sobs came in big, gulping waves that racked her frame. She felt like she'd never stop until strong hands took hold of her shoulders and she was turned on her chair to face Jack, who now knelt in front of her. He pulled her firmly against his hard chest and enveloped her in his warm, powerful arms. The kindness of his gesture and the fact that he knew what she needed in that moment made her heart crack, which made her cry harder.

How could she feel so safe in this man's embrace? She'd never felt like this with Darryl. In fact no man had ever had this effect on her before. Being in Jack's arms was like coming home; he made her feel like she belonged there. But that was silly. Eve hardly knew him and she'd always sworn that she'd never rely on anyone else for a sense of security. Darryl hadn't provided it; it just wasn't the type of man he was. Although she now wondered if she had been glad of that, as it meant she hadn't depended on him too much so she couldn't be let down. Her parents hadn't provided it, not when she was a child or at any point in her life, come to think of it. In fact the only person who'd ever given Eve anything remotely near to love and security was Aunt Mary.

And now there was Jack.

He smelt so good.

He felt so good.

The sound of his strong heartbeat was just so good.

He made Eve feel… so good.

She raised her face and his stubble grazed her forehead and nose. He gazed down at her and she melted into the chocolate-brown depths of his eyes, losing herself in his warmth as a delicious yearning flowed through her. It was like waking up after a long sleep.

She slid her arms around his neck, curled her hands in his hair then leaned closer, closer, until her lips found his.

For a moment, he didn't move.

Then he gently pulled away and slipped out of her embrace.

Eve froze. Blinked hard. Sniffed.

What did I just do?

'Oh my God, I'm so sorry!' She covered her mouth. 'I didn't mean to do that! I was just… You were just… Oh, I'm so embarrassed.' She jumped up and went to the sink. *What an idiot!* What had made her think he'd want her? But then she hadn't been thinking, had she? *Oh no!* She had just been feeling, giving in to the need that coursed through her whenever Jack was around. She turned and stared at him as though she could barely believe he was still there.

'Eve!' Jack's face was pale. 'It's okay. I didn't mean to hurt you. I did want to kiss you but I'm just… I just have… uh… some issues.'

Eve waved a hand. 'You don't have to explain anything to me. It was nothing but a blip! I was just emotional and you're so kind and I was totally out of order. Please, say no more about it!' Her heart pounded and blood whooshed through her ears.

Jack opened his mouth and seemed about to speak, then he shook his head and rubbed his big hands over his face.

'I'd better clean this up.' Eve gestured at the mess.

Jack nodded. 'Let me give you a hand.'

'No. Please. Just go.' *Go! Leave me with my shame.*

'Eve, friends help each other out, and I thought that was what we were becoming.'

She bit her lip. *Friends.* Of course.

'Yes. Okay. Thank you. That would be really kind.'

But I still wish you'd go.

She pulled on rubber gloves, then picked up a cake tin and started hacking at the burnt mess with a knife. She was mortified but she knew it wasn't Jack's fault. If he wanted to be her friend, then that was fine with her. Eve didn't have many friends and she should be grateful that Jack actually wanted to be one. After what she'd just done, he could have stormed out and never spoken to her again and she would have understood.

Because that was what she always did… she pushed people away.

But Jack wanted to stay. To help and support her.

So why did her chest ache as if she'd been punched? Why did she feel breathless as if that punch had left her winded? Was there a part of her that wanted more from Jack? Even if she did, he'd just made it perfectly clear that all she could ever hope for from him was a platonic relationship.

She'd have to make do with that.

But she didn't know if she could.

—

Jack finished drying the mixing bowl then tucked it into the correct cupboard. He'd eaten many meals at Mary's since moving in as her tenant and had always washed and dried the dishes to show his gratitude. It had been an hour since he'd found Eve in the disaster site that had been Mary's once spotless and organized cottage kitchen, but now it was finally clean and tidy.

As they'd worked, Eve hadn't said much to him but he'd sensed that she was hurt. He hadn't wanted to cause her any pain, but when she'd kissed him, something inside him had exploded and he'd panicked. He was attracted to her, of course he was, but she was wounded and here in Conwenna to heal. Then she would leave. And Jack would stay.

He wanted to get to know her but he was also becoming increasingly afraid. He really liked her, and the barriers he'd erected around himself to keep love out were weakening in her presence. If he let her in, what was there to stop her hurting him just like his wife had done?

Jack had rebuilt himself and his life once before; he didn't know if he could do it again. He didn't know if he *wanted* to do it again. It had been so hard the first time. He knew what it was like to try to maintain a long-distance relationship – he'd done it with Jodie when he was in Afghanistan – and though Bristol might not be that far away, it was far enough. He knew that Eve was a career woman, and that she might go back to her job. If something happened between them, how would he fit into her life? Would she ever have time to visit him here?

Because there was one thing Jack knew for certain: he couldn't face the idea of moving to a city. He needed to be near the sea, the open space of the horizon that allowed him to breathe. Being in a city would suffocate him with its noises, its towering buildings and its hustle and bustle. He'd tried it after his return from duty, when he'd lived in London for a while. He'd been able to see why other people loved the thriving capital with its proximity to everything a person could want, but it just wasn't for him. And it wasn't who he was any more. He needed the freedom of Conwenna Cove, of a seaside haven, and falling in love with a woman who worked in a big city wouldn't work for him. Or for her. So it was better that they remain just friends.

'You know, Eve. This one doesn't look too bad.' Jack poked at a circular sponge that Eve had tipped onto a plate.

'It's meant to be a Victoria sandwich.'

'So it is,' Jack replied, as he leaned closer and saw the jam in the middle of the two layers. 'Could I test it?'

Eve pursed her lips. 'I'm not sure that's a good idea...'

'Oh come on. I'm quite peckish now. Worked up an appetite with all that clearing up.' He patted his stomach.

Eve offered a small smile. 'Go on then.' She cut a slice of the cake, put it on a plate and handed it to him.

He bit into the cake and his mouth was flooded with the sweetness of a soft, light sponge followed by the summery taste of Mary's home-grown strawberries. He chewed, swallowed, then took another bite.

Eve stood in front of him, eyes wide. She watched every mouthful, until he'd eaten it all.

'And?' She raised her eyebrows and the vulnerability in her eyes made him want to reach out and hug her.

'Absolutely delicious.' He licked his lips.

'You're lying, Jack. It looks like a burnt Frisbee.'

'I'm not, I swear! It's light and crumbly. The flavour is perfect. And yes, the outside is slightly well done but I quite like that about it. It's tasty, I promise.'

Eve flushed, which made her even prettier, and he wondered for a moment if she coloured like that when she was aroused. He shook the wayward thought away. It was something he would never know.

'Okay then. Thank you.'

'No problem.' He watched as she flicked a tea towel over the Aga's front to dust away flour that had landed there, then tucked her hands into her jean pockets. She stood in the middle of the kitchen as if unsure about what came next. It was all Jack could do not to cross the room and pull her into his arms again. He'd liked holding her, cradling her petite frame against his chest. She was delicate, fragile, and it made something in him want to take care of her; to make her feel better. But it was dangerous territory. To get close to her, emotionally or physically, was risky for him and for her. He'd better make his exit now, while his willpower was still strong.

'I'd better get going now, Eve. Thanks for the cake. I'll uh… see you tomorrow.'

'Really? You don't have to go, Jack. I could make us a cup of tea.'

'No. I've got things to do. But thanks.'

Stay strong!

'Sure,' she replied. 'Okay. I'll see you tomorrow then.'

She turned away and left the kitchen, but not before Jack caught a glimpse of the hurt in her eyes. And it made him feel pretty bad. Being strong certainly had its drawbacks.

Chapter 10

When Eve woke in the morning, everything that had happened the previous day came back to her and she groaned. She should never have tried to kiss Jack. It was uncharacteristic of her; not the controlled, self-reliant woman she'd become. Perhaps the old Eve, the girl she'd once been, according to Aunt Mary, might have been *that* forward, that bohemian in her behaviour and attitude, but Eve Carpenter, head teacher, did not go around kissing random men then feeding them cake. And burnt cake at that!

But Jack had enjoyed the cake.

She believed him about that.

And she knew as clearly as she knew it was Tuesday morning that she wanted to be his friend. She'd go round there after breakfast and take him the rest of the Victoria sponge as a token of their burgeoning friendship. To show there were no hard feelings about him not wanting to ravish her last night… or ever, for that matter.

She pulled on her dressing gown and made her way downstairs, keen to find out what had happened to Aunt Mary last night. She'd heard her aunt coming home around eleven, which she'd been surprised at as it was quite late, but then why shouldn't Mary go out? It had been Irene's last night with them, so she hoped the two women had enjoyed themselves.

She found Irene and Mary at the kitchen table drinking tea. They were both dressed and Eve was surprised when she looked at the clock to find it was gone ten.

'I can't believe how well I'm sleeping here.'

Mary filled a mug then handed it to her. 'I'm glad you're resting, Eve. You need it.'

'So where did you two dirty stop-outs get to last night?' Eve winked at Irene to show she was joking.

'Your aunt took me for a stroll along the front, then we went for ice cream.'

'Until eleven?'

'Well, we might have popped in to Edward's for a nightcap.' Mary chuckled, then lowered her eyes to her mug.

'He had my favourite brandy.' Irene nodded. 'And we sang some old songs on his games computer thingy.'

Eve nearly inhaled her tea. 'You what?'

'Edward has a console with a musical game. You can play pretend instruments and sing karaoke.'

Irene nodded.

Eve watched them both. Were they pulling her leg? Edward had to be in his late sixties and he had a games console that he played on with her aunt and Irene?

'Don't look so surprised, Eve. He can't be out fishing all the time, you know. He has to have some down time.' Mary flashed her a big grin then stood up. 'Right, let's get you some breakfast. You look better than you did when you arrived, but it'll take more than a long weekend to build you up.'

Eve loosened the belt of her dressing gown. If Mary intended to make her breakfast, she suspected she'd need a bit of growing room.

Once she was washed and dressed in jeans and a pale blue T-shirt that was a bit on the big side but that she thought flattered her skin tone, Eve skipped down the stairs to the kitchen. She picked up the plate with the rest of the Victoria sponge on it, then covered it in foil.

Irene's daughter was due after lunch, so Mary and Irene were in the living room enjoying an antiques programme on the TV and drinking yet another cup of tea. It was the perfect opportunity for Eve to slip out and take the cake to Jack.

She went out the back door then right around Mary's house and past the front window. Eve moved quickly, hoping that her aunt and Irene would be too engrossed in the value of antiques to notice her. But when she knocked on Jack's front door, there was no answer.

She tried again. Her stomach flipped as she stood there wondering what to do. She was already a bit apprehensive after last night's embarrassment, but she believed it would be better to see him sooner rather than later, in order to put her silly attempt at kissing him behind her. But he wasn't answering the door. Did he know it was her? Was he avoiding her deliberately?

I could just go.

But no; that wasn't her. Eve confronted her fears. She didn't let things simmer. That was how things went wrong and she lost the people she cared about.

Hoping Jack hadn't heard her knocking, she went around the side of Jack's cottage then lifted the catch on the gate and let herself in to his back garden. It was a mirror image of Mary's in size and shape, but it didn't have the raised beds and fruit trees. Instead, there were a few barrel halves with a variety of wild flowers growing in them – for the bees, she guessed – and a beautiful carved bench under the kitchen window. She peered through the glass but she couldn't see any movement, so she tried the door. It was locked. Where was he? Perhaps he'd gone to the farm. She thought about leaving the cake on the bench but decided it would probably attract insects or even rodents. She'd have to bring it to him later.

As she was about to go back through the gate her eyes fell on the shed. What was it that Jack did in there? She almost laughed at her earlier suspicion that he might be growing marijuana. He didn't seem that type at all. But she was still curious. What did he get up to in there in just his jeans? Would it be open?

If it was, she could have a peek. It wouldn't hurt, would it?

She approached cautiously, aware that Jack could be inside. The padlock was off, hanging from the open clasp at an angle. She raised her hand and knocked. No answer. She took hold of the doorknob and turned it, and the door swung open. Still holding the plate in one hand, she entered the shed and waited for her eyes to adjust.

Tiny motes of dust floated in the air, catching the sunlight that filtered through a gap in the curtains covering a small window to her right. She paused as her first step caused the wooden planks of the floor to creak. She shouldn't be doing this, entering Jack's private property when he wasn't here and without his permission, but a desire to know more about him that burned brighter every minute pushed her on.

A smell greeted her nostrils and she tried to place it. Something to do with school... and the art rooms.

That was it. The chalky-earthy scents of paint, canvas and charcoal.

The small space was warm and stuffy, even mid-morning, and she could understand now why Jack often came out here in a state of undress. That was one part of the mystery solved. But the other – what he did out here – now became clear too. Balanced against the far wall and the one to her left were canvases. As she approached, she could see that they were all draped with what appeared to be white dust sheets. To her right, just before the window, stood an easel, and on it was another canvas, though this one was uncovered.

She moved closer, even as a voice at the back of her mind screamed at her not to do this; to leave and leave now. Before it was too late. But she couldn't. She was drawn to the canvas.

Her mouth fell open as she gazed at the charcoal sketch in front of her. Never before had she seen anything so beautiful, so lifelike, so pure yet so full of pain. She lifted her free hand, about to touch the surface just to check if it was real, if it was actually there before her, when she was startled by a sound behind her: the creaking of the floorboard at the entrance to the shed.

She turned, slowly, guiltily, to find Jack standing there, his feet apart, his huge body filling the doorway. The light was behind him, so she couldn't make out his expression clearly, but she could sense the anger and disappointment drifting off him like smoke from a fire. It filled the shed, stifling her and making her take small, desperate breaths. Her heart hammered and her vision blurred – just for a few seconds – and she cursed her own curiosity for getting her into this mess.

Not now! Not another panic attack. Not here!

'What the hell do you think you're doing, Eve?' Jack's voice was sharp as a blade as it sliced through the air.

Eve swallowed hard then held out the plate she carried. Her palms were sweaty and the cake suddenly seemed to be far heavier than it had been.

'I… I came to…' She swallowed again. Her mouth was as dry as sand and her throat constricted, choking her.

'Came to what? To pry? To spy?' He took a step into the room, then another, until he was so close she could have touched him. She stared up into his face and dismay filled her. He was furious and he had every right to be.

'No… I… Oh Jack, I'm so sorry. I didn't mean to come in here but I brought you the rest of the cake because you said you liked it and I wanted to see you smile again and… and…' To her horror, tears sprang into her eyes. It was as though all she did whenever Jack was around was cry. It had happened far too often for her liking since she'd arrived at Conwenna Cove and it was so uncharacteristic of her. This wasn't Eve Carpenter; this was an imposter. She had been invaded by some sort of strange emotional body-snatcher.

'This is my personal space, Eve. I might be your aunt's tenant but I have every right to privacy. *You* had no right at all to come in here… even if you were bringing me cake!' He waved at the plate and Eve took a step backwards as her legs wobbled.

'I know, Jack. I know I had no right, but this…' She gestured at the canvas on the easel. 'This is incredible. Beautiful. I didn't know you were an artist!'

'Why would you? We hardly know each other.' His voice was cold, his eyes now unreadable. This wasn't the Jack she knew, the Jack she'd been getting to know, the Jack who had said he wanted to be friends.

'No. Of course. You're right.' Eve lifted her head and stepped towards him, hoping that he'd move out of the way and let her pass. For a moment he didn't move. She wondered if she'd have to ask him to move aside, but then he took a step to his right to allow her to go.

She stepped out into the fresh air of the pretty cottage garden and gulped it down, trying to clear her head, to ward off the anxiety before it enveloped her in its agonizing darkness.

What have I done?

She didn't dare turn around to see if Jack was following her out. She couldn't bear to see the anger and disappointment in his gaze again.

As she hurried down the steps and towards the side gate, the cake slipped off the plate and landed on the ground, but she didn't stop to pick it up. The birds could have it, the ants could have it, the foxes that came down from the fields could have it. Eve had just been reminded of a very valuable lesson. It was foolish to start to care about someone, anyone, especially a man. Surely she should have learnt this by now. If you cared for your parents, they would hurt you. If you cared for a man, or he cared for you, something would change, and you would lose the bond you once thought you shared. *Or had hoped to share.* If you loved the babies growing inside you, you would lose them.

Eve had known that Jack didn't want her in a romantic way, but now she knew that there were even limits to the friendship he was offering. As there always were. Everything was limited, contained by boundaries that the eye didn't always see and the heart didn't always recognize.

Perhaps it was time for Eve to consider going back to Bristol, because it seemed that even here, in this beautiful idyll where she had hoped to heal and find peace, disaster could find her and fill her heart with pain.

Perhaps she had needed this lesson to remind her that no one could run from reality.

Not even her.

Especially not her.

Chapter 11

Despite Eve's best efforts and some pretty strong medication, the anxiety she had experienced brought on a blinding headache, and when the pain took hold, it set in worse than ever. She spent the rest of the day, then the whole of the following day, in bed with the curtains drawn. The only time she stirred was to accept the water that Aunt Mary brought her, along with more painkillers, which she swallowed dutifully.

In the solitary darkness, waves of guilt washed over her, making her nauseous: guilt that she was bedridden, guilt that she wasn't at work where she should be and guilt that she'd offended Jack by prying into his space. But she had to let the negative feelings go, she knew that, or she'd never recover.

By Thursday, she was well enough to sit up and accept some soup that Aunt Mary brought her, and she listened as her aunt relayed the story of Irene's departure for her daughter's home in Plymouth. She had even smiled when Aunt Mary described how Irene had been about to leave when she'd become concerned that she'd forgotten her glasses. Her daughter had told her to check her handbag, which she had, only to scream then empty its contents all over the floor in the hallway. Of course, a live mouse had fallen out and scampered across the floor and out through the front door, closely pursued by Tulip. It seemed that the cat was so fond of Irene that it had given her a parting gift to take home with her.

Her aunt hadn't stayed much longer, sensing that Eve was tired, and when she'd left, Eve had sat up in bed for a while thinking over her situation. She clearly wasn't well enough to return to Bristol yet, but she'd upset Jack badly. What if he was permanently furious with her for invading his privacy? And what about what she'd seen there on the canvas before her? Did he actually carry that around with him every day in his heart and his head?

Her initial reaction to his anger had been shock, then distress, then anger of her own. But that had faded quickly as she'd become fully aware of what Jack had been through. He was just so big, so strong and so sensible. To realize that he had his own troubles, such real, painful and evidently raw troubles, made her heart beat for him in a manner that made her want to hold him and make it all better. The emotions swirling around in Eve were puzzling her, yet not all in a bad way. She had been closed down for so long, shut off from love and devotion and even sexual attraction, but this man, with his ability to make her smile, with his strength and vitality – as well as his now not so secret vulnerability – was stirring her. The only way she could describe it to herself was as though she'd been in some form of stasis and now she was slowly, yet in full Technicolor, being brought back to consciousness.

Worn out by her musings, she'd fallen asleep again and when she'd woken it had been daylight. A quick glance at her mobile confirmed that it was now Friday morning. She still had a slight fuzziness around the edges from the migraine, a bit like a hangover, but she felt stronger than she had done in days. Today would be the day that she got up and tried to resolve matters with Jack. It was clear from what she'd seen that he could do with a friend too, whatever he believed, and she was determined to be that friend.

–

'It's good to see you up and about, Eve,' Aunt Mary said as she handed her a mug of tea that Eve accepted gratefully.

'It's good to *be* up and about, believe me.' Eve blew on the surface of the tea and cradled the mug in both hands. 'I went for years without suffering from a migraine, then they came back with a vengeance. I hope it's just temporary and linked to the anxiety I've been experiencing.'

Mary nodded. 'I recall your father suffering from them when he was a teenager. Of course, back then people weren't so understanding. Our parents thought he was either trying it on and being lazy, or using some illegal substance that made him ill.'

Eve wondered how her father had dealt with that. The man she knew had always been so aloof, so in control of his own world. Had he felt that his parents neglected him?

'What were your parents like?'

Mary paused and pressed her lips together. 'Didn't your father ever tell you about them?'

Eve shook her head. 'Whenever I asked, he never gave me much. He just said they were distant. Which is a bit ironic, I guess, in light of what he and my mother have been like.'

Mary nodded. 'Such a shame that they, uh, didn't appreciate you, dear. I'm sure they just never realized how you felt.'

'I'm not feeling sorry for myself, Aunt Mary. That passed a long time ago, that longing for doting parents who'd shower me with love.' She gave a wry laugh.

'Your parents were very lucky to have you, Eve. It's not my place to say, perhaps, but they should be here, even now, supporting you through all of this.'

'Maybe. But then I am a grown-up.'

Mary smiled. 'You'll always be little Eve to me; the pretty blonde girl who came to stay with me in the long, hot summers and taught me that there was fun to be had in the simple things.'

'I taught you that?'

Mary nodded. 'After I... well, after I went through my own... loss, you helped me come back to life again. I looked forward to our summers so much, Eve. You have no idea.'

'For my part, I just loved coming here. I felt cared about, spoilt, adored even. All children want and deserve that, don't they?' Eve sipped her tea. What was the loss that Mary had referred to? She couldn't recall her aunt being anything other than jovial when she'd been a child. Or having a boyfriend or anyone special around. 'You said you lost someone,' she said. 'I didn't know that.'

'Oh, it was a long time ago, dear. Such a long time, and so much has happened since then. I was going to tell you about your grandparents, wasn't I?'

'Please.' She realised her aunt was changing the subject, but she didn't want to push her on the subject of her loss. Not if she didn't want to discuss it. Besides, Eve was keen to know more about her grandparents.

–

Eve and Mary strolled down to the village. The morning was bright and breezy and Eve breathed deeply, enjoying the fresh salt-scented air. Her head was clearing by the minute as the remains of the migraine passed and she was relieved to be able to leave her bedroom and get outside. Being cooped up in the darkness didn't help her frame of mind, but when the pain had struck, she'd had no choice. Today she felt more positive, more capable, and she hoped that later on she would have the opportunity to speak to Jack and apologise. She just hoped he'd let her.

The discussion with Aunt Mary about her grand-parents hadn't revealed much more than she'd already known. Her aunt's version was the same as her father's: their parents had married young following an unplanned pregnancy. He worked in a factory and she kept house. When he'd died in his forties, following an accident at the factory, his wife had followed a year later, apparently just giving up after she lost her husband. It was a tragic story, especially as they'd left a son and daughter, but her father and Aunt Mary had built their own lives. It did give Eve a bit more insight into why her father wasn't a good parent; he hadn't, after all, been set a good example, but times were different then and the emphasis on nurturing children had somewhat changed. But she also believed that some people just shouldn't be parents; what was the point in having a child if you couldn't love it? Or give it the time it would need?

Her heart fluttered at the final thought and she rubbed a hand over her chest. This was not the time for painful memories.

'Here it is, Eve. Just along this street.'

They walked to the end of a narrow cobbled street and stood in front of iron railings that topped a stone wall.

The building was an old church that had been revamped to create a childcare facility, and it now displayed a large banner across the front: *Conwenna Kidz Daycare Centre: Open 8 til 8 weekdays.*

The windows were open as much as the security locks would allow, and the excited shouts and squeals of young children filtered out into the morning. Eve's stomach lurched.

'Shall we go in?' Mary asked, taking her arm.

'Uh… I don't know. I'm suddenly wondering if this is such a good idea after all.'

Mary had talked Eve into attending a reading hour at the daycare centre. When she had told Eve that she volunteered there once a fortnight and suggested that her niece accompany her this morning, Eve had been surprised yet pleased, but now she wondered if being around small people would be beneficial or detrimental.

'Eve, they're just children.'

'I don't have my CRB information. Surely they can't let me in without that?'

'You're a head teacher, for goodness' sake, and my niece. I can vouch for you, and if they need to check up on you, they can request a copy via email or even fax from your school.'

'Yes, but I'm… Oh, Aunt Mary, I'm nervous.'

'Why, dear?' Mary wrapped an arm around Eve's shoulders.

'I feel bad for leaving my own school, for not being there right now caring for the pupils I'm responsible for.'

'Eve, you are not indispensable, however hard it seems to accept it. That's something you need to learn. Your deputy head and the rest of your staff will be taking care of things there. You are, however, a human being with human frailties and that means that you need to rest and recover. Being around children is one way to remember why we're here.'

Eve nodded. What Mary said made sense. If only the butterflies in her stomach would listen to her aunt and calm down, she was sure she'd feel a lot better.

'I can do this.'

'Of course you can. You can even read them a story.'

They walked into the small front yard and Mary pressed the button on an intercom next to the front door. Once they were buzzed in, they entered a large open space painted in a bright sunflower yellow. Sunlight shone through the long stained-glass windows in the side wall and cast myriad colours across the busy room. The theme was open plan but there were smaller areas cordoned off with bookshelves and waist-high room dividers, and Eve noted that there was what appeared to be a lounge, a painting section and a library. Further back, there was a door that led to what she assumed was the kitchen, another that had a sign saying *Nursery* on it, with a picture of a cot, and to the right of that, two doors leading to the toilets.

And in amongst the bookshelves and the room dividers and the adults wearing purple T-shirts and matching lanyards featuring the centre's name were the little people. Lots and lots of tiny human beings, all intent on getting what they wanted, when they wanted it, from whatever target they zoomed in on.

'Come on, Eve. Steel yourself!' Mary said as she guided Eve to the reception desk, where she introduced her to the manager and some of the other members of staff.

An hour later, Eve found herself in the library area surrounded by children. Amanda had emailed through a copy of her CRB check – the manager had been apologetic but insisted that she had to abide by the rules – which had caused Eve some flutters of panic. She had spoken to Amanda on the phone and told her she didn't want her colleagues asking why she could be in Conwenna Kidz but not at her own school, but Amanda had told her that she needed to do as many ordinary things as possible in order to recover and that any doctor would tell her the same. Eve had done her best to believe her friend.

She gazed at the tiny faces of the children as they sat listening to Aunt Mary. She was reading a popular story to them about a terrible dragon that lived in a wood but tried to hide its phobia of squirrels. Eve held her breath as Mary neared the climax of the story, pausing for effect. A small girl with long brown hair in bunches moved closer to where Eve sat on a beanbag and sneaked her hand into Eve's. Eve started and almost pulled away, but then the girl popped a thumb into her mouth. Her big blue eyes were clear and innocent and she could only have been about four. Eve was used to working with tall, city-toughened teenagers, so to be with young children was very different. Yet nice and somehow soothing.

'Are you okay?' she whispered to the little girl, whose hand was rather clammy.

'It's a bit scary,' she whispered back.

'It'll be okay now,' Eve said, trying to adopt a reassuring expression. 'The dragon will be fine.'

'He will?' the girl asked.

Eve nodded, then placed a finger over her lips and pointed at her aunt. How did you explain the concept of learning to overcome your fears to a four-year-old with sticky hands?

Mary finished the story with a flourish and all the children cheered.

'I'm Joanne,' the little girl said. She stood up and touched Eve's hair. 'Your hair's short like a boy's.'

'Uh… I guess it is.'

'But I like it. It's soft.' Joanne stroked Eve's hair, then giggled.

'Thank you.' Eve smiled at her new friend, then gasped as the tiny girl threw herself at her and hugged her.

'Are you okay there?' It was Karen, the manager. 'Joanne not being too bossy, is she?'

'No. Not at all,' Eve replied. 'She's just being… friendly.'

'Time for some squash and fruit then, children?' Karen asked as Aunt Mary placed the book back on a shelf.

'Yay!' Joanne cheered as she ran with the other children over to a seating area decked out with small tables and chairs.

'See, that wasn't so bad, now was it?' Aunt Mary asked.

'No. I quite enjoyed it. But thanks for not making me read. I needed to see how it was done. I'd have been too nervous to do it justice,' Eve replied.

'Maybe next time, dear. Now, how about a coffee?'

'Sounds like a good plan.' Eve picked up her bag and followed Mary out into the sunshine, with thoughts of the brave dragon who learned to overcome his phobia of squirrels dancing around in her mind.

Chapter 12

Eve strolled along the street arm-in-arm with her aunt. Occasionally, they stopped to gaze in a shop window at the typical seaside gifts and souvenirs on offer, and Eve felt her spirits lifting as if the soft, warm breeze of the afternoon were capable of taking away her troubles and concerns.

They paused outside a small coffee shop and Mary asked, 'Shall we go in here? They serve the best lattes and the most delicious cakes.'

'Definitely,' Eve replied, her mouth watering at the prospect.

They entered the cafe and a small bell above the door tinkled. There were a few customers sitting at small round tables, chatting quietly or reading newspapers, but there were plenty of other tables to choose from. As they took a table near the window, Eve looked around at the pretty interior. It was painted buttercup yellow, giving it a warm atmosphere, and the walls featured hearts and boats made out of driftwood. On the far wall she spotted a greyhound painting. Her heart picked up its pace as she peered at it, realizing it resembled the ones Jack had pointed out at the art gallery.

'Hello, Mary! How are you today?' A man with a small goatee beard and messy blonde hair that looked as though it had been repeatedly bleached by the sun and never brushed appeared at their side with a notepad and pen.

'Ah, hello, Nate. I'm very well, thank you. How are you?'

The man smiled and nodded. 'I'm good too, thank you. Busy preparing for the buzz in two weeks' time, but it's good for business, so can't complain.'

'This is my niece, Eve.'

Nate held out a hand and shook Eve's firmly. 'Pleasure to meet you, and welcome to Conwenna Cafe! Not the most original name for a cafe in Conwenna Cove, but hey, it fits, right? Between you and me, it's my aunt and uncle's fault.' He grinned, and Eve smiled back; his enthusiasm was infectious, and she couldn't help noticing that he had the most piercing blue eyes.

'It's lovely in here and I love the name,' she replied. 'I also really like that painting you have… of the greyhound.' She gestured at the far wall.

'Ah, yes! From our local talent.'

'Local?' she asked.

'Yes, of course! Mary's tenant is quite the artist!' Nate twirled his pen around above the notepad as if imitating painting. 'You can purchase his works at the local gallery, or even commission one if you're feeling that way inclined.'

Eve swallowed hard. So Jack painted more than just the scenes she'd seen in the shed, and he was modest about it too. Yet what she'd seen there had made her heart ache and she wanted to speak to him about it and soon. Of course, he might not open up to her, he might just tell her to get stuffed, but she had to at least try.

'Anyway, lovely ladies, what can I get you?' Nate waved his hand at the chiller cabinet in front of the counter. 'We have a delicious lemon tart on special today, made with the finest local ingredients, or some good old-fashioned scones that I can serve with blackcurrant jam and clotted cream.'

Eve knew she wouldn't be able to resist the scones.

'Eve? Tea and scones?' Mary asked as if reading her mind.

'Please. Earl Grey tea if you have it.'

'Of course! For both of you?'

'Yes please.' Mary nodded.

Nate disappeared to sort their order and Mary settled back in her seat.

'He seems nice,' Eve said.

'Quite a dish, too!' Mary winked. 'He's about your age and, I think, quite single.'

'Aunt Mary!' Eve shot her aunt a warning glance.

Mary held up her hands in a show of surrender. 'What? Just letting you know what talent we have around here.' But her mischievous grin said otherwise. 'No, on a more serious note, Nate is a lovely young man. He's very friendly and kind. He's been in Conwenna for about five years and he helps his aunt and uncle out with the cafe. You remember Kevin and June Bryson?'

'The names do sound familiar.'

'Well they've been here for donkey's years but bought Conwenna Cafe about ten years ago. June worked locally as a secretary and Kevin used to commute for work, something to do with insurance, but they gave up their jobs when they bought the cafe and I don't think they've ever looked back.'

Eve nodded to show she was listening, but she was starting to notice a familiar theme here: that of leaving a city job to live and work in Conwenna Cove. She had to admit that it was tempting.

'What about Nate? Why did he come here?'

'To be with his family. His father passed away tragically young, and Nate packed in his job, sold his flat and came to Conwenna. Plus, of course, he's a surfer.'

'So he makes the most of living in Cornwall?'

'Indeed he does. Anyway, how are you feeling now, Eve?'

'Relaxed.'

'Your face looks better but... I don't know... you're still worrying about things, aren't you?'

Eve sighed. 'I can't help it. I have so much responsibility back in Bristol. I can't just switch off, even though I'm trying. I know I should be there, doing, rather than here... not doing.'

'All in good time.' Aunt Mary's voice was firm. 'If you go back too soon, you'll do more damage than good. Listen to your aunt!'

Eve smiled. 'Thank you.' It was soothing to have someone tell her what to do instead of her having to make all the big decisions herself. When she was around Mary, she didn't exactly feel like a child, but she did feel supported, as though the older woman had her back. It was a good feeling. She spent so much time trying to be strong that it was a relief to let go for a change.

'Here you are!' Nate said as he placed two teapots and cups on saucers in front of them. The cups were white with tiny blue sailing boats painted around the rim. 'I'll be back with the scones. They're fresh out of the oven.'

Eve poured milk into the cups then picked up each teapot and gently swirled it to give the tea bags a chance to steep. She lifted the lid of one to check the colour, then poured tea into each cup. She raised hers and stared down into the steaming liquid before taking a tentative sip.

'It's good to have you here, Eve. I've missed you a lot.'

'I've missed you too. And I'm…' She swallowed hard. 'I'm so sorry I didn't come earlier.'

'I didn't expect you to. You had your own busy life, and as long as you were happy, then I could sleep at night. When I realized things were going wrong for you, then I worried.'

'Oh Aunt Mary.' Eve reached over the table with her free hand and took her aunt's hand. 'I've been a bad niece and I don't deserve you.'

'Nonsense!' Mary shook her head. 'I should have come to you when things were rough. After you lost… suffered the…' Her eyes glistened and she waved a hand in front of her face. 'I just didn't know if you'd want me there. It had been so long since I'd seen you.'

'My graduation.' Eve pressed her lips together. 'Did I make you feel unwelcome?'

Mary lifted her bag and pulled out a tissue, then wiped her eyes and blew her nose.

'Aunt Mary? Please be honest.'

The older woman fixed her eyes on her. 'It wasn't that you made me feel unwelcome, dear. Just more that… I didn't think I'd fit in with your city lifestyle. I didn't know if you'd want me there or if you'd be a bit… well, you know, embarrassed by me. A short old woman from Cornwall. There you were, all beautiful, polished and successful, and here I am… an ageing stereotype.' She gave a small laugh, then blew her nose again and tucked the tissue into her sleeve.

'I can't believe you thought that.' Eve's heart was beating so hard she felt sure Mary could see it under her

T-shirt. 'You're not a stereotype. When did I make you think that? I must have done something...' She thought back to her graduation and before. Had she hurt her aunt at some point then?

'It doesn't matter, Eve. It's all water under the bridge, dear. You're here now.'

'No, it does matter!' Eve's clipped tone caught Nate's attention as he placed two plates on the table. Each held an enormous golden scone, a small pot of dark purple jam and one of thick yellow cream. The freshly baked aroma teased Eve's nose and she realized that in spite of the tension, she was hungry. Really hungry.

'Anything else?' Nate asked, concern crossing his handsome features as he gazed at Mary. Eve felt like shrinking down in her chair. He must be thinking she'd upset her aunt and wondering if he should say something.

'No, that's wonderful, thanks,' Mary replied. When he was out of earshot, she gestured at the scones. 'Eat up! They're still warm.'

'Not until you tell me what I did. I can't bear the thought that I hurt you.'

'Oh Eve. All right, I'll tell you, but you need to know that it no longer bothers me. I love you and have always been so proud of you.'

Eve waited, her mouth dry and her palms clammy.

'Okay... at your graduation, of course I was sad that you didn't have your parents there like most of the others, but I was grateful that I got to see you receive your teaching certificate.'

'I was glad to have you there.'

'Yes, but...'

'But what?'

'After the ceremony, I went to the ladies', and when I emerged, I saw you with a group of friends. I came over but you didn't see me approaching. I... uh... heard one of them asking what your plans were.'

Eve's cheeks filled with heat as the memory of the conversation returned. She was catapulted back to that August day in Bristol when the heat had been so intense and she'd been sweaty and uncomfortable in her cap and gown. When an acquaintance had asked if she'd go and live in Cornwall with Mary, her only local relative, she'd been keen to dismiss the idea. And that was what she'd done.

'You said that you had plans, you had ambitions and that you wouldn't become—'

'A stuffy old woman who lived with her dogs and parrot and didn't have any direction.' Eve finished Mary's sentence. 'Oh my goodness, Aunt Mary, I am so sorry! That was so wrong of me. I was hot and tired and it had been a stressful year. What I said was unforgivable. I was a total idiot.' She rubbed her eyes, furious with her former self for being so callous.

Mary squeezed her hand. 'I forgave you long ago. You were right really. I was lacking in drive and ambition. All I wanted was a quiet life.'

Eve nodded. 'Still, it was an awful thing to say. I was twenty-two and so young. But that doesn't excuse it. I just thought I knew what I wanted and how I'd get it.' Shame burned in her belly as she thought about how Aunt Mary must have felt hearing that after making the effort to travel to Bristol for her graduation. The poor woman. 'And you never let on.'

'You were young, Eve. And it's in the past. But I didn't ever want to be an embarrassment to you. I am who I am and I'm happy with that.'

Eve chewed her lip. Mary did know who she was and what she wanted. But since her panic attack – no, since she'd lost the babies – Eve had begun to wonder if she herself knew who she was. Or what she wanted any more. Her life had once seemed so vibrant and fulfilled. But had it been fulfilment or had she just filled the hours to escape the reality that the career she'd sacrificed so much for was no longer what it had been? Without a family, without love, the shine had faded and now here she was in her early thirties, questioning everything.

Perhaps this was her time to re-evaluate, to change direction. She was still young and she still had options.

'Again, I am deeply sorry. It was a stupid, thoughtless comment and if I could go back in time, I would punch myself in the mouth for saying it. I have never been embarrassed by you, Aunt Mary. Never. You're all I have!' As the words tripped off her tongue, Eve was struck by their truth. The one person she had always been able to rely on had been wounded by her arrogant comment and she'd been unaware of it all these years because she'd failed to come back to Conwenna to visit.

'Now, Eve, let's put it behind us. You've enough to worry about and life goes on. Tuck in! You'll soon feel better after one of Nate's cream teas. Although I suspect that Kevin actually made the scones; he's a dab hand with a bag of flour.'

They ate in silence, slathering the fat fluffy scones with jam and cream and watching the world go by through the cafe window. The sun shone on their table and Eve was lulled by the tinkling of cutlery and the comfort of good food. She couldn't quite push away the thought of how she'd hurt Mary, but she was glad that she knew the truth. At least now she could try to make up for the past. And that was what she intended to do.

–

Eve finished her cup of tea then dabbed at her lips with a napkin. 'That was delicious.'

Mary smiled. 'It's one of the reasons why I can't lose weight. The food in here's just too tempting.'

'You're gorgeous the way you are. And hopefully it will help me to gain a few pounds. I know I'm a bit scraggy at the moment.'

'I'll do my best to feed you up before you return to Bristol.'

Eve reached into her bag for her purse, took out a note and placed it on the table.

'I'll get this, Eve.'

'No, no!' She raised a hand. 'I won't hear of it. You've been feeding me all week so it's the least I can do.'

'It's a pleasure to have you home again.'

Home? If only…

Eve's bag started vibrating. She rummaged inside it and found her mobile, then pulled it out and stared at the screen. 'It's Amanda, my deputy. I'd better take this.'

Mary nodded, so Eve swiped the screen to answer the call. 'Hello?' She gestured at the window then pushed her chair back and went outside. The breeze caressed her warm cheeks as she moved away so that she wouldn't be standing right in front of anyone as they ate their food.

'Eve, sorry to bother you. Uh, did this morning go okay at the daycare centre?' Amanda's tone was cautious, as if she didn't want to be disturbing Eve at all.

'Yes, thank you. It was lovely. I was there for story time. A little girl took a shine to me and the staff were very welcoming. It was a bit strange being there when I should be in work, but you made me feel better when we spoke. Thank you for that.'

'No problem at all, sweetheart. And how are you feeling now?'

'I'm okay. Getting there!' Eve bit her lip. Just having contact from her life in Bristol made her heart pound, even though it was her closest friend.

'Good. Good.' Amanda sounded distant, as if she was multitasking. 'Look, I know you need a total break, but I was wondering… Well, actually that's a lie. It's not me, it's the damned governors. They want to know when you might be back.'

'Oh.' Eve began to pace back and forth. 'I've tried to make a decision about that, and although I'm feeling a bit better, I still don't think I'm ready. I've had two more… for want of a better word… funny turns since I arrived and I want to be strong enough to cope with it all again.'

'Of course you do, Eve. I feel like such a shit for ringing you. If it was up to me I'd tell you to take a year on full pay, but unfortunately it's not my decision. If you're going to be away long-term, then we need to put something in place, you know, have a bit of a reshuffle, and although I said they should give you a few weeks, they're conscious of having to answer to parents and the community and so on.'

'I know that, Amanda, and I also know that they're quite within their rights to want to know how the land lies. Look, I'm going to ring the doctor on Monday, then I can let you know more. Does that sound okay?'

'I guess I can fob them off until then. But it sounds like you're thinking you won't be back next week?'

Eve took a deep, shaky breath and peered through the window into the cafe. Aunt Mary was tidying their plates and wiping the table with a napkin. Typical: she couldn't even leave the cleaning alone when she was eating out. It was so good to be with her again and Eve realized that she wanted to spend more time with her. Apart from the fact that she knew, especially after speaking to Amanda, that she wasn't quite ready to go back to Bristol yet, she had to make things up to Mary. She wanted to. Mary was an important person to her, someone she loved, and Eve regretted hurting her all those years ago. If she left now, she knew she'd regret it.

'No. I'm thinking it could be another two weeks at least. Probably after half-term if I'm honest.' Her voice sounded stronger than she felt.

'That's absolutely fine, Eve. You take the time and get yourself back to one hundred per cent. The governors can like it or lump it. Besides, they've got me and Donovan to hold the fort.' She snorted.

'And how is Donovan?' Eve's stomach churned at the thought of the beady-eyed assistant head teacher with his hyena-like grin, lurking like a bad smell ready to tear the meat from her bones if he got the chance.

'Oh, you know... being an arse-wipe as usual!'

'Oh dear.'

'You know how he is, Eve. He sticks his head so far up the butt of anyone with an iota of power that he can see through their eyes. Thankfully Sandra seems to have no time for him. Whether it's her pregnancy or what, I'm not sure, but she sees him for what he is. It's not that he's a total waste of space; just that he can't seem to accept that he can climb the ladder gradually and based on his own merit rather than jumping up a few rungs by being a complete sycophant.'

'I know what you mean. He's reasonably bright and capable but it's hard to see that when he's being so darned annoying.'

'Anyway, forget him. I'll whip him into shape if necessary. How is Conwenna Cove?'

'In all honesty, it's delightful. The weather has been beautiful and I'm just enjoying the pace of life here. It's so different to what I'm used to, but that's a good thing. I needed to slow down. The problem is that I have more thinking time, which is tough, but I suppose I buried everything for too long and then look at what happened.'

'Exactly! You need to go through it all and process it. I've been worried about you for months and had a bad feeling that something like this might happen. Well you take care, and once you've spoken to your GP, text me. I don't expect to hear from you apart from that, unless it's to tell me that there are lots of really hot fishermen asking for your hand in marriage.'

Eve giggled. 'Not likely. The most dashing one I've seen is past sixty and has eyes only for my aunt.'

'Oh never mind! I'm sure you might come across a surfer or two.'

'Actually I've just been served by one in the local cafe.'

'You are living it up. Well get his number and take a selfie with him, then send it to me.'

'I'm not doing that!' Eve chuckled.

'Spoilsport! But I bet there are loads of gorgeous Cornish men just clamouring for your attention.'

'Not what I need right now, Amanda.' Eve's thoughts drifted to Jack's gentle brown eyes and soft pink lips. *Lips made for kissing.* Then she shivered as she remembered him pushing her away. There'd be no more of that. Besides, he'd been furious with her the last time she'd seen him, so she needed to try to find a way to apologize to him for prying. She just hoped he'd let her.

'Eve?'

'Oh... yeah?'

'I said take care and let me know if you need anything.'

'Thanks, chick, I will. You know, I wouldn't be able to cope without you.'

'The feeling's mutual, honey. TTFN!'

As Eve ended the call, she felt as if a weight had lifted, if only an inch or two. She'd made the decision to stay in Conwenna for two more weeks. Perhaps even three if she stayed for half-term too. Once she'd spoken to the doctor, she'd be able to relax a bit and allow herself to heal properly, as well as to enjoy several more delicious cream teas.

She might as well make the most of it while she was here.

Chapter 13

'What do you think of this one?' Eve asked as she showed her aunt a blue and green checked neckerchief.

'That's a nice colour.'

'Will it suit him?'

'Probably, with his dark hair and dark eyes. It should be lovely on him.'

Eve nodded. She could just picture it tied around his strong neck and the thought made her tingle. She took the scarf to the counter and paid for it, then tucked it into her handbag.

'Did you find everything you were looking for?' the assistant asked. Eve scanned the range of dog toys and treats behind the girl.

'Actually, give me a bag of those dental stick things too, would you? I'm sure he could do with something to keep his teeth clean.'

'What's his name? The lucky boy?'

'Gabe.' Eve smiled. 'He's gorgeous.'

'How long have you had him?'

'Oh… uh… he's not mine. I just helped out at the rescue sanctuary with him and he kind of stole my heart.'

'No doubt he'll be coming home with you soon then, Eve,' Aunt Mary said as she placed a hand on Eve's shoulder.

'Well, I don't know. I mean, I'd love to adopt a hound but is it really practical with me living alone and so far away?' She wished Aunt Mary could say what she wanted to hear, but she knew the practicalities of the situation made it impossible.

'Wait and see, dear. Things have a way of working out.'

Eve swallowed a sigh and nodded, then put the treats into her bag with the scarf. She wished she had Aunt Mary's quiet confidence that things would work out; it would be wonderful to feel the freedom of knowing it would all be okay, but how could it be? She was caught like lamb's wool on a wire fence, waving wildly in the breeze yet unable to extricate herself. And she didn't know which direction she would go in if she could.

As they strolled along the street, Eve gazed around her. Some of the people were already familiar, if only because she'd seen them once or twice when she'd wandered through the town. In two weeks' time, she might well know their names too, and they might know hers. What would it be like to live in a place where people knew her name and took the time to make conversation as the sun shone above them? If she did get to know the people of Conwenna, it could make leaving even harder.

Her aunt patted her hand. 'There's Jack, dear!'

Eve followed Mary's finger and sure enough, there he was at the rail along the side of the harbour, peering down at the water and apparently watching the boats bobbing on the afternoon tide.

'Oh! Eve!' Aunt Mary covered her mouth and raised her eyebrows. 'I've only gone and left my... uh... glasses at the cafe.'

'Really?' Eve tore her eyes from Jack.

'Yes. I'd better go back and get them. You go on ahead and speak to Jack. Don't wait for me, though. I'll probably get caught up talking to Nate. I'll see you back at the cottage.'

'Are you sure?' Eve kept looking back towards the harbour, afraid that Jack would disappear if she didn't keep watching him.

'Yes. Absolutely.' Aunt Mary waved at her. 'Go on!'

Eve nodded, then turned away and headed down to the harbour. She didn't have the heart to tell Aunt Mary that her glasses were, in fact, perched upon her head. Her aunt obviously sensed that she needed to speak to Jack alone, and she had manufactured the perfect opportunity.

Eve approached Jack cautiously, quietly, the way she imagined a photographer would a wild animal in a nature documentary. He was deep in thought, his strong arms bulging from the sleeves of his T-shirt as he leaned on the black iron rail and stared down at the water.

'Don't do it!' she whispered as she reached him.

He started and turned towards her. His face was golden and he looked handsome and healthy in his white T-shirt and faded blue jeans. He had a pair of battered trainers on his feet, and as Eve looked closer, she saw that there was mud on his jeans. He'd been gardening again.

'Hello.' He nodded at her then turned back to the rail.

'Jack. I need to apologize to you.'

He sighed deeply then faced her again. 'You do?'

'Yes.' Eve's cheeks burned under the intensity of his gaze and she wanted to cover them with her hands. She felt like a naughty child being carpeted by an angry teacher.

'You have nothing to apologize for. Don't worry about it.' He tucked his hands in his pockets. 'Are you feeling better?'

Eve frowned.

'Mary told me you'd been rough. I didn't want to bother you until you'd recovered.'

'I guess I just need to avoid all stressful situations.'

'I guess so.'

'Like creeping around my aunt's lodger's garden and snooping in his shed. Oh Jack, I'm so sorry.'

He shook his head. 'I overreacted, Eve. I'm sorry too. It's just no one's ever been in there except me. That stuff is... well it's...'

'Wonderful? Incredible? Heartbreaking?'

He ran a hand over his hair. 'I don't know about that. I was going to say personal, emotional, cathartic.'

'Cathartic?'

'Yeah. Tell you what, if you haven't got any other plans, why don't we grab a few things from the delicatessen then take a walk over to the cove? I bet it hasn't changed since you were a child. It's one of those places that seems to be protected from the outside world.'

Ten minutes later, they had purchased the basics for an impromptu picnic from the deli and were heading along the narrow path that wound over the cliffs and led down to the secluded beach. Tourists tended to swarm to the larger beaches a bit further along the coast, so the cove was used more by the locals. During the day, it was often busy with families with children who needed to burn off some energy, but at night it was a favourite with young courting couples. As Eve and Jack were neither, she wondered how they would appear there.

As the path began to descend, Eve slipped and landed with a thump on her behind. 'Ouch!'

Jack turned and relieved her of the carrier bag that held a fresh baguette and a block of creamy garlic cheese, then helped her up. 'Be careful, Eve! Stay close to me and you'll be fine.'

He placed her hands on his shoulders then moved slowly forward. Eve tried to keep her touch light, but the path was steep and she couldn't help tightening her grip on him. Beneath her hands, his shoulders were broad and muscular, and it was hard not to become distracted by how good he felt. But she needed to focus on staying upright rather than gazing at the impressive physique of her aunt's lodger.

As they neared the bottom, she pulled her hands away and waited as Jack carefully stepped down onto the sand. It wasn't a big drop, but she could see that the lower step that had carved into the rock had been worn away by the tide, so it was steeper than it used to be when she'd come here as a child. Unless she'd just been fearless then. She could recall throwing herself off the step and racing across the sand with the dogs, eager to dive into the foamy water to cool down. Jack hooked both bags on one hand, then turned and held out his free hand to her.

'I'm not the Queen, you know. Or an old lady.'

He smiled. 'I know that. But you are a lady and I want to help.'

'Okay then, but I'm tougher than I look.'

He nodded. 'I know you're strong, Eve.'

'Yes, I am. Usually…'

As she went to take his hand, he leaned forward and slid his arm around her waist then lifted her off her feet. She gasped and flung her arms around his neck as he turned and lowered her to the sand.

'You can let go now.'

'What?' Her voice was muffled from where it was pressed against the warm skin of his neck.

'Well you can stay like that if you want, but I'll have to carry you across to the shade.' Eve felt him shaking against her and realized that he was laughing. She slowly released him then took a step back.

'You startled me.'

'Sorry.'

'It's okay.' She could still smell his skin on hers, and when she licked her lips, she could taste him too. She couldn't recall the last time a man had affected her so much. Was it possible that Jack Adams was awakening some part of her that she'd shut down long ago? Or perhaps it was a part that she'd never actually met before.

'Come on.' He grabbed her hand before she could argue and they made their way across the golden sand towards the shaded area at the far end of the beach. Apart from a few teenagers playing football and an older couple sharing a flask of tea, the cove was quiet.

Jack placed the plastic bags on the ground, then sat down and patted the sand next to him. 'How about one of those beers we bought? Before they get too warm?'

'Sounds like a good plan,' Eve replied as she sat next to him.

'Then I'm going to try to apologize properly, and to explain why I paint those scenes that you saw in the shed.'

He pulled two bottles of beer from the bag, unscrewed them and handed one to Eve, then took a long draw from his. Eve watched his Adam's apple bob as he swallowed, before taking a deep slug from her own.

She had no idea why Jack felt he owed her an apology – it was she who had been in the wrong – but she knew she was about to find out.

–

Jack rubbed his thumb through the tiny beads of condensation on the neck of his beer bottle as he steeled himself to explain things to Eve. He felt like such an idiot for losing his temper with her when he'd found her in the shed. It wasn't her fault that he had painted so many of those damned scenes or that some of them were so... graphic.

He took another swig of beer then turned to her. His breath caught in his throat at her effortless beauty. She had removed her shoes and now sat on the sand, in her simple jeans and T-shirt, with her windswept cropped hair glowing like gold in the afternoon sunshine. Her skin was radiant and her green eyes were luminous, deep green pools that made Jack want to paint her in order to capture the way they appeared in that moment. She gazed out at the sea, watching the waves breaking against the shore, and the word that came to Jack's mind was *serenity*.

She could be my serenity...

'Eve.' He broke the spell.

She blinked then turned to him. 'Yes?'

'I'm so sorry for shouting at you in the shed. I completely overreacted.' Her green eyes roamed over his face and for a moment he wondered if she would refuse to forgive him. 'Will you accept my apology?'

'Of course, Jack. As I said earlier, you had every right to be annoyed with me. I didn't mean to but I guess I was... snooping.' Her cheeks coloured and before he knew what he was doing, he'd taken hold of her hand.

'No. Well, okay. You kind of were, but you were looking for me and only to bring me cake. Dammit!' He rubbed a hand over his face and shook his head. 'You were just being kind.'

'Bringing you burnt cake?' Eve's mouth twitched.

'I liked that cake very much. I was really disappointed to see it on the ground being consumed by ants.'

'I'm sorry too… for going into your shed.'

'Honestly, it doesn't matter. I was shocked that you were there, that was all. It's probably time I showed someone what I've been painting anyway.'

'Your work is incredible. You are extremely talented, Jack.'

He didn't know how to respond to the compliment, so he took a swig of beer. It was cold, refreshing and welcome.

'The paintings of greyhounds in the art gallery were yours too, weren't they?'

He nodded. 'There are a few of them scattered around the village.'

'I'd like one, if I may, to take back to Bristol with me.'

'So you are leaving?' His heart fluttered as he watched her face.

'Not yet. I'm going to stay at least until half-term. I thought I'd come to the village fair… if that's okay?'

Relief surged through him, relief that he shouldn't be feeling because it shouldn't matter if she stayed or not, but he couldn't help it. He didn't want her to go yet; he wanted to spend more time with her, to get to know her properly. He hadn't been interested in a woman in a long time and he knew he shouldn't allow himself to get attached to Eve, because before he knew it she'd be gone. But he liked her; he was drawn to her. Whether it was because they were both wounded, both scarred by their pasts, or just down to good old-fashioned attraction, he didn't know, but he couldn't deny it. He wanted her.

But I have no right to… I'm damaged goods.

'The painting you saw on the easel?'

'Yes.'

'It's real.'

Eve frowned. 'Real?'

'Things I saw… when I was in Afghanistan.'

'I did wonder if that was the case. Jack, that must have been so hard for you.'

'It was hard for all the troops out there, especially the ones with children back home. I mean… seeing the poverty, the way the ordinary people suffered, it was just so disturbing. Our lives here are so different to theirs.'

'I've seen things on the news, everyone has, but you've really captured the things the cameras might not see, or at least choose not to show. Unless it's after ten p.m., and even then things are censored, biased.'

Jack nodded. Some of the scenes he'd painted were horrific; they showed wounded children, houses blown apart, families destroyed by grief. 'Painting was like therapy for me. I mean, I did have counselling when I came back to England after I was injured, and that kind of helped, but I could talk about it all day and still never clear those images from my head. One counsellor suggested finding an artistic outlet to help me to deal with it all, and drawing and painting just seemed to work.'

'We try to build the self-esteem of some of our more troubled pupils in school by encouraging them to be creative. Whether it's painting or building things or writing poetry, it all helps.'

'It was as if, once I started painting, I couldn't stop, and now the images just pour out of me.'

'I saw you, you know? Going out to the shed… wearing just your jeans.' Eve lowered her eyes to her bottle and worried the label with her thumbnail.

'It gets hot when I'm working.' Had she been watching him?

'I'd like to watch you work.'

Jack raised his eyebrows.

'Oh my! Ah… what I meant was uh…' Eve's cheeks were bright red now and Jack started to laugh.

'You want to watch me, Eve? Are you a closet voyeur or something?'

'No!' Her eyes were wide. 'What I meant was that I'd like to watch how you start with an outline then fill it in. I find the whole creative process just amazing. I feel like such an idiot now!' She drained her beer then placed it on the sand next to her.

'Are you warm?' Jack asked as he took their empty bottles and put them into a carrier bag, tucking it into the sand so it wouldn't open and spill its contents. He removed his trainers and placed them next to it.

'I am a bit. Why?'

'Fancy a swim?'

Eve stared at him, then at the water, and he saw longing in her eyes.

'I can't. I don't have my costume.'

'You could go in in your T-shirt,' he suggested.

'There are other people here.' Eve gestured at the older couple, but they were packing up, and the teenagers had moved further up the beach and were inspecting some of the rock pools.

'There's no one to see… or to care.'

'I don't know.'

'Come on, Eve. Let your hair down.'

Eve laughed and ran a hand over her crop. 'That's a bit difficult.'

'You know what I mean.' Jack stood before he could overthink it and pulled off his T-shirt, then unbuttoned his jeans and let them fall to his feet. As he kicked them off, he felt Eve's eyes on him. It was with relief that he looked down to find he'd put a decent pair of boxers on that morning; he'd have been far more self-conscious in one of his scruffy old pairs. He held out a hand. 'Coming?'

Eve moved onto her knees then stopped as she caught sight of his left leg. He shifted a bit, aware that his scarring was a shock whenever someone saw it for the first time. Back at the cottage, when Eve had caught him in just a barely-there towel, she'd presumably been distracted by his nudity as he'd tried to tighten his towel, but now, in the bright sunshine, there was no avoiding it. So he let her look.

'Jack... is this why—'

'I limp a bit. Yeah.'

She reached out a hand but stopped just before she touched him. 'May I?'

She wanted to touch it? His horrific scar? One of the things that had made his ex-wife recoil in horror? He suddenly wanted to tell her about what had happened. 'We were doing a tour of the area one day. We stopped to check out a suspicious vehicle and when we...' He paused as the memories rushed in, vivid and painful, loud and horrifying.

Eve nodded. 'Yes?'

'When we were out in the open, away from our truck, a lone biker appeared from nowhere and threw a grenade at the parked vehicle. It all happened so fast... there wasn't time to react. I was hit by shrapnel; it tore right through my flesh.'

The pain, the smoke, the sickening smell of charred skin, muscle and bone.

'Oh God, Jack! How terrible!'

'It hit my chest and stomach,' he pointed at the smaller scars on his torso, 'then ripped through the front of my leg and severed my tibialis anterior muscle and tendon.' He stared down at the long scar. It was thick and red and ugly. He didn't care so much about how it looked, though, as about how it affected his mobility. 'It was weird. I collapsed when I was hit but I was so jacked up on adrenalin that I didn't know what had happened. I kept trying to get up but I just couldn't. And it was all still going on around me... men, women and children screaming and shouting. Guns being fired. The air choking everyone, thick with black smoke. Rubble still falling.' He shook his head. 'I had several operations to repair the area, but there's so much scar tissue that it pulls my skin whenever I flex my leg.'

It was hard saying it all out loud, as if keeping it in made it seem almost unreal, like something he'd seen on TV a long time ago. But it had happened and he had been there. His counsellor had worked through it all with him but also told him to be realistic about it. What he'd seen – the loss of his friends, the damage done to other people, especially children – would never leave him. He would just have to learn to live with it and there were strategies that would help him cope. He knew others who'd come home but been unable to deal with things, and that was sometimes harder to accept than anything.

The scar was the physical evidence of what he'd endured. Sure, most of the time it was covered up with clothing and he guessed he usually avoided looking at it when he dressed, as if ignoring it would help him to forget. Two of his troop had been killed by the explosion and another three seriously injured. The emotional repercussions were huge and he'd tried to stay in touch with the other men, but somehow they'd drifted apart, as if their shared memories were easier to block out if they didn't have any reminders of the past.

'I'm sorry you went through all that,' Eve said. Then she ran her cool fingers over his skin and he sighed, releasing the knot that had built in his stomach as he'd relived that awful day when his world had changed forever. She touched him tenderly, with interest, as she ran her fingers over the lumps and bumps, the hollows and swellings of knotted tissue. It was as if she was drawn to the scarring, intrigued by its source, and it made his heart swell. He'd seen things that no one should see, and at times, he'd done things in the line of duty that would reduce other people to quivering wrecks. But things had changed, his life had moved on and now he was set on a different course.

He'd enjoyed most of his time as a marine, in spite of the difficulties, and been proud to serve his country. Being a part of the Corps had made him feel, for the first time in his life, that he belonged, that he was part of a family. So his injury, then his decision to leave the marines – because any future tours would be difficult for him, and he knew that a weak link could mean death and danger for his brothers – had changed him.

Then things had gone wrong with Jodie and he'd packed up and set off with no idea where he was going.

For two years he'd travelled without purpose, going anywhere he felt like, picking up casual work when he needed to. He'd been alone again, but he hadn't minded. It gave him time to think, to try to find an inner peace. He'd come to Conwenna by chance, following the coastline of Cornwall with just a rucksack on his back and some of his pension in his pocket, going nowhere in particular, just knowing that he had to keep on moving. He'd literally bumped into Mary in the Conwenna Cafe when he'd been asking Nate if he knew of anywhere in the area to rent for a night or two. He hadn't wanted to stay at a hotel, finding them too formal, and had been thinking more of a hostel or campsite. Mary had insisted on buying him a coffee, then told him she was looking for someone to help out around her home with odd jobs and so on, and that she had a cottage to rent. He'd been able to provide her with phone numbers for references — which she'd used right there and then in the cafe — from his former commanding officer and a restaurant in Plymouth where he'd washed dishes for a few weeks, then Mary had invited him up to see the cottage.

Since then, Jack had spent time with the dogs, kept active and painted. It was a simple life and one that he enjoyed because he knew what to expect from each day. There had been no surprises.

But now... for the first time in ages, a woman he was drawn to was looking at him with acceptance; was touching him as if his scars were something to be revered. And Jack was having a mighty hard time keeping himself from bending down and kissing Eve hard.

'Eve?' His voice was husky. 'Shall we swim?'

'Yes.' She stood up.

'I'll go on ahead so you can have some privacy.' He ran down to the water before she could see how her touch had affected him, then waded through the shallows and dived into the waves. The cold water washed over him, cleansing him and cooling his blood. He loved how the sea had the power to make him feel renewed, as if it could remove all the bad things and let him start over.

When he surfaced, he spotted Eve immediately. She was ankle-deep in the water, stepping carefully as if afraid of splashing herself.

'It's freezing!' she gasped as the waves licked at her knees. She was clad in just her T-shirt and a pair of navy satin knickers. They were those shorts things, modern undies for a modern woman. She paused as the sea reached her thighs, her arms folded over her chest. 'I can't, Jack. It's too cold.'

He swam towards her then stood in front of her. 'It's okay. I understand.'

He made out that he was going to help her back to shore, then knelt and splashed her repeatedly. Eve screeched as she was covered from head to toe.

'Stop it! Jack, you animal!'

He reached out and grabbed her arms. 'What did you call me?'

She grinned and a drop of seawater plopped from her fringe onto her cheek. It trickled down until it reached her chin. Jack pulled her closer and saw her pupils dilate as their bodies met.

Something changed right then and there.

All the sounds of the beach faded away, from the shouts of the seagulls overhead to the crashing of the waves on the shore and the distant clattering of a bucket against the rocks.

All Jack could see was Eve, as if everything behind her had been smudged into some sort of soft focus. And all he could smell was her skin, her perfume, her shampoo.

All he could feel was her heat and the way her body fitted so well against his. He could even feel the goose bumps on her legs as they brushed his.

He slid his hands under her arms then lifted her so she was the right height. She folded her arms around his neck and pulled her close. Then he kissed her. Gently at first, feathering kisses over her lips and cheeks, but when she wrapped her legs around his waist, he was consumed by desire and he kissed her harder.

They were lost in each other, swept up in need and longing. Jack was completely overwhelmed by the sensations running through him and by the deep emotional connection that surged in his chest. This was right. At last, this was right.

A loud cheering dragged him from the brink, and he gently pulled his head back to peer along the beach. The teenagers had spotted them and were clapping and waving at their rather passionate display.

'Jack?' Eve whispered.

'Yeah.' He realized that he was cupping her little bottom in his hands and that they were as close as they could be without actually having sex.

'Perhaps I should get down.'

He nodded. 'Um… perhaps I should just go out a bit deeper first, though?'

'Oh. Of course!'

He kissed her gently, then lowered her to her feet and immersed himself in the water up to his chest. The waves lapped at his shoulders and the sandy seabed moved beneath him, but he wasn't aware of any of it as he watched Eve wade back to shore then walk to their belongings.

Calm down, he told himself as he tried to bring his body under control by thinking about boring things, anything other than how good Eve had felt in his arms, and how good he knew she would feel if he made love to her.

And he knew as he watched her opening another beer, then waving to him, that he was completely and utterly lost.

Chapter 14

Eve held tightly to Jack's hand as they walked back up through the lanes. She felt like she had sand everywhere; in her hair, her bra, her knickers and her shoes. Her skin was dry with salt and when she licked her lips she could taste it. But she also felt happy. Contented. And overwhelmed.

What had happened down in the cove had taken her breath away. Being there with Jack on the sand as the waves foamed against the shore, he had told her so much about himself, allowed her access to the inner workings of his mind, and she'd begun to open up to him too. Impossible to believe that it had only been a week since she'd first met him.

They crunched along the gravel road and Eve looked around her. How strange to think that seven days ago she had driven along here, unaware of how it would be to see her aunt after so long and carrying the tension of her job and her grief so tightly between her shoulders. Now she took a moment to think about how her body felt and the differences were clear. Though the tension hadn't gone completely, it wasn't as bad. Her left shoulder didn't hurt when she turned her head. She hadn't even realized how bad it had been, but now that she could move more freely, she knew just how stiff with tension and grief and loneliness she'd become.

Because she had been lonely. But being around Aunt Mary and around Jack had changed that.

They reached the end of the road and slowed, as if reading each other's minds.

'So...' Jack said as he gently caressed her cheek. 'What happens now?'

'Now?' Eve smiled. 'I need a shower to get rid of this sand.'

'Me too,' he said. 'You want...' He paused and licked his lips. 'Probably not a good idea.'

'If you mean to share a shower, then probably not.' *This is so difficult.* 'Jack, I enjoyed what happened down at the beach. A lot. But we shouldn't rush things. I really like you and I don't want to spoil how this is between us right now.'

'I like you too.' He swallowed and she watched his Adam's apple bob. 'But you'll be going back to Bristol in a few weeks. I can't pretend that's not going to happen, even though I'd like to.'

Eve nodded, hating that the thought made her stomach churn as if she'd swallowed seawater. 'Can we just... take this slowly? See what happens?'

'Sounds like a good plan. If I came on a bit strong then I'm sorry. I know you're fragile at the moment and it was wrong of me to muddle you up even further.'

Eve shook her head. 'I wanted that kiss as much as you did. For the first time in what feels like a lifetime, I was free. My body was alive with something other than sadness and stress, and it seemed in that moment that there were... possibilities!' She held her arms out and laughed, then frowned and scratched her head.

'What's wrong?' he asked, his face etched with concern.

'My head's really itchy. Must be the salt.'

'Could be. Give your hair a good wash to get it all out. So I'll see you later at dinner?'

'You will.'

Jack lifted her hand and kissed it gently and Eve's heart fluttered. She was relieved that he hadn't tried to kiss her on the lips again, because she knew that if he had, she'd probably have lost her tenuous hold on her willpower and gone with him to share that shower.

–

After dinner that evening, Jack helped Eve to clear away, then he excused himself. Eve and Mary had been reminiscing about the summers of her childhood and he thought they needed some time alone.

As for him, he had an overwhelming urge to go to the shed. It had been a good day and he wanted to continue with a project that, luckily, Eve hadn't spotted when she'd gone in there. He'd hidden it behind the rest, almost as if he was afraid to admit that he was doing it, as if it was an invasion of her privacy.

He grabbed a bottle of water then stripped off his shirt and headed up the garden path. The night was clear and cool but he knew the shed would be warm from a day of sunshine. He opened the door and switched on the light then padded across the wooden floor as the door swung shut behind him. The woody scent of his creative space was instantly comforting.

He carefully lifted the large sketchpad from behind his other work and flipped back the cover. There she was. Beautiful and pale. Her eyes were so big in her tiny face that they dominated the portrait. He stared at her, captivated by her beauty and her sweet essence of vulnerability. This woman was under his skin, in his heart, and he couldn't get her out of his head. It was as if an invisible thread had been fastened between them and now he couldn't sever it – or didn't want to.

He got to work, shading and highlighting, perfecting and shaping, until the Eve in the painting was at the pretty cove he'd taken her to today, sitting on the beach facing inwards, with the waves lapping at the sand behind her, their froth fluffy as candy floss. The sun sat low in the sky, illuminating the clouds and creating a glow around her. He shaded her hair so that it appeared roughly tousled, just like it had been today when she'd emerged from the water, then he smoothed around her breasts, making the nipples point through her top as they had done after he'd soaked her. She was, he knew in that moment, the most beautiful thing he had ever seen.

And his heart ached as he thought about how she'd soon be leaving.

Unless I can persuade her to stay.

But how did you ask someone you hadn't even known for that long if they'd give up everything and spend their life with you? It would take a lot of trust. Could Eve trust him to take care of her? Could he trust her not to break his heart?

'Hello?' There was a gentle knock at the door, then Eve called through the gap. 'Is it okay if I come in?'

Jack quickly pulled the cover back over the sketch, then tucked it behind a canvas under the window. He crossed to the door and opened it. 'Hello. I thought you and Mary were having a chat then you were going to watch that documentary together.'

'We were.' She smiled, her eyes flickering over his naked chest. 'We are... but it's not on for another half an hour, so I said I needed to check if it was okay for me to come up to the farm with you tomorrow. I want to take Gabe his treats.' She plucked at the hem of her knee-length dress. It was made of some lightweight crinkle material and the green leaf pattern brought out the colour of her eyes, while the spaghetti straps showed off a faint T-shirt mark from their time at the beach. Her feet were bare and he noticed that she'd painted her toenails a golden-green colour that shimmered in the light.

'Of course it is. Gabe will appreciate that, I'm sure.'

'How was your shower?' Eve asked. She licked her lips, and when she raised her eyes again he saw hunger. A hunger that echoed his own.

'It was... lonely.'

They laughed together, both embarrassed by his loaded comment, and he realized that they were also both a bit confused by their feelings. 'You want an art lesson?'

'Me?'

'There's no one else here.' He made a show of looking around him.

'No, I know that, but... uh... I've never been any good.'

'Come on, I'll show you. I'm a good teacher.'

Jack set up a new sketchpad on the easel then handed Eve a stick of charcoal. 'Now I want you to try to draw me. I need to see what you can do first, then I can assess how to help you improve.'

'Okay...' She frowned and a tiny line appeared between her brows.

'I'll stand here like this.' He stood beneath the light bulb and crossed his arms. 'Then you draw what you see.'

'Really?' Eve tilted her head. 'But I am *so* bad at art.'

'Humour me.'

'Okay, but let your arms hang down or stick your hands in your pockets.'

'Why?'

'Oh come on, Jack. At least let me admire the view.' Eve gave him a cheeky wink and Jack was amused to feel heat rush into his cheeks.

He stood there for about ten minutes, occasionally shifting his weight from one foot to the other, but trying to keep his face still.

'This isn't going well,' Eve said. She wiped a hand across her brow and sighed.

'Are you too hot?' Jack asked.

'It is warm in here.'

'That's why I work topless,' he said, shaking with laughter.

Eve peered at him from behind the easel. 'Oh no you don't. I see where you're going with this, Mr Charming Ex-Marine.'

'What?' He held up his hands in mock surrender. 'I don't know what you mean.'

'I can't take my top off because I'm wearing a dress. With nothing underneath.'

'What?' His heart raced. 'Nothing?'

'Ha ha! Now who's shocked? I ran out of underwear so it's all in the washing machine. I didn't bring that much with me because I didn't know how long I was going to stay.'

'So now you're – as they say – going commando?'

Eve nodded and continued working on her sketch. Jack tried not to think about the fact that she wasn't wearing anything under her dress, but it was impossible.

After another ten minutes, he couldn't stay still any more. 'Right, let me see!'

Eve stepped back and he turned the easel around. He had to bite the inside of his cheek. She hadn't been kidding; she really was awful at art.

'It's great, Eve.'

'No it's not.'

'It is. You've got my basic shape right and my face kind of looks… like a face.'

'It looks like a marshmallow.' She swayed from side to side, hanging her head.

'Hey, come here.' He positioned her in front of him so he could see the sketchpad over her shoulder, then lifted her right hand and gently wrapped his fingers around it. 'Let me guide you.'

He slid his left arm around her waist and moved her closer to the paper. As he guided the hand that held the charcoal over the page, the image began to take shape, and soon it looked more like him and less like a cartoon character. He used her forefinger to smudge and soften the shadows and tried hard to focus on the picture, but it was hard not to be distracted when she was so close. When she slipped her left hand over his where it rested on her waist, he buried his face in her neck and breathed deeply of her fresh apple-blossom scent. 'You smell so good, Eve.'

She tapped his face with the hand that still held the charcoal. 'Focus, Mr Artist!'

'I'm trying. Stop distracting me.'

'I'm not doing *anything*.'

He growled into her ear then nipped at her ear lobe, and she squealed and slipped out of his embrace.

'I'd say that looks a lot better now, wouldn't you?' he asked, taking a few deep breaths to try to slow his heart rate.

'It certainly does. Thank you for the lesson. How much do you charge?' Eve's eyes sparkled. She rubbed at her nose and Jack had to contain his laughter when he saw the charcoal smudge there. *Hazard of the job.*

'I'll have to think about that and let you know. Unless you have any suggestions?' He wiggled his eyebrows.

'Just because I'm not wearing underwear doesn't mean I'm fast and loose!' Eve wagged a finger at him. 'Now I'm going to watch that documentary with my aunt. You coming?'

Jack looked around the shed then back at Eve. It wasn't a difficult decision to make. Any excuse to spend another hour in her company, even if it did mean watching one of Mary's bizarre documentaries and being fed yet more cake. He flicked the light switch then followed Eve out into the night air. It was good to have a reason to spend time with people, to have someone want him around. Mary had always been warm and kind but he didn't like to overstay his welcome at her cottage. He was conscious of the fact that she probably wanted time alone, or with Edward, even though she always claimed to the contrary. But Eve had invited him and it made him glow inside, because right now he could imagine nothing better than squashing up next to her on the sofa with at least one dog, and just enjoying her company.

–

Eve could barely contain her delight when Jack agreed to come with her to watch TV. She hadn't wanted to leave

170

the shed but knew she had to because it was getting harder and harder to resist him. When she was with him, she just felt lighter, more vibrant, as if she'd been walking around seeing in shades of grey and now she was slowly noticing colour again. It was wonderful.

They entered the kitchen and she switched the kettle on.

'Tea or coffee?'

'Eve?' It was Aunt Mary.

'Yes?'

'I've made a pot of tea ready. You just need to bring some extra biscuits. Edward has eaten all the ones I brought through.'

Eve raised her eyebrows at Jack. So Edward was here.

'Okay! Be there in a minute.'

Jack opened the cupboard above the kettle. 'You want chocolate chip cookies or malted milk?'

Eve shook her head. 'I don't mind.'

He handed her the cookies. 'Hey, what is it?'

'Nothing.'

He stroked her face and she shivered with delight.

'Something's up.'

'I didn't know Edward was coming round.'

'He often comes to visit, especially in the evenings. They watch TV together or play cards. Sometimes Mary goes down to his house to play on his games console.'

Eve suppressed a smile. 'I just… I wish I'd known about him before, you know? That Aunt Mary had someone special in her life.'

'He's a good man, Eve. He makes her happy.'

'She seems to like him.'

'And I'm pretty sure the feeling is mutual.'

'I feel like I've missed so much.' Her throat tightened.

Jack nodded. 'That's natural, but you can't turn the clock back. All you can do is take it from here and make it good from now on.'

'You're so right.' She stepped closer then pressed her lips to his cheek. 'Thank you.'

They took the biscuits through to the lounge and found Mary and Edward sitting together on one of the squishy sofas with Harry wedged between them. The dog's head was hanging off the cushion and his legs pointed up into the air. The room was lit by two floor lamps, and a red candle burned in a clear glass jar on the table, making the room smell of spiced apple. It was warm and homely. So unlike Eve's lounge in her large, empty house in Bristol.

'Is he okay like that?' Eve asked.

'He's just roaching,' Edward replied.

'Roaching?'

'It's what we call this position. It means he's extremely comfortable and relaxed.' Edward smiled at her then rubbed Harry's ears gently and the dog let out a long, low grunt. 'See, he's happy.'

Jack sat on the other sofa next to Clio, then patted the seat next to him. There wasn't much space because the greyhound was taking up over half the sofa, but it meant that Eve got to snuggle up to Jack, so she didn't complain.

'How has your time at Conwenna been so far, Eve?' Edward asked as he leaned forward and retrieved his mug of tea from the tray on the table.

'Good, thank you. I'm enjoying being here.'

'You should consider staying around. I know Mary would love to have you here.'

Eve swallowed hard. Was he criticizing her or just making a kindly observation? His face was warm, his smile seemed genuine. In his faded jeans and AC/DC T-shirt, he looked cool and casual. Eve wasn't used to being around men of her father's age, except at work, and she wondered how it would be to live surrounded by a family like this.

Mary clapped her hands then pointed at the TV. 'Here it is! I've been waiting for this Mary Berry documentary since I first saw it advertised.'

The opening credits rolled and Eve accepted a mug of tea from Jack then settled back on the sofa. When he slid one arm around her shoulders and pulled her closer, she could barely contain her happiness. However long this lasted, even if it was just for tonight, she would be grateful that she'd had the chance to be a part of her aunt's life again, and that she'd had the chance to meet Jack.

—

Before Jack had left to return to his cottage, Eve had arranged to go with him to Foxglove Farm the following day. As they crossed the farmyard the next morning, her stomach flipped over. She was nervous about seeing Gabe again. Nervous in case he was still anxious around her, nervous in case he didn't like his presents and nervous that she wouldn't be able to contain her emotions around him. Since her arrival at Conwenna Cove, she had been catapulted from one emotion to another. It was as if, having had a lid on them for months, it had been blown off and now she couldn't contain them. Since university, she'd liked to think of herself as being strong, calm and in control, but now she was feeling things she hadn't felt, or allowed herself to feel, in years: guilt about her neglect of Aunt Mary, desire and affection for Jack, fear about her job, both losing it and returning; she was a boiling pot of emotion. Perhaps that was why her head was also so itchy right now. Some kind of stress-related skin condition. She'd have to get some antihistamine from the chemist later on.

Jack opened the door to the small office at the end of the stable block. 'After you.' He nodded at Eve and she entered. Neil was sitting at a desk in the far corner, his hands full of papers and a pair of smudged glasses perched on his nose. He grunted at them in acknowledgement.

'Hey, Neil. How're you?' Jack asked.

'Can't keep on top of all this damned paperwork, to be honest. I'm a practical man, me, not an office administrator, and I don't have time for all this. Plus it's getting worse the more dogs we take in and the more that I hear of needing homing, rehabilitation, fostering and adoption.'

'Well I'll help out if I can,' Jack said, approaching the desk.

'Think I'm going to need to get someone else in, to be honest; someone who's good with this type of thing. Vet's bills. Adoption certificates. Dog histories. Cases reported to the RSPCA. You know anyone wanting an admin job – part-time to start off with, and the pay won't be great – send them in my direction.'

'Sure,' Jack replied. Eve bit her lip to prevent herself from offering to help out. She could do the job standing on her head, she felt sure, after juggling so many things for so long as a head teacher. But she wasn't staying long, and she shouldn't start something she couldn't finish.

'How do you fund all this?' she asked.

'Partly through donations from those adopting the dogs, partly through a very generous donation left by an elderly lady who passed away two years ago and partly through fund-raising. Last year Nate Bryson got some of his surfing buddies involved and they did a sponsored surf. They all have contacts and managed to get an online sportswear company involved. It was brilliant.'

'I bet that was fun.' Eve looked at Jack.

'I wasn't around then but I've heard about it. Surf for Sighthounds, wasn't it?'

'That's right!' Neil smiled. 'Hoping he'll do another one this year, or maybe next. Then there's Oliver Davenport, the village vet. He does as much as he can for the charity pro bono, but at the end of the day he has children and needs to make a living. Especially since he lost his wife.'

'What happened?' Eve met Neil's eyes and saw sadness there.

'Tragic it was. Linda grew up round here. Lovely girl. They have two young children, a girl and a boy. Terrible thing when kids lose a mum like that. It was cancer. She fought it but it claimed her in the end and she was only thirty-one.' He shook his head.

'That's so sad.' Eve's eyes stung for the woman who'd lost her life, for the children without a mother and for Oliver, a man bringing up his family alone. Life could be so cruel.

Neil nodded. 'We're lucky here in Conwenna Cove, though. It's a real community and everyone chips in to do what they can. Oliver's had a lot of support, although nothing can make up for what he's lost. But like I was saying, the community here helps the hounds as much as it can… from funds raised at the annual village fair to generous tourists who donate when they're around. We've been quite lucky in that respect, and obviously Elena and I do what we can ourselves.'

'They're too soft sometimes.' Jack smiled. 'You should have seen it up here at Christmas.'

'Really? Why?'

'Not one dog without a present.'

Eve glanced back at Neil and noted his flushed cheeks. He evidently had a generous heart.

'That was down to the shoebox appeal. Gifts came from far and wide for that one.' Neil stood up. 'People can be very kind, especially at Christmas.'

'So who's up for some attention today?' Jack asked.

'Mainly Gabe. He needs some time in the assessment room to see how he reacts to normal surroundings.'

'What does that involve?' Eve asked.

'We want to see how he deals with objects that would be found in a normal family home. Most of these dogs have never been in a house before,' Neil explained. 'So they need to get used to similar surroundings before they can be homed.'

'Can I help with that?' Eve asked, toying with the handle of the bag containing Gabe's treats.

'That would be great. Thanks, Eve. Jack can explain the process to you in more detail.'

'Come on, I'll show you the assessment room.' Jack took her arm gently and her skin tingled where his fingers touched her.

They left the office and went around the back of the stables, then through a door at the end. Eve was surprised to find herself walking into someone's living room. Except it wasn't. It was a room in the barn made to look like someone's living room. It had two sofas draped in patch-work quilts, a table that held an old portable television, and a coffee table in the centre of the room. A small window with red curtains looked out onto the yard, and there was another window in the back wall next to a door.

'That door goes through to a room with a kettle and a toilet,' Jack explained. 'The window is there so that whoever's working with the dogs can keep an eye on them when they're left alone and see how they react to being in a home.'

Eve nodded. 'Do they behave?'

'Sometimes, though sometimes they mess things up a bit. We've had to replace the cushions and the coffee table a few times after they've had a good chew on them. It's like Neil said... many of the dogs don't know how to react in a home environment. It's all about helping them to adapt, kind of like rehabilitating them so they can be rehomed.'

Eve gazed around the room. 'So can I sit in here with Gabe?'

'Sure. Today we'll just let him have a good sniff around and try not to react to the things he does. We have to allow them to adapt.'

'How long can it take?'

'Depends on the dog. They're all different. I'll go get Gabe now and you make yourself a coffee if you like, then perhaps take a seat.' He gestured at the sofa.

'See you in a bit,' Eve replied as she headed to the kitchen area. She knew that she needed to mentally prepare herself to see Gabe again. Just like Jack, he'd been wounded by his past, and just like with Jack, she was apprehensive about startling him or scaring him away. She wanted them both to learn to trust her, though deep down she knew she had no right to do so when she'd be leaving soon. Where would that leave Jack and Gabe? And where would it leave her, especially if she gave them both access to her heart?

Chapter 15

Eve had finished her coffee and washed and dried the mug by the time she heard the door to the assessment room open. She popped her head out of the small kitchen and saw Jack holding a rather reticent-looking Gabe. He caught her eye and placed a finger over his lips, then led Gabe into the room and removed his lead.

'What should I do?' Eve asked.

'Just take a seat for now. He's been in here a few times already, but not for long and not alone. It will help having you in here for company.'

'Okay.' She perched on the sofa that sat against the back wall and watched. Gabe sniffed by the door, then around the edges of the room. He was nervous; his tail was down and his ears were flat against his head.

Eve bit her lip.

'Hey, don't be nervous. He'll sense it.'

She pushed further back onto the sofa and tried to relax.

'Be as normal as possible. Whatever normal is.' Jack grinned at her.

'Of course.' She placed her hands in her lap.

'I'll just make a cuppa.' Jack went through the door into the kitchen area.

Eve sighed. She had to loosen up a bit in order to allow Gabe a chance of being in a so-called normal environment. She would imagine that she was in a home, doing normal things while her dog wandered around the lounge.

But what did normal people do? Eve wasn't used to sitting still or spending time at home. If she was, would she watch TV? Do the ironing? Make dinner?

All these things were what other people did; people with husbands and families and lives. Eve didn't have that type of life. So how could she be normal?

Her heart raced and she leaned over her knees. *Breathe slowly. Calm down.*

She rested her chin on her hands and closed her eyes. *In and out. In and out. There... cool and calm.*

A sudden loud sniffing at her right ear startled her. She opened her eyes and there he was. Gabe. Right next to her, staring at her as if she was the most interesting thing he'd ever seen. His head was tilted to one side and his ears were pointing straight up.

'Hello.' Eve spoke softly, not wanting to frighten him away.

He tilted his head the other way.

'How are you, Gabe?'

She slowly reached out her hand and he took a step backwards.

'It's okay, boy. I promise I'm nice.'

She stretched her arm to get her hand closer to the large dog. He paused, then sniffed her fingers and her palm.

'That's it, boy. There you go.'

She remembered the things she'd bought him in the village. She leaned over and lifted the bag from the side of the sofa and opened it carefully to avoid making too much noise. Then she pulled out the dog treats and placed them on her lap.

Gabe watched her, his big black nose twitching.

'How about a treat?'

She opened the packet and took out a brown circle. As she raised it, the smell of meat met her nostrils. It must have met Gabe's too, because he approached her licking his lips.

'Go on. It's for you.' She opened her hand so that the treat sat on her fingers then held them out but not too far, so that Gabe had to move closer.

He eyed her for a moment, then his whiskers tickled her fingers as he took the treat gently. 'Such a good boy,' Eve praised him.

She gave him another two before putting the bag away again.

'You can have some more later, Gabe. You want me to stroke your ears now? Or give you a brush? I'm sure we can find a brush here somewhere.' She looked around the room and took in the paintings on the walls that she'd failed to notice earlier. She was certain they must be Jack's; they had his style written all over them.

'There's no milk left,' Jack said as he emerged from the kitchen area. 'I'll pop to the farmhouse to get some. Officially I shouldn't really leave you two alone, with you being new here, but I'll be quick as I can. Will you be okay?'

'I think so. We seem to be making friends.'

'I'll be right back.' Jack left the assessment room and quietly closed the door.

Eve gasped as a weight landed on the cushions to her left, making her bounce up and down. Gabe had joined her on the sofa. She watched him as he circled, round and round, until finally settling at the other end and letting out a long, satisfied grunt. She shifted slowly so that she faced him, and rested her head on the back of the sofa.

Gabe gazed at her, his white eyebrows moving in turn. She wasn't sure if this was allowed; hadn't even thought to ask about allowing the dog on the sofas in the assessment room. For now, it seemed that she had won a fraction of Gabe's trust, and she knew that trusting was a big deal for a dog who'd been through the ordeal he had endured. It was food for thought, she mused as she closed her eyes. If a dog like Gabe could begin to put the past behind him and learn to trust again, even if it was a slow process, then perhaps Eve could do the same. She knew that she'd already started to trust Jack. Her problem was learning to trust herself and her instincts; that was something that wouldn't be quite so straightforward.

–

Jack had got stuck in the farmhouse kitchen for longer than he'd been comfortable with, but Elena had started chatting and once she got going she was hard to stop. In the end, he'd had to interrupt to tell her he'd left Eve with Gabe but only to get some milk. Concern had crossed her face and she'd encouraged him to return to the assessment room immediately.

He approached the window quietly and peered through the glass. And what he saw made his heart soar.

There on the sofa were Eve and Gabe. Eve was facing away from the window but she was leaning back against the cushions and the slow movement of her chest told him that she was probably asleep. Gabe lay on his front facing her, watching her intently as if she was the most interesting thing he'd ever seen. Jack hated the idea of disturbing them, but it was better that he woke her than someone else. Better for Eve. Better for him. He didn't want anyone else to see her like that, all sleepy and sweet. He walked towards the door, then winced. What was wrong with him? He was getting all protective and even a bit possessive, it seemed. Eve wasn't his; she wasn't his woman, his lover, his wife. He had no more right to wake her up than any other man, and yet...

He wanted to be there when she woke, the first one to see her pretty smile that warmed him right through like the rays of the sun when they burst through the clouds on a winter's day. She had that power over him; she made him feel like he mattered, like she actually saw him and appreciated him for who he was.

He turned the door handle and entered the assessment room. Gabe watched as he approached. 'Hey, boy. How're you doing?' Jack spoke softly, keen to stop the large dog from jumping down and startling Eve.

Just then she opened her eyes and blinked, clearly confused by her surroundings, then she looked at Gabe and smiled. 'Hey, boy. Hey, Jack.'

'You okay? Sorry I took longer than expected, but Elena got talking.' He shrugged. 'I came back and saw you sleeping through the window.'

Eve scratched her head then rubbed her eyes. As she moved, Gabe shuffled around on the sofa, then slid off and stood in front of her. He shook himself suddenly, as if shaking water off, and Eve chuckled. 'I can't believe I nodded off, and so quickly. How'd he do that?'

'It's the greyhound effect,' Jack replied. 'Has he been all right?'

She nodded. 'He sniffed around for a while then came and had a few treats. Next thing I knew, he was on the sofa with me and... well, I wasn't going to argue with him.'

'That's fine. Whatever helps the hounds acclimatize is acceptable here. I didn't expect him to relax so soon. You must have the magic touch.'

Eve smiled and stretched. '*He* has the magic touch.'

'So it seems.' Jack held out his hand. Eve took it and he pulled her to her feet. One side of her hair was flat where it had pressed against the sofa and he had to tuck his hands in his pockets to avoid running his fingers through it to fluff it up for her. 'Your… uh… your hair's a bit flat there.'

'Oh!' Eve ran a hand through it. 'That's the problem with such a short haircut. If I had the patience I'd grow it out, but I never seem to get around to letting it get past my ears.'

'It suits you like it is. Kind of cute.'

A smile played on her lips. 'Cute, eh? Like a puppy cute?'

'If you like.' He shrugged and grinned. 'You hungry?'

'Always, with this sea air.'

'Come on then. Let's walk Gabe, then I'll take you into the village and we can grab a bite to eat.'

He put the lead back on Gabe then followed Eve out into the afternoon sunshine. Since she'd arrived, they hadn't had any rain and he was convinced that it was a good omen. Or he would be if he believed in such things. As it was, he just liked to believe that Eve brought the sunshine with her. And he was happy to bask in her rays.

–

Eve sat in the cosy booth and stared at the menu. There was so much choice. Jack had recommended the diner down by the harbour. Its floor-to-ceiling windows faced out across the sea, and Eve felt as if she was on a boat. The diner was decked out as though it was stuck in a time warp, with red and silver seats and a black and white checked floor. It even had an old jukebox near the bar.

The lighting was low and it added to the cosy appeal. A Sinatra tune played softly and the combined effect made Eve feel relaxed and happy. If only she could stay in Conwenna. The pace of life here was so much slower that she was used to, and better quality too. In the past, she'd believed that anything less than one hundred miles an hour would be too slow for her, but apparently not. Perhaps it was her age; perhaps it was everything she'd been through. But more and more she found herself wishing that she could remain in this idyllic part of Cornwall.

'Who owns this place?' she asked.

'Zoe Russell. I don't know if she's in today but she's really nice. I think Mary said she bought the diner about six months ago.'

'Looks like she's doing well.' Eve appraised her surroundings.

'Yeah, she did a bit of a refurb, and even off season it's quite popular. People from other towns drive in, some just for the milkshakes.'

'What'll you have?' A waitress appeared at their table in a pink and white checked tunic with a frilled apron tied around her waist. Her hair was up in a beehive and her lipstick matched the pink of her outfit.

'I'll take the house special with a banana milkshake, please,' Jack said as he handed over the menu.

'I'll have the same, thanks.' Eve closed her menu and met the waitress's curious eyes.

'You do know what the house special is, right?'

Eve looked at Jack and saw him smiling broadly. 'What? No, I… uh… I thought it was a burger or something. Isn't it?'

'It's a *monster* of a burger!' The waitress held her hands wide apart. 'It's like HUGE!'

'Oh. Uh… do you have something similar but not quite so… huge?'

'I'll get Chef to make you a smaller version if you like.' The waitress scribbled something on her notepad.

'That would be great, thanks.'

As the girl walked away, Jack let out a snort of laughter.

'What?' Eve's cheeks burned. 'I didn't know it would be some humongous meal, did I?'

'It's not that!' Jack laughed and slapped his hand on the table.

'Then what is it?'

'I saw what she wrote on her pad.'

'And?' Eve took a sip of her water to avoid pouting like a sulky teenager.

'She put you down for a child's version.'

'No!'

'Yeah!'

Eve shook her head.

'You are kind of tiny.'

'I can't help being short, can I?'

'I didn't mean that,' Jack said, his face serious now.

'You mean thin.' Eve's stomach sank. She knew how she looked. 'I'm working on that.'

'Look, Eve. You're beautiful. But you do look like you've been through a tough time. Mind you, you're already looking better than you did just last week.'

'It's doing me good being here.'

'It is.'

'I wish...' She stopped herself. Sinatra had been replaced by Elvis, who was singing about a hound dog. The song made her want to move in time, to click her fingers and even to dance. But people didn't do things like that in harbourside diners, did they? And there was no point in wishing for things either. She wasn't a child, even if she was being served a child's meal. She was an adult with adult responsibilities and she had to tend to them sooner or later.

'What, Eve? What do you wish?' Jack reached across the table and took her hand. He slid his thumb over her palm and stroked it, his touch so tender and gentle that it sent tiny delightful sparks all through her body. The song slowed down and Elvis crooned from the jukebox.

'I just wish... that food would hurry up! I'm starving.' She pressed her lips together, glad that she'd saved herself. But as she looked at Jack and saw the sadness in his eyes, she regretted lying. He knew what she'd been about to say and he'd needed to hear it.

So why couldn't she tell him?

–

'Ouch! I ate too much!' Eve slumped in her seat and rubbed her swollen belly.

Jack grinned at her then popped his last chip into his mouth. 'Good food, though?'

'Delicious!'

'I can't believe you ate two extra sides with your child's meal.'

'I told you it wouldn't be enough. But now I'm thinking I overdid it.'

'You'll digest it soon and you'll feel much better.'

'I'll have to undo my top button, though.'

'Carry on!' Jack waved a hand at her as if undoing her jeans was perfectly acceptable behaviour when out in public.

She popped the button and sighed as her stomach relaxed. 'That's a bit better.'

'A food baby.' Jack gestured at her stomach. 'That's what they call it, isn't it?'

Eve shuddered as a cold chill ran down her spine. 'I'm sorry?'

'A food baby. You know, you're so full you look pregnant.'

Eve's lunch churned in her gut. She reached for her water and took a sip.

'Eve, what is it? You've gone ashen.'

She shook her head. 'Nothing.'

The Platters' 'Only You' floated around the diner, and Eve felt emotion welling inside her.

Jack took her hand across the table. 'I've offended you, haven't I? I didn't mean that you look fat. Of course not! You're lovely. It's good to see you enjoying your food. I mean, I—'

Eve held up a hand. 'It's okay, Jack. I'm fine. Just full. A walk would help.'

'Of course.'

Ten minutes later, they strolled from the harbour back towards the village. Clouds had gathered during their time at the diner and Eve shivered at the drop in temperature.

'You want my jumper?' Jack asked, offering the sweat-shirt that was draped over his arm.

Eve was about to decline, but her T-shirt was thin, and although she'd been warm earlier, now she felt cold and tired. 'Thank you.'

They stopped walking while Jack helped her to pull it over her head. It smelt fresh, warm and masculine. She fought the urge to press her face into the sleeve in order to sniff it properly.

'Better?'

'Yes.' She nodded, though the jumper was huge on her.

Jack tucked his hands into his pockets and they carried on walking up the hill.

'What do you want to do now?' he asked.

'We should probably get back, I guess. But we could have a wander through the main street first if you fancy it?'

'I'd like that.'

'Do you have to go back to the farm later?'

Jack nodded. 'I'm on the late shift. Jerry asked me if I'd swap as he has a hot date!'

'Jerry?'

'He works at the farm and helps out with the dogs. He's about my age, I think. He's a quiet chap and really nice. He doesn't give much away but we went out for a pint one night and the beer loosened his tongue. To cut a long story short, he's been here for about ten years. He moved here with his wife but she left him last year. She'd been in contact with a holiday rep she met when they were on holiday in Spain and she went back out there to be with him.'

'Wow!'

'I know. Poor guy. But he seems okay. He's been out on a few dates recently. It's Elena, see. She keeps setting him up.'

'Did she do the same for you?' The question escaped before Eve could stop it.

'No. I politely declined. I'm not... I mean, I wasn't interested in getting to know any women.'

'And now?'

He released a deep breath. 'I think you know the answer to that, Eve.'

They started up the hill, passing the shops with their arrays of souvenirs and other wares. Outside Pebbles, the gift shop, wind chimes tinkled and driftwood garlands swayed in the breeze. Eve gazed at the colourful buckets and spades and the foil windmills that caught the light as they spun. The next shop was Riding the Wave, whose window display featured surfboards, wetsuits and some very skimpy bikinis. The breeze carried the scents of chips and bread, suncream and salt. It was the scent of summer and it tugged at Eve's heart, making her feel happy and sad simultaneously.

They passed Scoops and Sprinkles, then slowed down when they reached the Conwenna Bookshop. Eve perused the display of the latest best-sellers in the window but couldn't help noticing their reflections as they stood side by side: tall, broad Jack, with his tanned face and dark eyes, next to her, tiny in comparison, swamped in his sweatshirt but with some colour in her cheeks. Despite the height difference, they looked like a couple. A handsome couple, physical opposites perhaps, but that could be a good thing. Couldn't it?

'Will Gabe be okay?' she asked as they neared the top of the main street then turned left onto the country lane that would take them to the main road.

'What do you mean by okay?'

'Well... he's such a lovely dog. Will he find a family?' She glanced at Jack's profile and was stunned by how much she wanted to hold him. It wasn't just that he was handsome; he was so much more, and she was drawn to him just as she was drawn to Gabe.

'He probably will. He is a lovely dog. Most of our rescues find a home sooner or later. But I think Gabe's already chosen his new mum.'

Eve pressed a hand to her heart as she met Jack's eyes. He stopped walking and took hold of her upper arms. 'Eve, this is hard to explain without it sounding like a load of superstitious nonsense, but I really believe that these dogs choose us as much as we choose them. I've seen it happen before.'

'I can't adopt a dog. My life in Bristol is so different. I work all day and it wouldn't be fair.'

Jack nodded. 'I know. We'd never encourage someone to adopt if they're out all day and can't commit. That would be unfair on the dog. But Gabe has bonded with you, and if I'm not mistaken, you have with him.'

Eve nodded slowly and bit her lip hard.

A small group of teenagers passed them, laughing and joking. One of them held his mobile phone above his head and the beats of a popular chart tune filled the air around them. She wondered if the teenagers lived in Conwenna or if they were on holiday.

She waited until they'd walked away before answering.

'I do care about him. But I can't adopt him.'

She had taken to the dog and knew that she could love him, but she had to be practical. She had to be fair on Gabe and on herself.

'You could if your life changed, Eve. Nothing is impossible.'

Not when I'm with you... She didn't vocalize the thought. Instead it spun round and round in her head.

'Come on,' Jack said as he released her arms and placed his hand on her back. 'Let's get back to Mary's and make a cup of tea. Things have a way of working out.'

'I hope you're right.'

As they walked up the lane then crossed the road and took the gravel path to Mary's cottage, Eve thought she heard Jack mutter, 'Me too.'

Chapter 16

When Eve descended the stairs on Sunday morning, the house was unusually quiet. She'd become accustomed to hearing Mary pottering about in the kitchen and singing as she went about her routines, but today there was silence.

She walked into the kitchen and switched the kettle on, then peered out the window. The morning was darker than any she'd experienced since her arrival in Conwenna and it looked as though it might rain later. As the kettle bubbled away, she leaned against the unit and thought about yesterday. She learned more about Jack every day, and about herself. She'd never thought she'd ever consider adopting a dog, but now... now she was racking her brain to think of a way to make it work. Like Jack had said, nothing was impossible. The idea of going back to Bristol and leaving everything behind was something she was struggling with, but she didn't have to do it yet.

When she'd arrived back at the cottage yesterday, Jack had gone for a nap before his late shift at the farm and Aunt Mary had been out, so she'd taken advantage of the time alone to read and snuggle with the dogs on the sofa. Quiet time wasn't actually as bad as she'd come to believe. Being in Conwenna, she didn't have her usual commitments, so putting her feet up with a book and a mug of tea seemed acceptable. She was learning, slowly, how to relax and switch off. Mary still hadn't returned by teatime, so she'd made herself a sandwich, not needing anything more substantial after her huge lunch with Jack, and taken her book up to bed. She'd fallen asleep reading and not stirred until seven this morning.

She hadn't heard Mary come home but her shoes were by the front door so she must have come back at some point. She decided to make her aunt some tea and take it up to her. Who didn't like tea in bed in the morning?

Once the tea had brewed, she carried the mug upstairs and knocked gently on her door. 'Aunt Mary? Are you awake?'

There was no answer.

'Hello?'

Still no answer.

Eve's stomach churned with unease. This wasn't good. She didn't want to disturb her aunt's lie-in but she didn't want to leave her there if something was wrong. She knocked once more and heard a soft moan.

'I'm coming in, Aunt Mary!'

She pushed the door open and stepped inside. Her aunt's room was at the front of the cottage overlooking the yard. It was normally bright and airy, but this morning, with the curtains closed and the morning dark with the threat of a storm, it seemed small and stuffy. 'Sorry to wake you, but I was worried. I thought you might like some tea.' She placed the mug on the bedside table closest to where there was a shape under the duvet, then stood there waiting for a response.

Nothing.

'Aunt Mary? Are you all right?'

'Yes, dear. Thanks for the tea,' Mary mumbled from under the duvet.

'It's just that you're always up and about so early and this morning, well…'

Eve looked around the room, suddenly feeling awkward. This was her aunt's house and if Mary wanted to sleep in then that was up to her. But something about this wasn't right.

'Can I get you anything else? Some toast perhaps.'

'No thank you. I'll be down in a bit. I'm just tired, Eve.' Her aunt kept the quilt over her head and it muffled her voice.

'Really? Um… could you just let me see your face? I need to know you're okay. I'm getting worried.'

'Umphh!' came from beneath the duvet.

'Please?'

'Oh all right.'

The bed moved as Mary wriggled upright and sat against the headboard. Her hair was ruffled and she sniffed as she pushed it from her face.

Eve moved closer. 'Oh Aunt Mary, what happened?'

Mary shrugged as she rearranged the covers.

'Can I let some light in?'

'If you like, dear.'

'And some air?' Eve pulled the curtains apart then cracked the window open. The breeze blew in through the gap, fresh and cool, carrying with it the scents of salt and cut grass. She breathed deeply then turned back to Mary.

And gasped.

'I'm fine, dear. Really.' Mary lifted her mug and took a sip of tea. As she lowered it again, Eve saw that her hands were trembling.

'You are not! What on earth is wrong?' Eve approached the bed then perched on the edge and stared at her aunt.

Mary's face was red and her eyes were swollen, their edges white and puffy. 'Have you been crying?'

Mary nodded. 'Silly old fool that I am.'

'No. You're not old and you're no fool. But why are you so upset?'

Mary lifted her chin and met Eve's eyes. 'Men, eh?'

'What?' Eve was filled with sudden anger. 'Edward did this to you?'

'Not his fault.'

'Well if he's upset you this much, I think I'd better go and speak to him. I mean... how dare he? How *bloody* dare he?' As Eve stood up, she realized she didn't actually know what had happened, so she sat back down and took Mary's hand instead.

'Ah, love, it's just life, you know?' Mary gave a half-hearted chuckle. 'These things happen.'

'But what happened? What was so bad?'

'Edward... proposed.'

'He proposed?' Eve chewed a ragged fingernail. 'But that's a good thing. That's sweet and romantic and... not what you want?'

'Oh Eve, I'm too long in the tooth for all that.'

Eve paused for a moment. So her aunt was upset because the man she'd been seeing had asked her to marry him. She hadn't seen much of Mary and Edward together, but surely a proposal was evidence that they cared about each other. They clearly had that intimacy of a couple in love; it was clear for all around to see. 'But don't you love him?'

Mary drained her mug then placed it carefully on the bedside table. 'I do care for him very much. If we'd been younger, then maybe it would have been different.' She lowered her eyes to her hands then rubbed the fingers of the one over the raised veins on the other. 'But time has gone by so quickly, Eve. Too quickly if I'm honest. The time for such... stuff has passed for me.'

'Now that is absolute nonsense!' Eve snapped as she covered Mary's hands with her own. 'There's no age limit on love. You and Edward are in a relationship. You obviously care about each other, so why not get married?'

Mary lifted her head and smiled sadly. 'Eve, I do love him, I know that much. But getting married? That's for you youngsters.'

'I can't believe you would say that, Aunt Mary. You're normally so sensible and practical and...' Eve bit her lip as realization dawned. She'd always thought of Mary simply as her aunt, her caring, practical older relation who just got on with things. But she was also a person, a woman, and, it seemed, just as stubborn and irrational at times as Eve could be herself. Just because her aunt was older, it didn't mean that she had all the answers or all the common sense. She was a woman who'd once been a girl and who was now facing a big decision that could take her life in a very different direction. She needed help and advice, love and support, and Eve would do what she could to help her through this.

'I told him last night that I didn't want to get married and he asked if I'd at least think about it, but I shall meet him later today and tell him no. It won't work. We're too old.'

'Aunt Mary... Edward makes you happy when you're with him, right?'

Mary nodded.

'And do you miss him when he's not with you?'

'Well, you know me, Eve, always so busy and—'

Eve shook her head. 'Do you miss him when he's not here? Or you're not there?'

Mary sighed. 'Yes.'

'Then why not make it official? Life's too short to miss opportunities to be happy. You have to seize them when they come along.'

'But what about the practicalities?'

'Such as?'

'Where would we live? I've been here for years.'

'You could both live here, or even move into his house.'

'It's a bit small. It's a fisherman's cottage, what you might call a bachelor pad down in the village.'

'Well, move him in here then.'

'You think this could work?'

'Of course I do!' Eve said, her heart filled with hope and happiness for her aunt. 'Twenty-somethings don't have the monopoly on love, you know. What have you got to lose?'

Mary's expression turned serious. 'I lost a lot before, Eve. A long, long time ago. It makes one wary, you know?'

Eve didn't know what her aunt was referring to but she knew that everyone had scars from their pasts. 'But that shouldn't stop you seizing happiness now.'

Mary nodded. 'You've given me things to consider, Eve. In fact now that I've slept on it and spoken to you about it, I'm starting to wonder if I made a huge mistake. I do love Edward, old fool that I am. And the thought of being without him is just awful.'

'So if he knocked on the door right now and asked you again, what would you say?' Eve held her breath. Perhaps she was being too pushy, but it was worth a shot.

Aunt Mary licked her lips and closed her eyes for a moment.

Take a chance!

'If he asked me again…' she opened her eyes and held Eve's gaze, 'I would say… "I'll seriously consider it."'

'Seriously consider it? But Aunt Mary, you've turned him down once. You can't toy with his emotions.'

'Eve, dear, he might not even want to ask me again, so there's no point in me getting my hopes up.'

'So you would consider saying yes, then?'

Aunt Mary pursed her lips. 'Oh all right then. Have it your way. I love him, and yes, I would say yes. I don't want to be without him.'

Eve's stomach flipped. *Now we just have to hope he will ask you again.*

'You're quite wise, you know, Eve.'

'Perhaps.'

'If only you'd take some of your own advice, though.' Aunt Mary pushed back the duvet and swung her legs over the edge of the bed.

'Sorry?' Eve watched as her aunt slid her feet into her pink moccasins then pushed her arms into her dressing gown.

'Well you've been hurt too but there are new opportunities opening up for you right now. You just need to know where to look and be prepared to take a risk.'

Mary picked up her mug and crossed the room. 'Let's have some breakfast and I'll talk you through what happened last night. It was actually all rather romantic until my silly stubbornness got in the way and scared the hell out of me.'

Eve stood up and followed her aunt downstairs, Mary's words ringing in her ears: *…there are new opportunities opening up for you right now. You just need to know where to look and be prepared to take a risk.*

'So he proposed and she turned him down?' Jack handed Eve a mug of coffee then led her into his lounge. It was smaller than Mary's and only boasted one chair and a two-seater sofa. Eve sat on the sofa and swallowed her pleasure as Jack took the seat next to her. As he placed his mug on a side table, their knees brushed and she experienced the delicious electric shock that his touch always caused.

'Yes! Can you believe it?'

Jack shook his head. 'I knew they were close but I didn't know it was heading that way. It makes sense, though. Mary is very fond of him but she doesn't say too much; she tends to keep things close to her chest. It's habit, I guess.'

'Habit?'

'Well, when someone's been hurt, they protect themselves in a variety of ways, and not talking about a relationship can be one of those ways. As if keeping it low-key can prevent it becoming too serious.'

'Aunt Mary's been hurt? What, by a lover, do you think? She did mention that she'd suffered a loss a long time ago, but I didn't want to pry.'

'Seems we've all been hurt in the past.' Jack sipped his coffee thoughtfully.

'You were hurt? I know you told me about Jodie, but you said that... that it was for the best.'

'Still hurt, though, even if it was mainly my pride. I wanted it to be more than it was, and I did marry her after all, so I guess I was hoping it would work. No one really gets married thinking they'll divorce.'

'No, they don't. That would be madness.' Eve's thoughts strayed to Darryl and the solicitor's letter. She needed to visit her own solicitor to get the paperwork sorted. Why had she been delaying? It wasn't as if there was a chance they could work things out – it had gone too far for that – but her heart still ached when she thought of how hurt Darryl had been by it all. How angry he had become. He hadn't gone into their marriage believing it would end as it had, and neither had she. But then she hadn't ever fully committed either, had she? And why not? What exactly was she protecting herself from?

Rejection? Relying on someone else?

'But Aunt Mary's never been married before.'

Jack shook his head. 'Not that I know of, but I think there's something in her past that she's not telling us. I mean, I have no right to ask her about it, but you're family. You could ask.'

'Jack, I'm pretty certain that she sees you as family now; kind of the son she never had.'

'What if that's it?'

'A child?'

He nodded. 'Could be.'

'But she never said.'

'Why would she? Things were different years ago. Having a child if you were unmarried wasn't as common-place as it is today. It would have been more likely to have been frowned upon.'

'You think she might have had a child then had it… him or her adopted?'

'It's possible.'

'Or perhaps she lost the baby?' Eve went cold all over. She knew how that felt but she'd had her job to keep her busy. What had Mary had? Had her lovely aunt lost a child in her past? Was there a secret there that she was hiding?

'Again, anything's possible. But I'm assuming that whatever it was happened before you came along, otherwise you'd know about it. Didn't your parents ever say anything about it to you?'

'No. But then… we're not close.'

Jack finished his coffee then placed his mug on the table.

'So what're we going to do about Mary and Edward?'

'I think you should go and talk to him, invite him for dinner, and I'll take care of things here. I did get her to admit that if he asked her again, she would say yes. Perhaps if we get them together they can talk, and if need be, you could give him a nudge. Mary clearly isn't happy about declining his offer. I'm certain that she really loves him.'

'Then they should be together. It's ridiculous that two people who have fallen in love should deny themselves that happiness…' Jack stopped speaking and stared at Eve. She gazed back into the unfathomable depths of his eyes, conscious of her pulse racing and her body trembling.

Say something, Eve. Break the spell.

Instead she scratched her head furiously and the moment was over. Jack coughed and looked away and she had another good scratch.

'You need to get some after-sun or something on your scalp, Eve. All that scratching's going to make your head sore.'

'I don't know what's wrong with it. I've never had such an itchy head before.'

What a way to ruin an intense moment packed with romantic possibilities, Eve. You might just as well have gone and farted!

'I'll go and get Edward, then, and you sort Mary. Shall we reconvene at eighteen hundred hours?'

'Getting all military on me now? Should I expect you to start drilling me and putting me through my paces?' Eve held out a hand and he pulled her to her feet. She stumbled forward with the force of his tug and raised her free hand instinctively. Beneath her palm, his heartbeat was strong, powerful, fast.

As fast as hers.

He covered her hand with his and leaned towards her. For a moment she thought he was going to kiss her, but instead he stopped with his mouth just millimetres from hers. He was so close she could smell the vanilla aroma of the coffee on his lips and feel his warm breath on her skin.

'You have no idea,' he whispered before gently releasing her hand and taking a step backwards. 'If I started, Eve, I wouldn't want to stop.'

Chapter 17

Jack marched down to the village, cut across the main street then headed off along a small cobbled street to Fisherman's Row. The cottages were tightly packed together with tiny yards behind and front doors that opened straight onto the narrow pavement. The low windows set into the thick walls had small panes and some of the inhabitants had adorned the sills with window boxes of colourful flowers and sweet-smelling herbs.

When he reached Edward's small white cottage, he stood outside and waited to catch his breath. He couldn't see through the front window because it was dark inside but he did admire the way Edward had painted the window frames blue to match his door. As he peered more closely, he realized it was the same forget-me-not blue as Mary's door and window frames. Had they bought the paint together then? A seagull screeched, making him jump, and he glanced up to see its beady eyes glaring at him from the chimneypot on the slanting roof.

Was he doing the right thing here, interfering in someone else's relationship? Did he have the right to get involved? He paused, his hand raised above the door, ready to knock.

He cared about Mary; she'd been so good to him since his arrival in Conwenna. So yes, he should help out if he could. It was the right thing to do. He lifted his hand to knock and brought it down hard, but just before it hit the blue-painted wood, the door swung open and his fist met with human flesh.

'Ah!' Edward cried out as his nose was crushed under Jack's knuckles.

'Oh shit! Edward! I'm sorry!'

'Ahhhh!' Edward doubled over, his hands pressed to his face as blood gushed from between his fingers.

'I'm so sorry.'

'You didn't need to do this!' Edward slurred from behind his hands. 'I did nothing wrong!'

'Quick, let me help you!' Jack took the older man's arm and ushered him back into the cottage, ducking to avoid the low beam as he entered the doorway. As he shut the door behind them, he caught a glimpse of Mrs Bringle next door peering out with concern written all over her face.

Jack managed to get Edward into his small kitchen then sat him on a bench and went to the sink. He ran the cold tap then grabbed a tea towel and pushed it under the flow. When it was wet, he wrung it out and handed it to Edward. 'Here. Hold this over your nose for a bit to stem the bleeding.'

Edward removed his hands and Jack bit the inside of his cheek to stop himself gasping. There was so much blood and Edward's eyes were already swelling.

'Why did you hit me?' Edward asked, dabbing cautiously at his nose with the towel.

'It was an accident. I went to knock on the door but I was distracted and when my hand came down your face was there instead.'

Edward shook his head. 'Not exactly a fair fight with you being an ex-marine.'

'No, I know that. And I would never hit you deliberately.' He stepped closer to Edward and gently removed the towel. 'There you go. It's not as bad as it looks.' Bile curdled in his gut at the lie.

'It's not you with your nose plastered all over your face.' Edward sounded as if he had a heavy cold.

Jack shook his head. 'It's just a nosebleed caused by the impact. But I'm afraid you're going to have two shiners. God, Edward, I really am sorry.'

Edward shrugged. 'Whisky?'

Jack nodded. 'Good plan.'

He opened the cupboard that Edward pointed at and found a bottle of Scotch, then took two tumblers from a glass-fronted cupboard and set them on the table. He poured a finger's worth into each glass and handed one to Edward, then sat on the bench next to him.

'So why're you here?' Edward said as he removed the towel and took a sip of his whisky.

'To try to help.'

'Help be buggered! You just smashed my face in. I'll never pull looking like this.' Edward sounded shocked but his eyes twinkled.

'Pull?'

'Well… now that I'm single again.'

'Single?'

Edward threw the rest of his whisky down his throat and signalled to Jack to pour him another. 'Mary turned me down last night. She doesn't want to be with me.'

'Oh. Uh… I knew she'd declined your proposal, but I didn't know it was that final.'

'I don't know what else to think. She gave me some madcap excuse about age and being too late in the day, but like I said to her, we deserve a shot at happiness and

206

it's silly us living apart any longer. I love the woman, Jack, I really do, and I want to share my life with her. Neither of us is at death's door yet. I mean, bloody hell, we could have another thirty years together! That's more than a lot of couples have now, isn't it?'

Jack nodded as he refilled both their tumblers.

'I wish we'd met when we were younger, but we can't change that, and you know what?'

Jack shook his head.

'There's life in this old seadog yet!' Edward threw back his head and laughed. 'And in this old seadog too!' He gestured at his groin and Jack had to cover his mouth with his glass. He had absolutely no desire to know about Mary and Edward's sex life; the woman was like a mother to him!

'Well that's great to hear, Edward. But I came here to ask you to come up to the cottage for dinner. See, Mary might have said no but she's not happy about it.'

'She isn't?' Edward's eyes glittered but Jack wasn't sure if it was from the whisky or the punch to the nose.

'Nope. So Eve and I thought if you came for dinner it would give the two of you a chance to talk about things. Perhaps find a way forward.'

'I'd like that. But she hurt me last night, you know. I offered her everything, even my fishing boat to be at her disposal. I laid my heart on the line and she said no. That stung, Jack. Since I lost my wife all those years ago, I never thought I'd care about anyone again, but Mary... she's kind of special. You understand what I mean?'

Jack nodded. He certainly did. Eve had got under his skin in a way he'd never thought anyone would do. Perhaps there was a perfect someone out there for everyone, or perhaps he was getting soft living life as a civilian.

'So shall we get you cleaned up, then head to Mary's?'

'I'm not sure.' Edward stared down at his shoes.

'You're not sure?' Jack's heart sank. Had Mary blown it then?

'Well, no. You say she's not happy about it, but where does that leave me? She's not the kind of woman to live with a man if she's not married to him. And she didn't want to marry me last night, so why has she changed her mind?'

'Look, Edward, I have it on good authority that she regrets turning you down, okay? She said no instinctively, out of shock or surprise or on some sort of fear impulse. Marriage is a big step and she panicked, but she does love you.'

'She told you that?'

'She told Eve and Eve told me. I really think you should give it one more shot. If you love her and want her to be your wife, that is.'

Edward nodded, his white eyebrows going up and down as he listened. Then he sighed. 'I don't want to be without her. She's a ray of sunshine in my life, and since we started seeing each other, I've been so happy. It was just as friends for a while, you know, but it slowly morphed into something more.'

'As often happens.' Jack smiled.

'Indeed it does.'

'So shall we get you back to Mary's?'

'Sure thing!' Edward agreed as he drained his second whisky then thumped his glass onto the table. 'And on the way there, you can tell me a bit more about you and Mary's niece, because I saw the way you were looking at her the other day, and the way you slid your arm around her shoulders when you thought we weren't looking when we were watching TV. There's something going on there, maybe more than you realize. You mark my words.' He wagged a finger at Jack, then got to his feet. 'But first things first, I need to change this shirt.'

Jack followed his eyes and winced at the blood spatters over Edward's front. He'd never hit someone deliberately in his life outside of combat, and it was just typical that this should happen today, when he'd only come to lend a hand.

—

Eve placed the bottle of wine on the table then stood back and admired the view. There'd be no traditional Sunday lunch for the men when they arrived, but she'd done the best with what was in the fridge and the cupboards.

'Oh, it looks delicious, Eve,' Mary said as she entered the kitchen and paused next to the table.

'You look beautiful!' Eve exclaimed as she took in Mary's cream linen trousers and short-sleeved fawn silk blouse. Her aunt had clipped her bobbed hair at the nape of her neck and it showed off the silver feather earrings that she wore. She'd also added a touch of blusher and a slick of shimmering copper lip gloss that showed off her golden tan.

'Thank you, dear. I think I could do with a drop of that wine to steady my nerves, though.'

'Of course. But you don't need to be nervous. You just need to be honest.' *Not so easy to do when your heart's involved.*

'Yes, you're right, dear. I know that. But what if Edward doesn't want to come? What if I hurt him badly and he doesn't want to... you know... make up now?'

'He will. If he loves you.' Eve saw fear flitter across Mary's features. 'And he does love you or he wouldn't have proposed, now would he?'

'No. Oh Eve, I hope he still wants me, because now I've decided to accept him, I couldn't bear it if he didn't.'

Eve lifted the bottle and poured some wine into a glass. As the honey-coloured liquid glugged out, the scents of strawberry and Turkish delight teased her nostrils. 'Here.' She handed the glass to Mary.

Her aunt took it, and as she raised it to her lips, Eve saw that her hand was trembling.

'Aunt Mary, it will all be fine, I promise. I'll make sure that it is.' She wrapped an arm around her aunt's shoulders and hugged her, hoping that she hadn't just made a promise she couldn't keep. 'Now let's get this meal prepared.'

–

'Hello!'

Ten minutes later, Eve's heart flipped when she heard Jack's voice. As he walked into the kitchen, she turned slowly from the sink where she was rinsing spinach leaves, hoping that Edward would be there too.

And he was.

'This looks fabulous, Mary!' Jack said as he admired the spread of cold meats, cheeses and potato salad.

'Nothing to do with me. It seems that my niece actually can rustle up a meal when she wants to.' Mary smiled at Eve and winked.

Eve's cheeks glowed. 'It was all in the fridge; I just laid it out.'

'And made the potato salad from scratch.' Mary pointed at the bowl of home-grown new potatoes coated in mayonnaise and chives.

'Hello, Mary.' Edward approached her and Mary gasped.

'My goodness, Edward! Whatever happened to your face?'

Eve peered around Jack to see what had caused her aunt's reaction.

'Uh… a slight miscalculation,' Edward replied.

'Miscalculation?' Mary took hold of his chin and stared at his black eyes and the swelling on the bridge of his nose. 'What, someone swung a wrecking ball at a building and it missed and hit you instead?'

Edward shook his head and chuckled. 'Not quite, my love.'

'It was me,' Jack said, hanging his head. 'I'm so sorry. I went to knock on the door but Edward opened it and I hit him by mistake.'

Eve's mouth fell open. 'If that was by mistake, I'd hate to see what you can do if you deliberately punch someone.'

Mary and Edward took seats at the table, and as Mary fussed over Edward's face, Jack stepped closer to Eve. 'You don't think I'd do something like that deliberately, do you?'

Eve turned and met his eyes. She could drown in their chocolate depths; lose herself forever in their warmth and intensity. 'I don't think you would, no. But then I don't know you all that well, do I?'

'Eve...' He took her shoulders gently and gazed into her eyes. 'You know me better than you realize. I've shared more with you in the time we've known each other than I have done with anyone else in years.'

Eve's mouth was dry, and as she gazed at Jack, the rest of the kitchen blurred out of focus. 'What do we do now?'

'We eat, then give these two some space.'

She nodded. 'You think they'll be okay?'

Jack smiled. 'Of course they will. Now pour me a glass of wine, beautiful lady, and come sit with me at the table. I'm ravenous.'

—

'Eve, are you all right?' asked Mary.

'Sorry?' Eve scratched her head again.

'You just seem to be scratching quite a lot.'

'I think it's from being in the sea.' Jack raised his eyes from his food and met Eve's warning look.

'You've been in the sea?' Mary grinned. 'And when was this, Eve? You didn't tell me you'd been swimming.'

Eve's cheeks flamed as she thought about what she'd actually been doing in the sea. 'Yes. I went down to the cove and felt like going in for a swim. The water looked so inviting.'

As did Jack.

'You always did enjoy swimming, didn't you? When you were a child, we'd head down to the beach and picnic there often. They were some of the happiest days of my life.'

'Mine too,' Eve replied as she watched her aunt's eyes misting over. 'Those summers were precious.'

'We should all go down there together soon,' Edward said. 'Take a picnic, have a swim and make the most of this lovely weather before the tourists really pour in.'

'Yes, high summer gets so busy now,' Mary said. 'Not so much the cove, as the visitors tend to head to the larger beaches further along the coast, but some days the village is packed tight as a can of sardines.'

'I'll miss all of th—' The words were out before Eve had really thought them through. She glanced at Jack and saw him grimace. Why was this so difficult? The thought of not being in Conwenna in July and August to witness the mass of tourists enjoying the picturesque village, not seeing Edward and her aunt enjoying their relationship, not being with Gabe and Jack, was just unbearable. It made her feel physically sick.

'Well perhaps you can come back for the wedding,' Edward said as he removed his napkin from his lap and stood up.

'Pardon?' Mary asked as Edward slowly lowered himself to one knee in front of her and took her hands. 'Oh my! Edward, get up or you might get stuck.'

'I'm not that old yet, thank you.'

'Yes, but you have that sticky knee!' Mary laughed as Edward shook his head.

'Shush, woman! Let me do this properly and don't break my heart all over again.'

'Okay.' Mary dabbed at her eyes and gazed at him.

Eve held her breath. She couldn't believe this was happening right here in front of her eyes.

'What I was trying to say was that Eve can come back for our August wedding. I've arranged for us to marry down in the cove. I thought it would be beautiful at twilight on the sixth of August.'

'My birthday?'

Edward nodded.

'How have you arranged that? When?'

'I'd already done it, but after last night I cancelled it. Then, after Jack came and spoke to me today, I made a few telephone calls and set it all up again. Risky perhaps, but you're worth it. I'd do it a thousand times over, Mary, if it meant that there was a chance of you saying yes.' He coughed. 'As long as I knew you would actually say yes in the end, that is. I'm no fool. Well, I guess I am, but only where you're concerned.'

'Edward!' Mary cupped his face and pressed a kiss to his lips. 'I'm waiting.'

'Yes, so you are. Well then. With no further ado... Mary, I love you. You make me smile every day. I love how you walk, how you talk, how you light up a room when you enter it. I am grateful with all my heart that you entered my life. Without you there is no joy for me. I don't want to spend another day without telling the world officially that you're mine. If you can stand looking at me with my blackened eyes and swollen nose,' he flashed a scowl at Jack, 'I would be thrilled if you'd honour me by becoming my wife.'

'Oh darling, of course I will!' Mary leaned forward and kissed him gently, lingering there with her forehead against his as she stroked his cheeks.

Eve blinked but she couldn't see. Everything had blurred.

'Hey, softy!' Jack squeezed the back of her neck. 'This is a happy occasion.'

Eve nodded and used her napkin to dab at her nose.

'Now,' Edward said when Mary had released him. 'If you could just help me up, Jack, that would be wonderful.'

214

Jack took his hand from Eve's neck and stood up.

'Careful, young man. It's my knee, you see. Old fishing injury... got tangled in the damned nets in a storm and went down heavy. Almost broke my leg in two. Now it tends to lock in position if I bend it for too long.'

'Better?' Jack asked as he helped Edward to his chair.

'Much. Thank you kindly.'

Jack and Eve cleared the dinner things away and told Aunt Mary and Edward to take the rest of the wine into the garden and celebrate. When the kitchen was tidy, Eve made two coffees and they took them into the lounge. The dogs had gone outside to sit with the newly engaged couple, so there was space on the sofas for a change.

'So will you come back for the wedding?' Jack asked, without looking at Eve. Instead he stared into his mug.

'I hope so. I'd hate to miss it.'

'They'll want you here, you know.'

Eve nodded. 'I know.'

Jack took her hand and stroked the palm.

'I'm not going just yet anyway. I'll speak to my GP tomorrow and extend the sick note. I'm not ready to go back yet, I'm sure about that now.'

'Good.'

'Jack, I—'

'Shhh!' He placed his mug on the coffee table and shuffled closer to her.

Eve's heart rate picked up at the intensity in his expression. He was staring at her as if it would kill him to tear his gaze away. But he wasn't looking into her eyes. He was staring at her head.

'Jack?'

'Hold on!' He pulled her to his chest and she moaned softly.

'Jack, we shouldn't. I mean, I… *Ouch!*' She reached up to rub her head. 'You pinched me. Why'd you do that?'

He batted her hand away. 'Hold on!'

Eve wriggled as he pushed her head down onto his lap, all the while running the fingers of his other hand through her hair. Firmly. 'Jack!' Her nose was just above his crotch now. 'Jack, if you're trying to tell me about an erotic preference here, there are better ways of asking.'

She felt him shake before she heard his laughter. 'What?'

He released her and she sat up and straightened her T-shirt.

'I thought you were trying to get me to… you know.' She nodded at his groin.

'What? You think I'd ask for… that by pushing your head down there!' His eyes were wide and his jaw twitched. 'Is that what you expect of your men?'

'My men? What men?'

'Oh I didn't mean it like that. But is that what you've experienced in the past?'

'No. No it isn't. What were you doing then?'

'Eve, I'm really sorry to have to break this to you, but I think you've got… The reason you've been scratching so much is…'

She stared at him, watching his lips move. 'Oh no!' She covered her mouth. 'Please not that!'

He nodded. 'Yup. Seems you've got yourself a case of head lice.'

She gasped. 'But how? Where? Why?'

'Been around any small children recently?'

Eve shook her head. Then nodded as the memory of being hugged by the little girl at the Conwenna Kidz popped into her mind. 'Yeah… actually I have.' Her head began to itch viciously. 'Eurgh! I have to get these vile little creatures out right now!' She jumped up and shuddered. 'I can't believe this has happened. I've got nits!'

Jack's face was red now as he tried to contain his laughter. It burst from him in a snort, followed by loud gasps.

'Stop laughing!' Eve scowled. 'It's not funny. Anyway, you've probably got them too!'

'What?' His face dropped. 'But how?'

'Well,' she folded her arms across her chest, 'let's be honest, you have been up close to me recently.'

'Urgh!' He grimaced.

'Thanks for that.'

'No! No, I didn't mean urgh I've been close to you but urgh I could have head lice.'

'Come on! Let's get to the chemist.'

Jack shook his head. 'Can't.'

'What? But I can't sit here knowing that Mr Nit and his family have set up home in my hair and are doing God knows what with each other. They could be having sexy nit parties for all I know, while I scratch away. I just can't bear it!' She shook her arms and legs as if hoping that would dislodge the tiny creatures.

'The chemist is closed. It's Sunday.'

'Then what are we going to do?' Eve stared at Jack in horror. 'I can't wait until tomorrow.'

Jack chewed his lip for a moment. 'I have an idea. Come with me.'

He stood and seized Eve's hand, then led her out the front door and round to his cottage. 'I saw something on TV once. It might just work and it's worth a try.'

As they went into his lounge, Eve gave her head a good scratch. 'I hope you're right.'

'Me too. I can't stand the thought of a sexy nit party happening in your hair.'

'This isn't funny!' She tapped his arm, but as she closed the door behind them, she couldn't help the smile that played on her lips.

Chapter 18

'Are you sure about this?' Eve said as Jack made her sit on a kitchen chair then wrapped a towel around her shoulders.

'Sure as I can be. I definitely heard about this being an alternative treatment somewhere. It might have been on morning television when I was at Mary's having breakfast. Of course, I could also have dreamt it, but it's worth a shot.'

'So you're not really sure at all. *Great*. And it just seems so… yucky!'

'Well seeing as how the chemist is closed, it's this or just sit there scratching.'

'Okay then, go for it. But I'm doing you next.'

'Do you really think I need it? Chances of me catching them are pretty slim, although,' he scratched his head vigorously, 'my head does feel really itchy all of a sudden. It could be psychosomatic?' Jack raised his eyebrows as he looked at Eve, but she shook her head.

'Both of us or none at all. No point treating just me if you're already infested.'

'But what day did the girl hug you? They can't breed that quickly, surely?'

'I have no idea about their breeding habits, but the way they spread through schools and nurseries, I'm guessing they're prolific. Besides, even if they haven't had sex, laid eggs or done whatever it is they do, it's likely that more than one of them crawled from her head to mine and the same could have happened with you. Come on, Jack, man up and let's get on with it.'

'Yes, ma'am!' He saluted her. 'You're forceful when you want to be.'

Eve shook her head then shivered as he stuck a spoon into the large jar of mayonnaise on the kitchen table. As he pulled the spoon out, it squelched. Eve cowered as he spooned the creamy substance onto his hand then approached her.

'Here goes!'

As the cold mayonnaise met her scalp, Eve squealed.

'It feels horrible.'

'Cold?'

'Yes, freezing!'

'Just think about how it's suffocating those bugs.'

'And it smells!'

'It's nice! Creamy, sweet and… ooohhhh!' He rubbed the mayonnaise all over her head and started to massage her scalp. 'There you are, Mr and Mrs Nit. How's that for your sexy party?'

'What?' Eve screeched. 'Don't encourage them! They're meant to be deterred by this, not enjoying it.'

Jack laughed and Eve peered at him from under his hands. 'I don't even know how head lice breed, Eve. They're not likely to be in there rolling around and discussing the benefits of increased lubrication, now are they?'

'Too much! Stop it!'

Jack stopped massaging.

'Not stop that; I meant stop telling me nit horror stories.'

'Ha ha! Okay.'

He continued slathering the mayonnaise over her head until Eve's entire scalp was cold and wet, then he stood back. 'Looks pretty cool, though.'

'I bet it doesn't.'

'Kind of like one of those bald caps.'

'That is not the look I was hoping for.'

'Now for the best bit.'

He went to the sink and swilled his hands, then pulled a length of cling film off the roll and wrapped it around Eve's head. 'Ta da!'

'Thank you. How long does it need to stay on for?'

'As long as it takes for them to run out of oxygen, I assume.'

'And how long's that?'

Jack shrugged. 'I'd leave it on overnight just to be sure.'

'They can hold their breath for eight hours?'

'Doubt it, but don't take any chances by washing it off too soon.'

'All right.' Eve sighed. 'Your turn.'

She stood up and Jack sat on the chair, then she spooned mayonnaise onto her hand and smeared it over his head.

'You're right, that is cold.'

'I know.'

'Feels kind of nice in a weird way.'

She covered Jack's hair, running a finger all the way around his hairline to create a barrier to prevent any lice escaping. 'Now for the wrap.' She washed her hands, then pulled off a length of cling film and bound it round his head. 'And you've got a baldy too.'

'Thanks. So we're like twins?'

'I guess so.'

'What now?'

'I think we should stay indoors. I don't think going out in public is a good idea.'

'Me neither.'

'Game of cards?'

'Sure, why not!'

–

It was four hours later when Jack finally admitted defeat. Eve had won more games than she could count and they were both yawning through the final game. She was so comfortable on Jack's sofa and knew that if she stayed much longer she'd be tempted to lie down and go to sleep. The duck-down cushions were full and soft and the fluffy throw hanging over the arm was calling to her.

'I should get going,' she said reluctantly. 'Check on the lovebirds and have a shower.'

'No cheating, mind!'

'Don't worry, I won't wash it off until the morning.'

'Promise?'

'Cross my heart.' They stood up and walked to the front door. 'What will you do now?' Eve asked.

'Well I don't really want to get too warm, so gardening's out of the question. I've a book I'd like to finish and I might head out to the shed for a bit later too.'

'You read?'

'Of course! I love reading. Thrillers are my favourite but I also enjoy biographies.' His cheeks coloured. 'And not ones about sports stars either.'

'I didn't assume that. What ones have you read?'

'Recently I read one about an RAF pilot from the Second World War, but I've read all sorts, from books about captains in the Italian mafia to those about artists from all over the world and throughout history. To be honest, if I enter a bookshop, I'm done for!'

'I need to take you back to school with me when I go. You can come and give the boys a talk about the joy of reading. It can be so difficult sometimes to encourage them to read, and when they don't, literacy suffers.'

'I could do that.'

'Really?'

'If you think it would help.'

'Jack, you're an ex-marine who loves reading. You'd be their role model.'

He shrugged. 'I don't know about that. But I'd be happy to help if I could.'

Eve took a slow breath. Thinking about returning to Bristol hurt, but imagining Jack there too made it seem better. 'Do you think you would like to visit Bristol?'

He stared down at his feet and Eve watched him carefully. 'I'd consider coming. But not for long, because I just can't bear the thought of leaving the sea. City life isn't for me.'

He met her eyes and she saw his pain.

'I understand.'

'Look at us baldies having a serious conversation!' He grinned.

'See you tomorrow then.' Eve took her cue to leave before their mutual sadness permeated the evening air like a brewing storm.

'I'll be gone early... my shift at the sanctuary, but I'll see you later. Just mind you keep that mayo on your head.'

'I swear it's sweating already. I'm going to stink by morning.'

'Eggs and vinegar.'

'Yum!' Eve tapped her cling-film-covered scalp, then left Jack's cottage and walked around to Aunt Mary's back door.

She made herself a cup of tea and took it up to her room. The house was calm and quiet and she assumed that Mary and Edward must have gone for an early night. After such an eventful afternoon, coupled with a strange if relaxing head massage, Eve thought that seemed like a good idea.

–

The next morning, Eve walked into the kitchen to find Mary and Edward at the kitchen table, their faces glowing with happiness, their hands clasped on the tabletop.

'Well good morning, both!' She sat down opposite them and glanced discreetly at Edward's black eyes. The swelling on his nose had gone down a bit.

'Good morning to you too!' Mary replied, then started to giggle.

Eve frowned at her, then at Edward, who had also started laughing.

'What?' Heat flooded her cheeks. Were they sharing some secret joke?

'Eve, dear, whatever happened to your hair?'

Eve felt her head and groaned. She hadn't even bothered to glance in the mirror before heading downstairs, but now she remembered the mayonnaise. 'Long story.'

'We have time.' Edward grinned as he poured her a mug of tea then gestured at the plate of fresh pancakes on the table.

'Well… you know my head has been itchy? Turns out I must have picked up head lice when we went to Conwenna Kidz.'

Her aunt frowned and scratched her own head.

'And yesterday was Sunday, so there weren't any shops open for me to buy a treatment. Jack suggested using mayonnaise to suffocate the bugs and he said leave it on overnight, so, well, that's what I did.'

'Wrapped in cling film?' Mary asked.

'I know, it looks like a bald cap, doesn't it?'

Mary nodded.

'I just hope it worked. I'm not keen on using a chemical treatment anyway.'

'I think I have an old nit comb here somewhere that you can use. Wash all that out when you shower, then condition it, and while the conditioner's still on, drag the comb through. Should do the job.'

'Thanks, Aunt Mary.'

They sat in silence for a while as they drank tea and ate pancakes doused in maple syrup.

'Eve, how do you fancy a bit of a shopping trip?' Edward asked.

'Shopping?'

'Edward wants me to go and look at cakes and dresses. He's afraid I'll change my mind.'

'That's not going to happen.' Eve smiled at them both and nodded at their hands, still clasped tightly together.

'Of course not.' Mary kissed Edward's cheek. 'But I think I'd like a few hours browsing around the shops with my favourite niece.'

'Where did you want to go?'

'How about we take a drive and see where we end up?' Mary asked.

'Okay, lovely. I need to ring my GP first, but I'm happy to come with you for some retail therapy.'

After breakfast, Eve went and made the necessary telephone call. Her stomach churned as she rang the familiar number, but when the receptionist put her through, the GP's soothing, professional tone put her at ease. Eve explained that she felt she wanted to go back to her job but that she wasn't quite ready, and the doctor was understanding, telling her to ensure that she was fully recovered before heading back to Bristol. She gave Eve a note for another two weeks then told her to make an appointment to see her before returning to work.

When she ended the call, Eve stretched out on the bed and waited for her heart rate to slow. Stress was a horrid feeling; it flooded her with fight-or-flight symptoms and she didn't know whether she wanted to throw up, burst into tears or run to the toilet. It was so important that she got stronger before going back to work, but she couldn't go on like this indefinitely. She'd set herself a goal now – to return after half-term – and stick to it.

But now she needed to wash off the rather smelly and congealed mayonnaise and give her hair a thorough combing as Aunt Mary had suggested. Then she would feel ready to help her aunt look for a suitably beautiful wedding dress.

–

As they strolled arm-in-arm around the pretty streets of Truro, Eve felt her heart lift again. Time out of her usual existence was certainly a tonic. She couldn't recall the last time she'd just walked around a town and browsed in the shops. Whenever she did shop for clothes, it was a hurried affair, often after work before heading home for a microwave meal and a sleepless night. But this... it was so different. Here she was, with a woman she adored, just savouring the day. Enjoying the moment. And it was wonderful.

'Shall we look in there, Eve?' Mary pointed at a surf shop.

'They won't have wedding dresses in there!'

'Who cares? I'm enjoying myself.' Mary pulled Eve towards the shop and into its air-conditioned interior.

They walked around the clothing and Mary kept pointing out things that she thought would look good on Eve. 'What about this?' She held up a lavender shift dress with tiny white flowers embroidered over the bust and around the knee-length hem. 'This would look beautiful on you, Eve.'

'It is pretty.' Eve fingered the cool cotton of the dress.

'Then you must get it.'

'Okay then.'

'And what about this?'

She smiled as Mary handed her various garments to try on. It was lovely to have another woman's company and she could hardly believe that Aunt Mary was over sixty. Her energy and enthusiasm were infectious and Eve loved how her aunt made her feel that anything was possible.

'Oooh! Look, Eve!' Mary dragged her to the men's clothing. 'What do you think about this?' She took a green shirt down from the rail and held it out. It was plain, yet a beautiful colour; it reminded Eve of a mix between freshly cut grass and mint leaves.

'Are you getting it for Edward?'

Mary frowned at her. 'Of course not! I was thinking that it would suit Jack. Why don't you get it for him?'

'Buy him a gift?'

'Why not?'

'Well isn't that a bit—'

Mary placed a cool hand on Eve's arm. 'Are you friends?'

'Of course.'

'And there's nothing wrong with buying a gift for a friend. Especially when he helped you to treat your... *little problem.*' She leaned in to whisper the final two words as if it were part of some great conspiracy.

'You're right. I'll get it for him. But I don't know what size he is.'

Mary grinned. 'Big and broad.' Then she winked.

Eve felt heat rise up her neck. 'That's not very specific, is it?'

Mary looked through the shirts on the rail then pulled one out. 'Here you are. I know his size because I pinch his ironing some days to thank him for all he does for me. I just wondered if you knew.'

'Aunt Mary!'

Mary shrugged. 'Well, you can't blame your aunt for wanting to see you happy.'

Eve paid for her garments then they headed back into the sunshine.

'Time for a coffee and a bite to eat?' Mary asked.

'Great idea.'

They found a cafe with its own walled garden and sat at a small corner table outside so they could enjoy the fine weather. When they were settled, a waitress took their order.

'This place has great reviews.' Mary looked around at the pretty garden with its array of colourful flowers in pots and hanging baskets and its eclectic range of tables and chairs.

'The food I've seen people ordering so far looks amazing. Did you see the size of the portions?' Eve asked, her mouth watering.

'I couldn't resist the cherry pie. It's a summery delight,' Mary said, licking her lips.

Their coffee and food arrived quickly. Eve enjoyed every light, flaky, buttery mouthful of her cheese and onion quiche. The accompanying salad was drizzled in a creamy dressing and it made the spinach, peashoots and round red baby tomatoes even more delicious.

When they'd cleared their plates, she sat back and crossed her ankles. 'Aunt Mary...'

'Yes, dear.'

'I've been thinking a lot recently about my life and what I've done... what I've missed out on.'

Mary nodded.

'I have some regrets but I also have some things that give me hope. I mean... look at you. You didn't have children or marry, but now you've found love.'

'Edward and I have been friends for a few years. The falling-in-love bit developed slowly with us. He'd been through some tough times and in some ways so had I. But we are lucky to have found happiness together at our time of life.'

'Yes, but you have years ahead to enjoy being together.' Eve smiled.

'I hope so, Eve. Life passes so quickly. You must grab it with both hands and enjoy it while you can. It seems just yesterday that I was your age and just the day before that I was eighteen, a young woman with a lifetime full of possibilities ahead of me.' She sipped her coffee then wiped the rim with her napkin to remove her lipstick smudge.

'I can't believe I'm thirty-four. But I also feel like I'm still twenty-two. The years I've been in teaching have disappeared like smoke on the breeze. I plough through the terms then hit the holidays – most of which I spend working – then I start the next term. My life is an annual cycle and I try to cram as much as possible into it.'

'But are you cramming the right stuff in?'

Eve took a deep breath. 'What do you mean?'

'I'm not saying that you're not. I'm just asking you to consider it carefully. If you can look back at your life when you get to my age and happily say that you did all the things you wanted to do, then wonderful! No one can tell you what you want and need. Only you know that… deep down in your heart. However,' she held up a finger, 'if you look back in years to come and have regrets, then that would be so very sad.'

'You mean that I should decide what it is that really makes me happy?'

'Of course.'

'More coffee?' It was the pretty young waitress.

'Please,' Eve replied and Mary nodded. The waitress removed their plates and cutlery.

'If it's work that makes you fulfilled, then there is nothing wrong with that.'

Eve chewed her bottom lip. 'If you'd asked me two years ago what made me happy, my automatic reply would have been my job.'

'But things change. People change, dear.'

'And now, after my episode in the governors' meeting… I'm not so sure that it is work any more. Oh Aunt Mary… I lost everything.'

Mary reached out and took her hand. She squeezed Eve's fingers tightly. 'You did lose such a lot, darling girl, but there's still so much you can have if you want it… if you're prepared to do what it takes to get it.'

Eve bit the inside of her cheek hard and waited for the emotion to subside.

'Your stress attack, little episode or whatever you want to call it, was your body's way – heck, your mind and heart's way – of sending you a warning signal.'

She nodded, not trusting herself to speak.

'You know, Eve, it might seem as though I have everything I want now, but there were things… like a family of my own… that I never got to have.'

'You did want children?'

'Hundreds of them.'

'Really?'

'Well, five or six at least.'

'Why didn't you?'

Mary paused while the waitress brought their coffees, then she sat back in her chair and closed her eyes. Eve watched as the sunlight brightened her aunt's face, seeming to smooth out the wrinkles and to make her hair glow with golden tints. In that moment, she could see Mary as she once had been, a young and beautiful girl with her whole life ahead of her. Then a cloud passed over the sun and her face was back to normal. Still beautiful, still lovely, but a woman with a lifetime of experience and wisdom.

'I fell in love at just twenty years old. It was 1975 and the world seemed full of possibilities. I had money coming in, I had my youth and I fell head over heels in love.'

'You did?' Eve put her cup down on the saucer. 'With whom?'

'Oh, a very dashing, gallant and slightly older man. In fact, he was my boss at the factory where I worked. He was so handsome, Eve. I wish I had a photograph to show you.' Her expression softened as she reminisced.

'What happened?'

Mary's face changed then, as if she'd bitten something sour. 'He wasn't all he seemed to be. I was foolish, naïve... Back then we didn't have the kinds of things you women do now. We didn't have daytime chat shows where women discussed everything about their lives from sex to leg waxing. We didn't have the biological knowledge that most schools teach children now. Things were more... *mysterious*. At least for me, anyway. So Frank... that was his name... he seduced me.'

'Took advantage of you?'

'In some ways, yes, but then I didn't put up a fight. I felt so grown up and I wanted to be with him, to learn the ways of the world. I fell for him hard.'

'Did he love you?'

Mary shook her head. 'No. He was already married. Something he omitted to tell me. So when I missed my period, then another, and I went to him to tell him, he was furious. Called me all sorts of names.'

'Oh Aunt Mary, I'm so sorry.'

'It's all right, dear. Not your fault, now is it? Besides, it was a long, long time ago.'

'And the baby?'

Mary blinked slowly and clasped her hands in her lap. 'He asked me to meet him that night. In a quiet place where we'd met up before. I went, young fool that I was, hoping that he would propose or tell me he loved me and we could run away to be together.'

'But he didn't?'

'No. Instead he told me he wanted nothing more to do with me. He said I was a whore and that there was no way the baby was his. In that moment, my heart broke and I felt such a fool. Such a stupid, naïve fool.'

She took a sip of her coffee then dabbed at her lips with her napkin. A small brown bird landed on the wall next to their table, then fluttered down by Mary's feet and pecked at a few crumbs that had fallen from the table. Mary smiled at it.

'I turned away, about to leave, but he grabbed me. He was so strong and I was so tiny, like you are now. The morning sickness had kicked in and I couldn't keep a thing down. I tried to push him off, I tried so hard, Eve, but he said I needed to learn a lesson. He was an angry man. I hadn't seen that side of him before. I suppose these days he'd be offered some form of counselling.'

'Did you manage to escape or did someone come to help you?' Eve's armpits prickled with anger as she thought about this man who'd hurt her aunt.

'No. He punched me, very hard... several times.'

'Oh God!' Eve gasped then covered her mouth. 'That's so awful. Did the police get him?'

Mary shook her head. 'I didn't tell anyone. I was too embarrassed and too afraid of the shame it would have brought. I started bleeding that night and the next day I miscarried. It was early in the pregnancy, so I dealt with it myself as best I could and told no one.'

'Were you all right... physically?'

Mary pressed her lips together so hard they went white. 'It took a while for my body to recover. As you know, Eve, when you've been pregnant but not had a baby at the end of it, your body is a bit confused for a while.'

Eve nodded, remembering the milk that had leaked from her breasts in expectation of providing for two tiny babies that would never take a breath. 'Nature can be cruel.'

'Mankind can be cruel. Nature just does what it should do. At the end of the day, we're all just animals.'

'What happened to him? That brute?' Eve wanted to find Frank and punish him for what he'd done to her young and innocent aunt.

'I have no idea. I left my job and took the money I'd saved, then ran away. That was when I came here. To Cornwall, to Conwenna Cove. At just twenty, I left everything behind and made my life somewhere else. I couldn't stay there to think about what might have been. I had to leave, to change, to set myself free.'

'You were so young.'

'People far younger than I was make their own way in life, dear. Look at you and all you achieved by putting yourself through university and getting such a good job.'

The air around them seemed to thicken and Eve struggled for a moment to breathe. How had something so awful happened to her lovely aunt, to the woman who was not just a relative but a friend?

'Did you ever try to have another child?'

Mary shook her head. 'I didn't. I mean, I had a few relationships but they never worked out. Some with tourists flitting through, others with local men, but something held me back. I couldn't commit, especially not to having a baby. But I had one comfort in all of that.'

'You did?'

'My summers with you. Eve, you were like my own dear child. I loved you deeply, still do, and our time together was so precious. I looked forward to that hedonistic six weeks that I got every year. You filled my heart enough for me to go on. You were my little girl.'

Eve sprang from her chair and threw herself into Mary's arms. 'I love you too!'

Mary patted her back gently and they laughed and cried as they hugged, oblivious to the smiles being cast their way by other diners enjoying the walled garden.

When Eve returned to her seat, she asked, 'But now you're in love?'

Mary's face brightened. 'Oh yes, dear. Very much so.'

'Then there is hope for me too.'

'Plenty of it, Eve. It might be closer than you think.'

Eve smiled but didn't reply. Her belly fluttered. She'd just learnt things about her aunt that she could never have imagined. She would never cease to wonder at how much people went through and how much they could endure. Mary's loss had been great, and had impacted upon her enormously. Yet she had learnt to live with it and moved on.

Eve's own losses were different because she had made different choices; in retrospect, not always the right ones. But whatever else happened from now on, she knew that she was closer to Mary than ever before, and that they would have each other's backs.

No matter what.

Chapter 19

'So how did dress shopping go?' Jack asked later that day as they walked the dogs along the sandy shore of the cove.

'Well, Mary looked at quite a few dresses and tried some on but she didn't settle on anything.'

'Too fussy?'

Eve shook her head. 'Not really fussy. I think she's just taking her time. After all, it'll be the only wedding she's had.'

'I know. I can't believe that she never married. She's such a lovely person and she's attractive now, so when she was your age she must have been a knockout.'

'You trying to tell me you have a crush on Mary?' Eve nudged him.

'No, no. Of course not! That would be too weird. She's been like a mother to me.'

'Me too. My own mother being sadly lacking in maternal feelings.'

'Is she really that bad?'

Eve chewed her lip. 'She married my father when she was quite young but they were both so ambitious and had plans for their own business. They didn't really want children; I was kind of a surprise. Whenever they could palm me off on someone, they did. That was why I never wanted kids of my own.'

'You still feel that way?'

Eve stared out at the sea and watched a boat bobbing on the horizon. Sometimes she felt like that, small and alone, vulnerable, but she never allowed herself to dwell on it for long.

Jack took her hand and she felt instantly anchored.

'You mean do I want children?'

'Yes.' He squeezed her hand.

'I don't know, to be honest. At one point it seemed like a possibility, then things changed and now... there's so much else to consider. What about you?'

Jack smiled. 'Maybe one day. When I find the right woman.'

Did he just squeeze her hand a bit harder, or had she imagined it?

She nodded. The right time, the right woman, the right man, the right home, the right lifestyle, the right amount of savings... It could all seem right at certain points in life, but in reality there could be something not quite right lurking beneath the surface. And look what happened then!

A vibration from Eve's pocket broke into her thoughts and she pulled her phone out to look at it.

'I need to take this,' she said.

Jack nodded and released her hand, then took the dog's lead from her. Eve swiped the phone to answer and took a deep breath.

'Hello?'

'Eve, it's me.'

Her stomach churned at the familiar voice.

'Hello, Darryl.'

'How are you?'

'Oh, you know—'

'Look, Eve. I know what happened to you. I bumped into Amanda at the supermarket. I went round to the house at the weekend and you weren't there. I didn't like to let myself in, it just didn't seem right. I asked Amanda if she knew where you were.'

'I just needed a bit of a break.'

'I'm not surprised.' His tone was cold but Eve couldn't blame him. She'd hurt him and pushed him away when they should have been clinging together. 'But are you all right?'

'Yes. It's helping being away, taking some time.'

'So there's nothing *seriously* wrong?'

'No. I promise.'

'Phew! I know things have been tough between us, but I still wouldn't want to see you ill.'

Eve's throat closed over and she swallowed hard. Darryl had his faults just like everyone else, but he also had a kind and caring side. After all they'd been through, he was still concerned about her welfare.

'How long are you staying there?'

'A few weeks, I think. Until half-term, maybe a bit longer.'

'Okay. Look, Eve, uh… I don't want to add to your worries, but we need to talk… face to face. We have things to sort out. It's all dragging on a bit really, isn't it?'

Eve had wandered slowly away from Jack, but now she glanced up and saw him crouching next to the dogs. The three of them were gazing out to sea and the tide was creeping in, almost touching their feet each time a wave rolled in. Jack was a good man too, just like Darryl. But Eve didn't deserve to have a good man in her life. Jack had already been through so much; imagine if he fell in love with her and she hurt him.

'When were you thinking?' she asked.

'Well as soon as possible really. Time is money in the land of solicitors, and having this hanging over our heads… it's not exactly doing either of us any good, is it?'

'You mean you need some closure.'

'Emotionally as well as financially, Eve. We need to decide what we're doing with the house, our savings and the rest of our things.'

'I know. I'm sorry. I've just been trying not to think about it. Pushing it all away like one big sad memory.'

'I know you need your time out, but…'

'It's okay, Darryl. I'll come back this week and we can sort it out. Make a plan of action.'

'Are you sure?'

'Yes, of course. I'll drive back tomorrow and you can come over on Wednesday evening if you like.'

Give me a chance to tidy up a bit first!

'Sounds good.'

'See you Wednesday about six?'

'Six it is. And Eve…'

'Yes?'

'Drive carefully, won't you?'

'Sure.' Eve ended the call and slid her phone back into her pocket. The last thing she wanted was to go back to Bristol right now, but she also knew that she couldn't really move on until she'd put everything else behind her.

Jack looked up as she approached. 'You okay?'

'Yeah. I guess. It was… my husband.'

'Oh!' Jack stood up suddenly.

'He wants to sort everything out.'

Jack shifted uncomfortably. 'As in get back together?' His face had fallen.

239

'No! As in finalize the divorce and sort the house and finances.'

'But right now? Before you've had time to recover? It's not a good idea to go back until you're strong enough to deal with it all, surely?'

'To be honest, Jack, I think having all this hanging over me has been contributing to the pressure. I'm always pushing worries away, trying to store them at the back of my mind, when what I should be doing is living for today.'

'I can't argue with that. So when will you go?'

'Tomorrow.'

'So soon?' He raised his eyebrows.

'Sooner the better. I'll get it done and dusted then come back to Conwenna as soon as I can.'

'Okay.' Jack looked away and Eve watched as his Adam's apple bobbed furiously.

'I will come back,' she said, as she slid her hand into his.

Jack just nodded.

They walked the rest of the length of the beach in silence and Eve felt as if something had shifted between them. She wanted to talk more but she was afraid that Jack might say something to stop her going back to Bristol, and she knew that she had to go, had to get it all done, or she'd never be able to look to the future.

–

Eve dropped her handbag onto the passenger seat of her car then closed the door. She hadn't driven it since she'd arrived ten days ago. Just ten days, but it felt like ten months. Things inside her had already begun to change –

she felt healthier, happier, more herself – but she knew she had to get her life in order because she'd never relax fully with the shadows threatening to loom at any moment.

Jack had disappeared after they'd returned to the cottages the previous evening and she hadn't seen him since. She was hoping that he'd show his face before she left because she didn't like the thought of going without saying goodbye. Although she knew that saying goodbye was going to be tough.

She went back into the cottage and found her aunt in the kitchen filling plastic tubs with food.

'What're you doing?' she asked.

'I can't see you go off without giving you something to keep you going.'

'There are plenty of shops in Bristol.'

'Yes, but I worry that you won't eat properly. You weren't looking after yourself at all before and when you arrived you didn't look well. You do look better now but you've still a way to go before you'll be back to your fighting weight.'

Eve laughed. 'I'll be fine. I promise I'll eat.'

'Well I'll give you some cakes and some home-cooked meals for the freezer just in case. All you need to do is heat them up in the microwave and hey presto, you'll have delicious healthy meals… Oh, Eve!' Mary stopped what she was doing and turned around, then opened her arms.

Eve stepped into her embrace. 'I'll miss you, Aunt Mary.'

'And I shall miss you, my darling girl. You must take care of yourself and please come back soon. You know, I could have visited you in Bristol before… when you… but to be honest, I didn't think you'd want me there.' Mary raised shiny eyes to meet Eve's.

'That's my fault because of what you overheard at my graduation. But I was an idiot and I have always loved you and been proud of you.'

'Rejection is hard to take, and after all that happened in my past...'

Eve nodded. 'I know. That bastard knocked your confidence and you've been insecure ever since.'

Mary shrugged. 'I didn't want to be a burden. I just always hoped you'd come to me if you needed me.'

'And I did.'

'Yes, dear. I do love you so much.'

'And I love you. Look... I'm not planning on missing the village fair. I'm going to sort things out with Darryl, but I'll be back as soon as I can. I have my doctor's note and I know I'm not ready to return to work just yet. I'm not sure when I will be ready, but one step at a time, right? Sort my marriage and house, then deal with the next issue.'

'That's right, Eve. One thing at a time. You can't do it all in one go.'

Mary released Eve then tucked all the plastic pots into a big shopping bag and carried it out to the car. Eve patted the dogs' heads and waved at the cats. 'It's as if they know I'm going.'

'They do. Very intuitive these animals are. They'll miss you too.'

Eve glanced at Jack's cottage. But there was no sign of him.

Will Jack miss me too?

'Why don't you go and knock?' Mary asked.

Eve worried her bottom lip. 'I don't know if I should.'

'He'll be upset if you don't.'

'Okay.' Eve reached into the boot of her car and brought out a package wrapped in silver tissue paper. It was the green shirt she'd bought in Truro. She had considered keeping it and giving it to him when she returned, but it seemed more fitting for him to have it now, before she left. 'I won't be long.'

She walked to Jack's front door and tapped it lightly. Her stomach somersaulted. The thought of saying goodbye was physically painful and part of her just wanted to run away, to avoid seeing him in case it proved too much. Yet part of her was screaming that she was being irrational; there was nothing serious between them. They were friends, he was her aunt's tenant and she'd enjoyed his company. He was extremely attractive and kind and funny and talented, but circumstances had thrown them together and it was just that. Once she'd gone home, she'd forget all about him. Wouldn't she?

She knew she wouldn't.

She knew she'd ache to return as soon as possible.

She tried his door again but there was still no answer, so she waved at Mary then went around the side of the cottage and let herself in to the back garden. The shed door hung slightly ajar, so she went up the steps and knocked gently.

'Hello?'

'Jack?'

'Come in.'

She pulled open the door and stepped into the musky heat of Jack's studio. He stood before her in just his jeans. Her breath caught as she gazed at him. He was majestic. A ray of sunlight streamed through the window and illuminated his sculpted torso, which shone with perspiration. His hair was tousled where he'd run his fingers through it and his face bore a shadow of stubble. And his eyes… his eyes were as dark and deep as wells.

'You're going now?' he asked, and Eve saw the muscle in his jaw twitching.

'Yes. I need to get on the road.'

'Oh.'

'Jack, I…'

'You'll drive carefully?' His voice was husky.

'Of course.'

'I… uh… have something for you. But I don't want you to open it until you get home.'

'Right.' Eve stepped closer to him. She could smell his scent, warm and male, and she wanted to throw herself into his arms and never let go.

'Here.' He lifted a rectangle wrapped in brown paper and handed it to her.

'When did you do this? I mean, I'm assuming it's a drawing.'

'Last night. I couldn't sleep. It was in my head and I needed to get it out.'

'I got you something too.' Eve passed him the silver package. 'There's a note in there as well.'

'A note?' He frowned.

'Just to say thanks.'

'Oh, okay.' He rubbed his forehead and pushed back his hair.

The silence hung between them as they stood just two paces apart. Eve wondered if Jack felt as she did, or was he relieved? His life could go back to normal and he could find peace again. She knew that her arrival had turned the routine at Mary's cottages upside-down. Jack and her aunt had tended to her through her moments of bleakness and helped her to begin to mend. It couldn't be easy doing that. And she didn't want to be a burden on anyone. That would be horrendous. Her growing feelings for Jack needed reciprocity, in terms of desire and love, or they would drive her mad. Better to have a break now and get control of her heart before it led her towards territory she had no right straying into.

'So, um… take care.'

'You too.' He nodded and she saw that the tissue paper had puckered under his fingers. He was tense as a coiled spring.

Like her.

'I will come back. Soon. I want to be here for the summer fair.'

'I hope you do.' His voice was quiet and he'd lowered his gaze to the floor.

'Bye then.'

Please hug me or kiss me or just give me something!

'Bye.'

She turned and left the shed, feeling as if her heart would explode into a thousand tiny shards. Her throat throbbed and her blood whooshed through her ears. She knew she wanted too much from this man, but with his kindness and his innate goodness he'd made his way into her heart. She walked down the steps, careful not to bump the parcel, and around the side of the house.

Just as she was about to turn the corner, she felt a hand clutch at her arm.

'Eve!'

She turned and there he was. His chest heaving, his eyes full of emotion. Full of her.

'Jack.'

He reached out tentatively and stroked her cheek with his thumb. She copied his action, then he leant down and covered her lips with his. His kiss was warm and soft and she returned it eagerly. The corner of the parcel dug into her belly so she lowered it to the ground. When her hands were free, she slid her arms around Jack's neck and he lifted her, pulling her tight against him. When he finally broke away and stared into her eyes, Eve was so light-headed with desire and emotion that she felt as if she would float away.

He gently lowered her to the ground. 'Something for you to remember me by.'

'Thank you.'

She placed a hand on his chest, over his heart. 'I'm coming back. I promise.'

Jack raised her hand and kissed its palm. 'I hope so.'

Then he turned and went back to his shed, leaving Eve to fluff up her hair and straighten her shirt before picking up the package and walking back to her car.

–

Jack waited outside the shed until he heard Eve's car heading off along the gravel, then he opened the door and reached inside for the silver parcel she'd given him. He sank onto the top step and turned the gift over in his hands. He was tired and had that strange woozy feeling that came from a sleepless night. But he'd known when he returned from the beach that he wouldn't rest. Eve's announcement that she was leaving had thrown him into turmoil. He was such a fool. He'd known she wasn't staying in Conwenna; the woman was a head teacher with a home and job to return to, for crying out loud. Yet he'd hoped that she'd fall in love with the place and wouldn't want to leave. Just as he had.

And now she'd gone. But he'd sketched out something for her that he thought she'd like. Something to remind her of her time here. He hoped she'd be okay, that she had managed to relax enough to avoid any more anxiety attacks. Because that was what she'd been experiencing really. He'd had them himself and seen friends go through them. Sometimes avoiding the situation that brought them on in the first place was the only way to completely heal, but sometimes that wasn't possible, and at those times you just had to learn how to control them. Hopefully Eve's time at Conwenna would give her something to help whenever the tension mounted again. He hoped she'd come back but he also knew that if she did, it would be hard for him. He was falling for her, and seeing her regularly, during school holidays or on long weekends, would not help his feelings to abate.

He shook his head. He had work to do for Mary and a shift up at the sanctuary later. It wasn't as if he was going to be sitting around twiddling his thumbs. The hounds needed him and he was glad of it.

He picked at the Sellotape on one corner of the silver tissue paper and pulled the end of the package apart. He didn't want to tear it right open; it seemed wrong. Eve had taken the time to wrap this, and although it was probably silly, the silver tissue reminded him of her. She was bright and delicate, soft and luminous. She could be easily hurt, yet she had a strength about her, a determination that he admired deeply.

He slipped his fingers into the tissue and pulled out some green material. As he held it out, he could see that it was a green shirt from a surf shop brand that he liked. The shirt was lightweight and his size. How had she known? Then he noticed the chest pocket and it

247

brought a smile to his face. Embroidered there in dark green cotton was a greyhound, side on, standing proud. It was a thoughtful gift and one that he would certainly wear. He folded the shirt and laid it on top of the tissue paper, then opened the small envelope that had fallen out of the package. It bore his name in looped black handwriting; Eve's handwriting. His heart flipped as he ran his finger over it, admiring the way she'd written his name without taking the pen from the paper.

When he opened the envelope and removed the card, he smiled again. It was a print of Conwenna harbour by a local artist that he'd seen thousands of times on items such as postcards, mugs and T-shirts. Inside, Eve had written a message that brought a lump to his throat.

> *Jack,*
> *Thank you so much for everything you've done and been since I came to Conwenna. We've known each other such a short time yet I feel I know you better than many people I've encountered in my life. You've been a friend, such a good friend, and I will always treasure that. You've also been more, and although I'm a bit confused right now, I'm also happier than I've been in an age.*
> *I will return.*
> *Love and hugs,*
> *Eve x*

Chapter 20

Eve turned the key in the lock and the door swung inwards. She walked into the hallway and was greeted by a stale smell that was a mixture of damp washing and old food. She sighed as she closed the door and dumped her holdall and handbag on the floor next to the downstairs cloakroom, then carefully propped Jack's parcel and the bag of food from Mary next to them. She'd left her suitcase at Mary's with some of her belongings; it made her feel a bit better, as if it was some kind of security measure. She'd have to return if her things were still there, wouldn't she?

She picked up the post that had scattered on the hall mat and went through to the kitchen. Everything was as she had left it following her hasty departure. She'd done a quick clean-through before leaving but she must have missed a few things because there was something mysterious growing mould in the fruit bowl and the smell of damp washing was even stronger. A quick glance in the utility room made her groan. She recalled opening the washing machine door before leaving, meaning to take out the towels she'd washed, but she'd been distracted and forgotten about them. She filled the cap with non-biological liquid and flung it into the drum, then poured fabric softener into the drawer and put the machine on a sixty-degree wash.

As the drum filled with water, Eve went around the house opening windows, as well as the French doors that led from the dining room into the garden. She didn't want Darryl thinking she was living in conditions resembling a student house in the eighties. Once a breeze was blowing through the house, she placed the plastic boxes of food in the fridge and freezer, then sat at the kitchen table and went through the post. Nothing of any real interest, just bills and a letter from the bank offering her an extension on her credit card limit – she was the perfect customer, paying off her entire balance each month – until she got to one with the school's stamp on it.

Her bowels seized up.

Her mouth went dry.

Her heart began to pound.

What do they want?

She stuck a shaking finger under the seal and pulled out the page inside. It was a formal and courteous letter from Sandra Winters enquiring after her health and asking if there was anything that the school and governors could do to help. It stated that they'd received her sick note and that they were keen to do all they could to support her. Eve had seen such letters before – hell, she'd sent them out herself to staff with long-term absences as part of the managing sickness absence policy – so she knew it was just a formality, but being on the receiving end of one was horrific.

How had she got to this place? This sorry state of affairs?

Eve didn't do sick and she didn't get into trouble with her employer.

She flung the letter across the table then followed it with the envelope. This couldn't be good for her health.

She'd been back all of half an hour and already she could feel the pressure closing in like a pack of hungry wolves. She didn't want to feel this way. But she was trapped.

Or was she?

She had savings. She had no debt except for the credit card, which her salary covered easily, and the mortgage, but they'd put down a healthy deposit on the house after making money on their first house sale and had paid the mortgage monthly without fail. That meant there was a considerable amount of equity in the property, which was only just three years old and on a coveted estate near two of the best primary schools in Bristol. In spite of the housing slump, it would surely sell if they put it on the market. Besides, she needed to consider it or she'd have to buy Darryl out, and although she could afford that, she didn't really want to stay here alone any longer. It was a house of shadows, a house of shattered dreams, and Eve was becoming convinced that it was adding to her worries. When she spoke to Darryl tomorrow, she'd agree to sell it, and quickly.

Then she would have more cash to squirrel away. Even without her salary she could buy a smaller place and, if she lived carefully, survive easily for a year or longer. So she was lucky, she reassured herself. Unlike some people, she wasn't trapped; she had choices. It was just up to her now to make the biggest choice of all: did she return to work after the break, or should she quit? It was a terrifying prospect for a woman who'd worked all her life and striven to be independent.

Her thoughts drifted to her aunt's cottages set on the hill overlooking Conwenna, with the tree-covered gravel driveway bordered on both sides by pretty bluebells, and the colourful roses about to bloom on the trellises around the cottage doors. Where she could hear the squawk of seagulls and the cooing of wood pigeons as well as the hoot of an owl at night. Where she could smell the salt in the air and gaze out to sea; sense the freedom of the open horizon even when she was indoors. Where she could sit with Aunt Mary and chat about life over tea and cake. Where she could see Gabe and rub his silky ears as he leaned against her legs.

Where she could wrap her arms around Jack and bury her face in his neck, breathe deeply of his special scent and feel at once safe and exhilarated. Where she'd felt for the first time in her life that she was finally home.

Eve had experienced a different kind of existence in Conwenna, a life that *was* a life and not just an existence.

She knew what she wanted now; she just had to summon the courage to make it happen.

–

When Eve had showered and pulled on her softest pyjamas, she went back downstairs and picked up the parcel from Jack. She'd been afraid to open it earlier, had worried that it would deepen her heartache, but she couldn't postpone it any longer.

She laid it on the kitchen table and gently undid the string Jack had tied around it to keep the paper in place. She held it for a moment, conscious that his hands had touched it, had tied the knot and bow. Then she carefully opened the paper and allowed herself to look at what Jack had created.

For a moment, she just gazed at the charcoal sketch, but soon tears welled in her eyes and she let out a strangled moan.

The drawing showed her and Gabe facing each other on the sofa in the assessment room. What stunned her most was how peaceful her expression was as she snoozed. She looked more serene than she thought possible. And as for Gabe... the big black hound was watching her closely, as if he was guarding her while she was at her most vulnerable. As if he was her dog.

But of course; he is my dog!

The thought came out of nowhere and pierced Eve's chest. She covered her thudding heart with both hands. How could she leave Gabe there? Yes, he was well taken care of at the sanctuary, but he had bonded with her after all he had been through. After all the loneliness and pain and hurt. He had chosen to trust her, and such trust was a gift, to be valued and treasured, not ignored and left behind.

Gabe had chosen Eve.

She went to the kitchen drawer and took out a notepad and pen, then began making a to-do list. She needed to get everything in order, for her sake and for Gabe's.

And for Jack's too.

Because he had drawn this sketch, he had captured this precious moment forever, and that was something else that Eve shouldn't forget. He had taken the time to do this then given it to her as a parting gift. So surely there was something there, something more lasting than physical attraction and deeper than pity and concern. There was a bond between Eve and Jack just as there was between Eve and Gabe, but would it be enough of a foundation to build a life on?

I hope so with all my heart.

–

There was a knock at the front door. Eve paused in the kitchen and checked the clock. It was ten minutes to six. If it was Darryl, he was early. She'd kept herself busy all day, kept moving as a way to fight the tiredness after a restless night in her own bed. She'd been sleeping so well in Conwenna and being back in the big empty house had left her jumping at every noise. But now, it was time to deal with matters she'd delayed for too long.

She checked her appearance in the hallway mirror. She'd changed five times, not knowing what was appropriate clothing for a serious meeting with your ex-husband. She'd ended up settling on black linen trousers and a black vest top. Cool and comfortable yet still smart. She'd tamed her hair with a touch of serum that she'd found in her bathroom cupboard and now it shone. It was lighter from her time in the sun in Conwenna and her skin also had a light golden glow. She did look better than she had just two weeks ago. Even she could see that.

She took a deep breath then opened the door.

'Darryl, hi!' She stood back to let him in, then jumped as he placed a hand on her shoulder and leaned in to kiss her cheek.

'Oh… sorry. I just, uh…'

'No, it's okay, really. Don't worry about it.' Eve patted his hand.

'I'm not sure what the correct etiquette is when you meet up with your soon-to-be-ex-wife.' He flushed then handed her a bunch of flowers. 'And I brought these for the same reason.'

'Thank you. That's very kind of you. And I didn't mean to jump but you took me by surprise. It's been a while since I last saw you.'

He nodded, a flush creeping up his throat. This was uncomfortable for both of them.

'Come on, let's go through to the kitchen and I'll make us a coffee.'

Eve switched the kettle on. She'd cleaned around thoroughly that morning and hoped that the musty smell had gone completely now.

Darryl sat at the table and folded his hands on its shiny surface. Then he put them under the table. Then he folded them on top again.

Eve smiled. 'Nervous?'

'Yes. It's ridiculous but I can't help it. This is so weird.'

'I know. But try not to worry. It's just you and me. No one else here to criticize.'

'No. Of course not.'

Eve poured water onto the coffee grains then added milk and two sugars to Darryl's mug.

'Here you go. You want a biscuit or a slice of cake? I have scones from Aunt Mary?'

'No.' Darryl shook his head. 'But thanks. I don't think I could swallow food right now.'

'So how have things been?' Eve asked as she watched him carefully. He'd lost weight in the months since she'd last seen him and she thought he had more grey spreading through his brown hair, but it could just be that she hadn't noticed it before.

'Oh, you know, I'm okay. It's been tough, but with work and... and other things, I keep going.'

'Other things?' Eve asked.

'Things like... I'm seeing someone.' He let out a deep breath, as if it had taken him a lot of effort to say the words.

'Oh?' Eve tried to maintain a calm expression. She wasn't really surprised, had expected it at some point, but now it was there in front of her, she didn't know how to react. 'Do I know her?'

He shook his head. 'She's a teaching assistant at one of the local primary schools. I met her through a mutual friend. She has… um… a little boy.'

'A child?'

'Yes.'

'Well that's… that's wonderful. I hope she's good to you.' *Not like me.*

'She's very nice but it's early days. I can't move on properly while we're still married, Eve, if I'm honest. I mean, things are done between us, aren't they? There's no going back?'

'You left, Darryl. Months ago.' Eve spoke as gently as she could, but she saw Darryl's blue eyes cloud with hurt at the reproach.

'True. But you wanted me gone. It wasn't just me.'

Eve sipped her coffee. He was right. It had been over between them for a while before he left. If it hadn't been for the pregnancy, it might well have happened sooner.

'You're right. It wasn't just you. I guess it's strange knowing that you're with someone else now.'

'How about you?'

Eve's cheeks flushed and she considered telling a fib, but it felt mean to deceive him. 'There wasn't anyone… until I went to Cornwall.'

'You met someone in Conwenna?'

She nodded. 'But it's not like a relationship or anything.'

'It's not?' Darryl smiled. 'What's it like then?'

'Oh I don't know how to explain it.' How could she describe her hotchpotch of emotions to the man she was still legally married to? It didn't seem right, and yet…

'I met someone kind, someone who hasn't been through what I... what *we*... went through but who has been through his own tragedy in life. He kind of gets where I'm coming from.'

Darryl stared at her for a moment, then licked his lips and took a breath as if he was going to say something, but instead he released it slowly and sipped his coffee instead.

'So how do we sort all this? I know the solicitors will make things legal, but if we can hammer out the details then it will be easier in the long run.'

Eve nodded. 'I've made a list.' She pushed the notepad in front of him and he read it in silence then gave a low whistle. 'Very organized!'

'You know me.'

'And you're sure that this is what you want? To sell the house, split our joint savings to pay the legal fees then go our separate ways?'

'Yes, I think it's for the best. Unless you want the house? If you do, we can arrange that instead.'

Darryl leaned back in his chair and folded his arms then gazed around the room. 'It's a great house, Eve, but there are too many memories here. It needs a family and a fresh start. Just like we do.'

'So we sell.'

'You want me to ring the estate agent?'

'No, it's okay. I'm still off work so I'll contact them tomorrow and arrange it all.'

'Thanks. Now, how about I come over at the weekend with my brother's van and take away whatever you don't want or need? I'm kind of rattling around in my rented place at the moment and it's embarrassing having to offer visitors a deckchair.'

'Oh no! You don't have furniture?'

He laughed but shook his head. 'I didn't want to buy anything because I knew if I moved again it might not fit. Some of the houses out there have tiny lounges!'

'Oh Darryl, there's not much here I really want to keep. You make a list and we can split it all. Hell, you can have most of it!'

'Very generous of you. But don't sell yourself short.'

Eve bit her lip. She hadn't known what to expect but was surprised that things were so civil. There was a lot of pain between them but there were also good memories. They'd both said hurtful things when their relationship had deteriorated and they'd both been angry, but Darryl was seeing someone he liked now and Eve was just glad to be able to end things properly. The last thing she wanted was to make life more difficult for him; he didn't deserve that.

Chapter 21

The next few days flew past as Eve contacted several local estate agents, signed the divorce forms from Darryl and spoke to her solicitor. Then she began, with a heavy heart, to sort out the house.

She started downstairs by packing kitchen items into boxes that she placed in two piles, one for her and one for Darryl. As she emptied cupboards, she couldn't help letting out gasps and sighs at the things they'd accumulated over the years. It was difficult seeing wedding presents they'd received, like a herb board with a special curved blade that a colleague had given them, and a set of steak knives still in their packaging. They'd both been full of hope when they'd opened these gifts together, and Eve's throat ached as she remembered that time.

But she also knew that she couldn't carry on as she was; they couldn't continue as they were. Darryl already had a chance at happiness and she was glad for him. A woman with a child, a chance at being part of a family; that was what he had wanted so desperately all along.

In between packing and cleaning, she sneaked glances at the picture of her and Gabe, and every time she saw something new there, some detail Jack had captured that made her look at the drawing with fresh awe. He had such a talent. And she missed him, every minute of every hour of every day that passed.

She had never felt this way about Darryl. Not even when they were first together. She'd happily gone off on education conferences for days at a time, been relaxed when he'd gone away on trips with the lads; even when he'd gone to Cyprus for a week on a stag do. Looking back, she could see that it wasn't that she had trusted him implicitly or that they'd had an easy-going relationship; it was more that she just hadn't minded being separated from him. They should never have got married and certainly never attempted to have a family together. It had all been wrong.

But her feelings for Jack were sharp, intense and palpable.

It terrified her yet it lifted her. She could love and be loved. And Jack could be the man she spent her life with, if only they could both surrender their fears and commit.

But can I take that risk?

She dealt with her feelings by working her way through downstairs, then the spare bedrooms and her own room. It was an arduous process, but as the days passed, she made progress, and soon there was just one place left to deal with.

The one place she had deliberately left until last.

The attic.

Because that was where the baby things were.

She pushed her hair back from her face, then climbed the staircase at the end of the landing. Before moving into the house, they'd had the loft converted into an extra room, because who knew when they'd need more space? Darryl had nursed dreams of needing somewhere to escape his noisy family as they grew. Of having a hideaway where he could go with an ice-cold beer and a book when it all proved too exhausting. At the time,

Eve had barely registered the implication – that she would be left with their brood – but now it made her smile sadly. Knowing Darryl as she did, he'd have been there in the thick of it, making more noise than any child ever could. She experienced a twinge then – of regret or grief or… something she couldn't quite pinpoint. But this was natural, surely; the end of any relationship was difficult, especially a marriage that hadn't worked out. If she didn't feel sad, it would mean that she was devoid of all emotion, and she knew that wasn't true. Yet in spite of it all, she also experienced a sense of relief. This would pass, everything would be dealt with, and they could move on with their lives.

She pushed the attic door open and stepped into the bright open space. It was a large conversion with four windows set in the roof that opened up to the sky. The room was warm and slightly stuffy, so she pushed open all the windows and breathed deeply of the morning air, which carried the aromas of coffee and freshly baked bread, and beneath that the tang of fumes from the traffic that would be making its way around the bustling city.

She steeled herself.

In the far corner of the room was a pile draped with several large white sheets: old bed linen that she hadn't minded using to cover up the things they'd bought for the twins. She had been reluctant to purchase anything early in the pregnancy, but once she'd passed the twelve-week mark, then the fourteen, Darryl had been unable to contain himself any longer. He'd gone out and bought nappies in a variety of sizes – *never too soon to stock up* – car seats – *in case they come early; we need to be prepared* – and a sterilizer kit – *you might find breastfeeding too exhausting, then you can express and I'll give it to them in bottles.*

At the time, it had all felt a bit surreal to Eve, as if they were playing a game of let's pretend and there wouldn't really be babies at the end of it.

And there weren't. Because of me.

The things she dreaded seeing more than anything were the tiny outfits Darryl had been unable to resist buying; the beautiful matching outfits that their twin boys would have worn.

She approached the pile cautiously, as if she was afraid that something would jump out from under it, and pulled the covers away. Her heart pounded and her hands were clammy. She hadn't looked at this stuff in months, had hidden it away, buried it beneath the sheets as if that would help.

Just like your grief. Buried. Covered up. Yet still there… waiting.

She sank to her knees, her legs trembling violently, and took the top box from the pile. It was filled with clothes. Though she felt light-headed and nauseous, she knew that she had to go through with this. It was time. No more delaying.

She removed the outfits one by one. Two blue babygros with an elephant print. She ran a finger over the poppers on each one, imagining how it would have been to do them up after she'd bathed her little boys. Next came two small cream cardigans with pearly buttons, to keep the babies warm and cosy. To go with these, a set of cream crocheted booties.

Something inside Eve snapped.

It was like the uncoiling of a spring that had been wound impossibly tightly, its unravelling an explosion of acid in her chest. She cried out as it surged through her, piercing, aching, breaking, and she buried her face in the tiny cardigans and finally released everything she'd been holding in.

–

Gabe followed Jack around the pen while he picked up the pieces of a ball Gabe had dismantled with his strong jaws, then swept the smaller bits into a dustpan. The hound had come along impressively the past week and Jack was delighted with his progress.

'Not long now, boy, and we'll go for a walk, eh?'

Gabe's ears pricked up and he turned his head slightly to one side.

'Oh, so you fancy a walk, do you?'

The dog gave a small jump then started circling next to Jack with his long tail arching upwards. Jack laughed at his enthusiasm. To see a dog go from a state of anxiety to being so pleased to be around a human was a rewarding experience. He'd seen it more than once during his time at the rescue sanctuary. Sometimes it took a long time; it depended upon the dog. One thing he knew for certain, though: greyhounds had a huge capacity for love and forgiveness. He was aware that certain things would remind Gabe of his previous experiences, but come what may, he'd ensure that the dog went to a home where he was able to move on with his life and hopefully live to a good old age.

He'd hoped for a moment, when he'd seen Eve with Gabe, that she might adopt him. The dog had taken to her and she had clearly grown attached to him. But Eve had been gone six days now and he'd heard nothing from her. Jack had kept himself busy, of course, finishing off in Mary's garden and working with the rescue dogs, but he couldn't stop thinking about Eve, especially at night when he tried to fall asleep. He'd ended up in the shed every night until his muscles ached and his brain turned fuzzy, and only then had he been able to drift off into a doze. The feelings he was experiencing were unlike anything he'd ever been through before. He'd cared about his ex-wife and been hurt when she left him, but it had been nothing like this.

And yet... Jack knew that he could contact Eve; that he could text her, ring her or email her, but he didn't. Partly because he believed that she needed time and space to deal with her husband and whatever they needed to sort out, and to decide what it was she really wanted. He didn't want to be some sort of holiday romance for her, but chances were he'd been just that. He'd felt drawn to her for a variety of reasons and he knew that she felt something for him, but it could just have been because she was in a vulnerable state. She needed some room to breathe, time to reassess, and Jack didn't want to crowd her. If she decided that she wanted him, that she wanted to leave Bristol and move to Conwenna Cove, then he would be thrilled. If not... he'd deal with that when the time came.

But he hoped that outcome wasn't the one he'd be faced with.

'Okay, that's the last of it, Gabe. Let's stretch our legs!' He grabbed the harness and lead he'd brought into the pen with him and put them on Gabe, then led him out through the yard and headed towards the fields. An hour of exercise should wear both him and the dog out, and maybe, just maybe, he'd be able to get to sleep before four in the morning.

Eve placed the last of the babygros in the box and folded the lid over them, then Sellotaped it down. She used a marker pen to write *Baby Clothes* on the side, then she stood up and stretched. It had been a difficult day. She'd been delayed by her emotional state when she'd first come into the attic, but once she'd released her grief, she'd felt quite a bit better. She'd been afraid of letting it all out. Afraid that if she started to cry, she'd never stop. This had to be cathartic. She'd always carry the guilt around – she suspected she'd have to come to terms with that – but letting go of some of the grief did make her feel somewhat lighter.

Now she had to be practical. She couldn't hold on to the baby stuff any longer. She'd ask Darryl if he wanted it, and if not, she'd take it to a charity shop. Last time she'd been in the city centre she'd seen a greyhound rescue shop, and that seemed the most fitting place to donate to now. She pictured beautiful Gabe with his dark soulful eyes and his gentle nature. She wanted to help him and dogs like him; she knew she'd never stop loving the breed now that she'd experienced being around them first-hand.

'Oh lordy, am I getting like Aunt Mary?' she asked herself out loud. It seemed strange to hear her own voice, alone, in the attic room. She giggled. 'I'm going to be an old lady with lots of rescue dogs and cats to keep me company. Won't that be fun!' She clapped her hands together. It didn't seem like such a bad future, although it would be better if there was someone to share it with... someone like Jack. *Actually, just Jack.*

She shook her head. Too much to do now, no time for daydreaming about handsome ex-marines!

She folded the white sheets one at a time and laid them in a pile on the floor, then dusted her hands off on her jeans. She'd take the smaller things down to the dining room, but Darryl would have to help her with the bigger boxes tomorrow.

When she got downstairs, she saw that she had two missed calls on her mobile from Amanda. She listened to the voicemail her friend had left her.

'Hey, Eve! It's only me! Thanks for the text to let me know you were home. I'm glad to hear you've made some decisions about Darryl and the house. Fancy some company tonight? Only hubs intends to watch the match on TV and the kids are having their own friends round. You can tell me all about what happened in Conwenna Cove! I'll bring wine and chocolate! Mwah!'

Eve smiled. It would be nice to have a girls' night in. She should spend some quality time with Amanda to thank her for her friendship and support; it would also give her a chance to talk about her time in Conwenna and articulate her thoughts and feelings about work and what she'd learnt about herself today. A second opinion was always a good thing, right?

She headed back up to the bathroom. A bubble bath would be perfect to wash the dust off and help her to relax. She turned on the hot tap, poured some fragranced foam under the flow, then perched on the edge as the tub filled.

It was as she stared at the bubbles that she realized something. She'd been in this house for two years and had taken only a handful of baths during that time, always jumping into the shower because it was faster. Well, not any more. The new Eve that was emerging from under the layers of self-preservation would be taking time out to enjoy life's pleasures. She'd start with a long, hot soak then have a good chat with her best friend over a few glasses of wine. Small steps, seemingly ridiculous to some, but for Eve it was a big deal to come to terms with how much she'd denied herself over the years. And how unhappy that had made her.

—

'So tell me all about Conwenna Cove!' Amanda said as she filled two glasses with Prosecco, then passed one to Eve.

Eve took a sip of the cool, crisp wine, enjoying the way the bubbles tickled her lips. She tucked her legs beneath her on the sofa and leaned back. 'Not much to tell really.'

'Eve Carpenter, you're a big fat liar! I can see the difference in you. It's amazing! Was Aunt Mary's cooking really that good, or was it the sea air? Or did someone else in Conwenna make this difference?'

Eve smiled. 'It was good to get away and I do feel a lot better. I would've stayed on longer but Darryl called and said we needed to get things settled here. That's why I came back.'

'You're evading my question.' Amanda pushed up her sleeves and turned on the sofa to face Eve.

Eve took another sip of her wine. 'You're staying over, right?'

Amanda nodded. 'I told the family that they could cope without me for a night, and as I left, I swear I heard them whispering that they were going to get pizza delivered. As if they can't do that when I'm there!' She shrugged. 'Anyone would think I rule over my brood with an iron fist and that my husband is completely hen-pecked.'

Eve shook her head. '*I* know he's not. He just adores you.'

'I'm lucky.' Amanda nodded. 'But what about you? Did you meet someone?'

'My aunt has a tenant in the cottage adjoining hers.' Eve looked into her glass as her cheeks warmed.

'I knew it!' Amanda bounced on the sofa. 'And?'

'And he's… well, he's lovely.'

'Lovely how? Come on, Eve. I'm an old married woman. Let me live vicariously through you for a moment!'

Eve laughed. 'You have everything, Amanda. You do not want to live my complicated life, believe me.'

'Oh honey.' Amanda squeezed her hand. 'I know you've been through it, but to see you looking so well after I've been so worried about you means the world to me.'

'I know. Thank you. I don't know how I'd have managed without you.'

'So? At least give me his name.'

'It's Jack.' Eve sipped her wine. 'He's thirty-six. He has dark brown hair and the biggest, darkest eyes. Sometimes I gaze into them and I just…' She bit her lip. 'Nope. I can't do it. I feel silly talking about it. I shouldn't be falling for anyone.'

'That is the most ridiculous thing I've ever heard, Eve. You have every right to be happy, and this Jack, he sounds like a good one.'

'He *is* a good man, Amanda. He's warm, sensitive, caring and helpful. That's not very romantic-sounding, but I had a panic attack when we went into Conwenna one evening and he knew exactly what to do. I guess it's because he's been through so much himself.'

'Why? What happened to him?'

'He's an ex-marine. He was injured in the line of duty in Afghanistan.'

'A marine?' Amanda's eyes widened.

'Yes.'

'Is he… I mean, I don't want to sound crass, but is he fit?'

Eve nodded. 'But that's not what draws me to him. It's just *him*, you know? Who he is. He's so deep and so understanding.'

Amanda nodded. 'How does he feel about you?'

Eve paused and took a deep breath. 'I think he cares. I mean, I feel a bit like a teenager because we've only known each other for such a short time, but it's like I *know* him. Does that make sense?'

'It absolutely does!' Amanda drained her glass. 'But what will you do? Your job is here, and your house, although,' she eyed the empty shelves and nodded at the dining room, 'it looks like that's going to change.'

'We've agreed to sell the house. I can't rattle around here any longer and Darryl needs closure. We both do.'

'That makes sense. So what about work?'

'I'm not sure yet, but I have some more time to get my head around it all. Sometimes I'm convinced I need to resign, and other times I panic because it's all I've ever known.'

'You're a fantastic head teacher, Eve, and it would be a massive loss to the school and the profession if you left. But only you can decide what you need. If you feel better after half-term, come back and we'll all be thrilled. Well, except for Donovan, that is.' She pulled a face. 'But if you decide otherwise, then bloody good for you!'

'Thank you.' Eve shuffled closer to Amanda and opened her arms. They hugged for a moment, then she leaned back to meet her friend's eyes. 'Things are clearer than they've been in a long time. I'm not fully there yet, wherever *there* is, but I'm getting there.' She giggled, aware of how confusing her words were.

'You'll get there, Eve, I don't doubt it. Now let's have a refill, because it's not often that I get a night off, and I've a thirst for more!'

Amanda filled their glasses again then clinked hers against Eve's. 'To the future, my friend! May it bring you whatever your heart desires. Especially if that includes a gorgeous ex-marine with a sensitive side.'

Eve smiled then drank to the toast, silently wishing Jack and Gabe a restful weekend. She wondered if they were out walking now, and if they were thinking about her as much as she was about them.

Chapter 22

'Oh. Morning.' Eve peered around the front door at Darryl. Outside, it was already bright and warm and the light made her eyes sting.

'Wow! Rough night?' Darryl asked as she let him in to the hallway.

She tightened her dressing gown belt and folded her arms over her chest. 'Not exactly rough; more like a lot of fun, but Prosecco has a lot to answer for.'

'As do I! Sorry.' Amanda came down the stairs, fully dressed and looking as fresh as if she'd just returned from a spa weekend. 'Hi, Darryl, good to see you again. How're you doing?'

Darryl shook her hand. 'Not bad, thanks. You?'

'I'm good. Just glad to see this one looking a bit better.' She nodded at Eve.

'Me too. Well… she was looking better until you filled her with too much wine.' He laughed and Amanda joined in.

'Oh thanks very much, you two, let's all laugh at Eve's expense. I just can't drink much, all right?'

'It's because you're so tiny!' Amanda held her thumb and forefinger a centimetre apart.

'I've put on weight.'

'You have a bit, but there's a way to go.' Amanda smiled. 'Who's for coffee?'

'Please,' Darryl replied.

She headed for the kitchen, leaving the two of them standing in the hall.

'I'll just jump in the shower and freshen up, if you don't mind. Sorry I'm not ready; I overslept because of Princess Pours-a-lot in there.' Eve gestured at the kitchen.

'Of course. No rush,' Darryl said. 'I could do with that coffee anyway.'

'Won't be long!' Eve headed up the stairs.

As she showered, she thought back through the previous evening. Amanda had opened two bottles of wine, or was it three? Eve had lost count as the warm Prosecco buzz had settled in and relaxed her. She'd told her friend all about Conwenna, Aunt Mary and Edward and their wedding, as well as Gabe and how drawn she'd been to him. Talking about Gabe and then Jack had made them seem so real. When she'd been in Conwenna, they'd been real enough, but as the days had passed since her return, they'd taken on a kind of haziness, as if they'd been part of a lovely dream she'd once had. But describing them to Amanda had brought home to her how grateful she was to know them. It had also made her miss them even more. And she'd wanted to call Jack; even thought about it...

She froze.

Shit!

She *had* called Jack. When she'd crawled up the stairs to bed, too tipsy to walk, she'd found her mobile on her bedside table and pressed dial.

Gah!

What had she said? She couldn't remember him answering. But she'd heard his voice. His lovely soft voice. *Ah!* She'd left him a message.

Oh bloody hell!

272

She suspected that she'd get fragments of memories throughout the day, that the hours to come would be filled with cringing as she experienced flashbacks.

Damn Amanda and her Prosecco!

Once she'd dried herself and wrapped a towel around her hair, she went into her bedroom and checked the recent calls on her phone.

Ten?

Ten calls to Jack's number. Had she left ten messages?

Heat washed over her and her armpits prickled.

'I am never drinking again,' she vowed, as she dressed and combed her hair.

But as she stared at her reflection in the mirror, she caught sight of something there, twinkling in her eyes. It wasn't fear or panic.

It was mischief.

–

Jack sat on the sand and pulled his mobile out of his pocket. He'd left it in the shed last night by mistake, and when he'd gone out there this morning, the battery was dead. He'd plugged it in and let it charge for a while, and as the battery filled with life, the phone kept buzzing. Each time he checked the screen, there was another alert from voicemail.

When it finally fell silent, he saw that he'd missed ten calls from Eve. His heart had sunk and he'd been struck by panic. What if she'd needed him? What if she was hurt?

He had tried to ring her back but his signal had started playing up, like in one of those awful nightmares, so he'd gone round to Mary's to see if she knew what was wrong. She told him before he had a chance to ask that she'd had

273

a lovely text from Eve during the night telling her how much she loved her and Conwenna Cove. It had come through in the early hours, so, she'd said with a smile, she suspected that Eve might have been a bit squiffy.

Jack had released the breath he'd been holding. Eve was all right. That was good. He couldn't have borne it if she'd been hurt or afraid. He wanted to be there for her; to care for her and to protect her.

Shit!

He really did. He wanted to be the one she came home to, that she looked to for support, that she cuddled up to at night.

He'd accepted a cup of tea and some toast from Mary then taken the dogs down to the cove so he could get some air and thinking time. Which was why he was sitting on the sand with his phone out. The signal arcs were full now, so he should be able to access his voicemail.

And he could listen to Eve's messages.

But he was anxious. What if she had rung to tell him that she was reconciling with her ex? It could have happened. She'd come to Conwenna all mixed up, but going back to Bristol and the life she had there, she might have been swept back into it and now, this very moment, she could be lying in Darryl's arms.

His body tensed and his hands curled into fists. The thought of anyone else holding Eve was unbearable. Even if it was her husband.

But she'd said things were over between them. She'd said she'd be back.

Hadn't she?

He uncurled his hands and smoothed the dogs' silky heads. They both flashed him a glance then turned back to gaze at the sea. Harry and Clio were warm and contented

274

and Jack wished he could be as relaxed as they were; that he didn't have this terrible churning in his guts as he thought of the woman he adored.

Adored…

He was in deep.

It was better to listen to the messages and get this over with; no sense delaying any longer. He wouldn't run away from this; he wasn't a coward. He'd rather feel the pain now than spend his life wondering.

He swiped the screen of his mobile then raised it to his ear.

Time stood still. The sound of the gulls circling overhead dimmed, the waves froze mid-roll and the sporadic white clouds paused in the bright blue sky.

Then he started to laugh, a great heaving sound that began deep inside him and bubbled insistently out of his mouth, until his eyes were wet and his stomach muscles ached.

Each message grew more and more insistent and more drunkenly sincere. Each message carved out a passage across his heart. And each message made him long to see Eve Carpenter again, as soon as possible.

Because now he knew.

–

'That's the last of it,' Darryl said as he closed the doors of the van and pushed his hands into his pockets. 'I'll drop the bab… I mean the things off at that greyhound charity shop on the way.'

'Are you sure you don't want to keep any of it?' Eve asked as she peered at him from under her hand. The sun was making her eyes water and her head still throbbed dully with a hangover.

'I'm sure. No point hanging on to the past, is there?'

'No.'

'If things had been different and the twins had... I suspect we'd have kept some of their baby things for sentimental reasons and given whatever wasn't needed to charity. So this is kind of the same. Just sadder.' He looked back at the house. 'When's the sign going up?'

'Monday. The estate agents all gave similar estimates, so I went with the first one. She's certain we'll get an offer soon; said the catchment area alone will sell the house.'

'And what will you do then?'

'I'm still not entirely certain. The sale could take a while to go through, especially if the buyers are in a chain, but I've had some thoughts about how I might progress. Time to move on and all that.'

'Keep in touch?'

'Of course. We've the divorce to finalize as well as the finances.'

'No, Eve. I just mean, stay in touch. Let me know how you are, what you decide to do and so on. I don't want to make life hard for you or to hang around like a bad smell.' He flashed a small smile. 'But we do have a past and I would like to know that you're safe and well.'

'Same here.' She swallowed hard. This was more difficult than she'd anticipated. Their marriage hadn't been right, she was certain about it now, but even so they had shared a life for a while and been through some difficult times. Whatever happened from here on, they would always have a shared past, and nothing would change that for either of them. But they were heading in different directions now, and hopefully this time they'd both find happiness.

Darryl opened his arms and Eve walked into his embrace. They hugged for a moment then he released her. 'Take care now.'

'You too. Hope it works out for you with…'

Darryl nodded. 'Early days. Not counting my chickens.' He tapped the side of his nose. 'Speak soon!'

He climbed into the van, then started the engine. Eve stood at the edge of the driveway and watched as he drove away, feeling a strange mixture of sadness and hope. She had managed to leave things on a positive note with her ex-husband. The house was cleared out, their belongings divided, and the divorce would be finalized within weeks, since neither of them would contest anything.

They really were closing a door.

She jumped as arms encircled her and she turned to find Amanda standing beside her. 'You okay, chick?'

She nodded. 'Just about.'

'Good. Kettle's on.'

'Great idea. I'm parched.'

'Me too. All that wine dehydrated me terribly. Good thing I didn't try to drive home this morning; not worth the risk. I'd still have been over the limit.'

They headed into the house.

'Amanda?'

'Yeah?'

'Did you do that deliberately so you could stay here while Darryl moved his things out?'

'What, me? Come up with such a devious plan so I'd be here if my best friend was in need?' She shook her head. 'Never!' Then she winked.

'Thank you.'

Amanda waved at her. 'Now where d'you keep the biscuits?'

Chapter 23

Eve sauntered around the supermarket. The comforting aromas of freshly baked bread and fresh fruit and vegetables lifted her spirits. The smells reminded her of Aunt Mary's house and how happy she had always been there. As she picked up a bag of lemons, she pictured the first lemon drizzle cake she'd made and the following culinary disasters that Jack had helped her to clean up. It seemed such a long time ago now.

She'd thought about ringing him again to try to find out what she'd said in her messages – all ten of them – but just the idea made her cringe. She'd recalled snippets of what she'd said and had flashbacks of emotions, but the Prosecco haze had, perhaps thankfully, kept most of her drunken messages from her.

Jack had sent her a brief text teasing her about no doubt having a hangover and to say that he hoped she was getting on okay and that Gabe sent his love. Eve had found it reassuring and was grateful that he hadn't asked any questions, so she hadn't felt under pressure to provide him with answers. That was typical of how thoughtful he was. He knew she needed some space to sort out her life, but he also clearly wanted her to know that she was still in his thoughts.

'Well hello there!' A sing-song voice snapped her out of her musing and a shiver ran down her spine.

I know who that is...

She turned slowly and took a deep breath.

'Hello, Donovan.'

It was a school day and just gone one p.m. She shouldn't be at risk of bumping into anyone from work. What was he doing out and about?

'I didn't expect to see you looking so well, Eve. My, my...' He ran his eyes from her head to her feet and back again in such a way that Eve felt instantly uncomfortable.

'I'm... I'm certainly feeling a bit better.'

'Yesssss!' He dragged out the sound between his teeth and Eve was reminded of a snake hissing. 'Does this mean you'll be joining us back at school soon? Tomorrow, perhaps?' He ran a finger over one perfectly groomed brow, then rested his hands on his hips.

'Not yet, no.' Eve felt perspiration pop out on her upper lip and her heart began to thud.

'Not yet? Oh but Eve, we all miss you so much.' The way he said it made Eve certain that he didn't miss her at all, and that he was in fact enjoying her absence immensely.

'Well that's nice to hear. I will be back... after half-term.'

'Right!' He snapped his fingers and Eve jumped. 'But much as we want you back, are you sure you should risk it? After that rather unfortunate little incident.' He lowered his gaze and shook his head as if remembering the details of Eve's projectile vomiting.

Something about his tone and his smug expression made Eve's blood boil. She knew she should contain her feelings, that she should filter her words before her anger burst forth, but she couldn't; it was just too powerful. 'Now look, you weaselly little maggot! I've just about had it with you and your sodding snaky ways. How *dare* you stand there and look down your pointy nose at me!'

'Wha—' He raised his hands in alarm, but Eve cut him off.

'*No!* Oh no you don't, Donovan! I've had an absolute gutful of you being such a sly worm. Always sneaking around behind my back trying to find some dirt on me or Amanda, putting me down in front of the governors and staff. All I have ever done is strive to do my job and do it well. I'm not bloody perfect. Believe me, I know that very well.' She paused to take a deep breath, and out of the corner of her eye saw that she'd attracted a small audience of shoppers and supermarket staff, but she was too angry to care. 'But I am a human being, and although I love my job, I am not made of steel!' Her voice broke on the last word and she gasped as she tried to fill her lungs.

'Eve!' Donovan squealed as he waved his hands either side of his blotchy face. 'Oh my God, I'm so sorry.'

'Are you, though?' She gulped down air then took a step towards him. 'Are you really? I know you're ambitious and I know that your job means the world to you. You're not a bad teacher, far from it, but you are still quite inexperienced, and believe me, in teaching, experience counts for a lot. You've climbed the ladder quickly, and good on you for that, but you mustn't forget that you still have a lot to learn. I *never* forget that, Donovan, and if I had any intention of staying in teaching then I would remind myself of it every day.'

Donovan stared at her, his mouth opening and closing like a landed fish. 'You're not staying in teaching?'

'What?' Eve frowned at him.

'You just said that if you had any intention of staying in teaching—'

'Oh shit!' Eve covered her mouth. So she had! As she'd vented her long-building frustration with her assistant head, her inner decision had been released.

'Do other people think I'm a snake?' Donovan asked, hanging his head and toeing the speckled supermarket floor with a shiny loafer. She noticed how the gel in his hair had turned white and how some of the strands clung together in a sticky clump.

'Sorry? What?'

'You said I'm snaky. I never wanted to be snaky. I just thought I was being kind of... clever. You know... Machiavellian.' His cheeks reddened and Eve started to giggle.

'Oh Donovan, really?'

'Honestly. I was just trying to get on. Playing the game, as one of my heads of department once told me. I just want to do well, Eve. Like you.'

Eve stared hard at him, seeing for the first time exactly how young he actually was. While she was in head teacher mode, which she was fast recognizing as her battle mode, she saw practically everyone as some sort of threat. Poor Donovan had been one of those threats, and rather than being brutally honest with him about his behaviour, and trying to guide him, she'd let him carry on while resenting him. As his line manager, she hadn't been fair at all. He needed nurturing, not resentment and the cold shoulder of authority.

'Donovan, do you want to grab a coffee?'

The gratitude that flashed over his face made Eve feel even guiltier. 'That would be great, thanks. I only have about half an hour, though. I came to order a cake for Sandra.'

'You did?'

'Yeah. She had her baby.'

Eve smiled. 'Everything okay with them?'

He nodded. 'A healthy girl. Mother and baby doing well.'

'Oh that's great news,' Eve said as they entered the store cafe and went to the counter.

'Eve, are you really going to quit? I just can't imagine the school without you there.'

'Oh Donovan,' she replied as she handed him a mug of coffee and went to pay, '*I* just can't imagine being there any more. So yes, I'm going to resign. But first let me tell you a few things I've learnt along the way, and who knows? You could be the next super head teacher to make the local news.'

–

Eve stood in front of the postbox.

What she was about to do would alter the course of her life forever.

It was an enormous decision to make.

But it was the right one. She was certain of that now.

She ran a finger over Amanda's name, then over the school address. She could have gone to see Amanda and given her the resignation letter in person, but she'd worried that her friend might try to dissuade her, or delay her, and she knew she wouldn't be free until she did this.

Of course, this was just the start of proceedings; she'd have to negotiate with the school a way of working out her notice. But she suspected they'd be able to sort something out for her, some sort of flexi working plan, to run down her time as head teacher.

She raised the letter to the opening in the red postbox that reminded her of an open mouth just waiting to swallow up her past. Her hand was steady; no trembling at all.

'See. It's the right thing to do,' she said out loud. Then she pushed the letter through the slot and heard it land on top of other post.

She dusted off her hands and walked away.

It was a beautiful summer morning. Flowers bloomed in gardens and someone was mowing their lawn. When she reached her house, she stopped and stared at the *For Sale* sign that stood proudly in the front garden. She'd given the estate agent the keys so she could show interested parties around in her absence, and now that Darryl had taken his things and removed a lot of their unwanted possessions, the house had a showroom feel to it: a blank canvas just waiting for its new owners.

She unlocked the front door and entered, conscious of how her footsteps echoed in the empty hallway. She'd scrubbed the house thoroughly and everything shone; there wasn't an empty wine bottle, takeaway carton or pair of pants hanging from a cupboard door handle to be seen.

The house really was just a house now. It needed a family; then it could become a home.

As for Eve, she was heading to *her* home.

Home to Conwenna Cove.

Home to Aunt Mary.

And home to find out if Jack felt the same way as she did.

Her stomach fizzed with excitement and she placed a hand over it. She couldn't allow herself to get too far ahead. He might have decided that she was too crazy, too neurotic, too needy... hell, too much of everything for him.

But she had to find out. She had learnt that recently; that honesty was best, whether with yourself or with those around you. Even if it wasn't always the easiest route.

Chapter 24

As she pulled up in front of Mary's cottages, Eve was trembling. She couldn't believe she was back. She'd only been away eleven days, but it had been long enough. She yanked on the handbrake and removed the key from the ignition, trying not to stare at Jack's cottage to see if he was there, wondering if he would come out to greet her.

Or not…

She got out of the car and stretched. The journey had seemed interminably long, as she'd got stuck in traffic jams with everyone else who hadn't set off for the bank holiday weekend on Friday evening, choosing to leave on Saturday morning instead. Like them, she'd hoped to miss the rush; like them, she'd ended up stuck in it.

But she was here now. The late-afternoon air smelt woody and fresh, a mixture of laburnum, cut grass and salt. Eve went to the boot and pulled out her holdall, then shuffled it across the gravel towards Aunt Mary's cottage.

As she reached the door, it swung open and her aunt beamed at her. 'Oh Eve! It's so good to see you! When I got your text last night, I was thrilled!'

'It's wonderful to be here, Aunt Mary. I'm so glad to be back.'

Mary hugged Eve so tightly that she wheezed.

'Oh sorry, Eve. I'm small, I know, but I'm stronger than I realize.'

'That's fine! Never apologize for hugging me.' She glanced around once more but there was no sign of movement from Jack's cottage, so she followed her aunt inside, leaving her holdall in the hallway.

As she went through the lounge, the dogs raised their heads in greeting and she gave them both a quick ear rub, then did the same to the cats, who were curled up together on an armchair.

'Okay, the kettle is on and I've a fresh lemon drizzle cake here, so we can sit down and catch up.'

Eve nodded. She sat at the table and took the plate her aunt offered.

'How've you been?' she asked.

'Very good, dear.' Aunt Mary smiled and Eve noticed that she was, in fact, glowing. As she placed the milk carton on the table, a sparkling on her left hand caught Eve's eye.

'Oooh! Let me see!'

Mary chuckled. 'I asked for something quite cheap and, you know, not fussy, but Edward had other plans.' She held out her hand and Eve gazed at the diamond engagement ring. It was a square solitaire set in a platinum band.

'It's beautiful and it's not at all fussy.'

'With all the cooking and gardening I do, I'm terrified it'll fall off or get dirty, but Edward said it's quite hard-wearing, so I'm trying to relax about it. I'll be honest, though, Eve, it's strange wearing a ring on my finger. Anyway, enough about me. I want to know how you're faring, Eve.'

'Much better, thanks.'

'You said you'd done something drastic?' Her aunt paused at the table with the teapot in both hands.

'That's right.'

'You haven't…' Aunt Mary chewed her bottom lip, her eyes wide.

'I did. I gave in my notice yesterday.' Her stomach flipped; saying it out loud made it real. 'I posted it, which is a bit cowardly perhaps, but I'd made up my mind and wanted to get it done.'

'And you're certain about it?' Aunt Mary asked as she poured tea into their mugs.

Eve nodded. 'It was bumping into a colleague that helped me make the final decision.' She decided not to go into detail; it was a long story that would keep for another time. 'And so it's done.'

Aunt Mary cut two slices of lemon drizzle cake and placed one on the plate in front of Eve. 'What will you do now?'

'Now I will allow myself some time to just *be*. Coming back here a few weeks ago was one of the best decisions I've ever made. It's helped me to come to terms with what's been wrong in my life.'

'I told you Conwenna Cove has magical elements, dear.' Aunt Mary smiled with satisfaction.

'I believe you now, Aunt Mary.' Eve paused and bit into her cake. It was moist and light and the tartness of the lemon was complemented by the crusty sugar glaze. 'How's… uh… Jack?'

'I thought you'd never ask!' Mary laughed and tapped the tabletop. 'He's been like a sad puppy around the place since you went.'

'What?' Eve sat up straight. 'But why?'

'Why d'you think?'

Eve shrugged. She knew she should feel bad for Jack, but knowing that he'd missed her made her smile inwardly.

'Is he there now?' She nodded at the wall, indicating the cottage next door.

'No, dear.' Mary shook her head. 'He had to go up to the farm.' Her face fell. 'There was an emergency with one of the dogs.'

'Which one?' Eve's stomach flipped.

'I'm not sure. One of the male greyhounds, I think. The vet told him on the phone that it didn't look good.'

'Oh God! That's awful. Should I ring him?' Eve's mind filled with images of the big black dog she'd grown so fond of. She couldn't bear it if something had happened to Gabe and she hadn't been there. She'd missed him so much, it was almost as if he was hers and she was his.

'I doubt he'll answer if they're in the middle of something.'

Eve drummed her fingers on the table. She'd only just arrived but she didn't know if she could sit here chatting with her aunt when Gabe needed her. She knew the dog had formed an attachment to her. What if he'd thought she'd abandoned him, that she would never return?

'I have to go up there!'

'I understand, dear.'

'Sorry about this.' Eve dusted the cake crumbs off her fingers, pecked Mary's cheek then grabbed her bag from underneath the table.

'Let me know how you get on!' Mary called after her as Eve rushed out to the car and jumped in, quickly fastening her seat belt before doing a three-point turn and heading off along the gravel road.

–

Jack shook the vet's hand. 'Thanks, Oliver.'

'I'm sorry I couldn't do more,' Oliver Davenport replied. 'Sometimes this happens, even to relatively young dogs; their hearts just give out. It could be due to a variety of factors, but I think in this case it's most likely a congenital defect.' His tone was neutral, his eyes kind.

Jack swallowed hard. Losing a dog was always rough, but the male greyhound had been making good progress. It seemed so unfair that it hadn't worked out for him.

'If you get him out to my Land Rover, I'll take him in with me and sort out the cremation.'

'Of course.' Jack nodded. He glanced at Neil, but his boss was staring out of the window. Neil had been silent throughout the vet's examination of the dog, unable to speak for emotion. For a farmer, a man who'd grown up with animals, viewing life and death as intertwined, he had an unwonted soft side when it came to the rescue dogs.

Once Jack had wrapped the dog in a large grey blanket and carefully placed him in the back of the vet's vehicle, he turned and gazed out across the fields. It didn't get easier losing a dog and he doubted it ever would. At the rescue sanctuary they strove to help the greyhounds in every way they could. So losing one, especially a young one, was the worst possible scenario, although he knew that at times it was inevitable.

He watched as Oliver got in his car then gave a brief wave before driving away.

'I'm off for a cuppa. You want one?' Neil asked.

Jack shook his head. 'No, I'm all right. Need some air if I'm honest.'

Neil nodded, then patted Jack's shoulder before walking away.

Jack leaned against the low wall in front of the office and gazed into the distance, out in the direction of the sea. He imagined that he could hear it, the waves crashing against the shore, rolling up and down the beach, possessing then rejecting the sand as they had done for what must have been forever. There was some comfort to be found in that knowledge, that even after you'd gone, the world would carry on: the wind would blow, the clouds would race across the sky and the trees and plants would continue to grow.

Life was short and he knew he should grab happiness while he could. And with that thought came another that pierced his heart: he missed Eve so damned much.

—

Eve drove through the farm gates then got out of the car to close them behind her. As she entered the yard, she spotted Jack by the wall in front of the office and her heart leapt. Then she saw his expression and it plummeted.

What was wrong? Had the dog travelled over the rainbow bridge? It was a comforting euphemism that they used at the sanctuary; a beautiful image of the hounds following the rainbow across the sky. It was easier to imagine them heading that way than the alternative. Eve wasn't a religious person but she could accept any idea that helped people to deal with grief. Besides, why shouldn't lovely dogs be able to go to a beautiful, peaceful place after they left their owners?

Has Gabe gone over the rainbow bridge?

Her throat tightened as she pictured his big brown eyes, his long muscular legs and waggy tail.

Oh please no…

She got out of the car and approached Jack. Her heart hammered as she took in his handsome face, his strong physique and the deep line that now sat between his black brows. Something was wrong.

'Jack?'

No answer.

'Jack? Are you okay?'

He stared into the distance, not seeing her, not hearing her, and Eve was consumed by panic.

'Jack?' She'd reached him now, and she took hold of his upper arms and looked into his eyes. He jumped and blinked.

'Eve?' His face contorted and Eve saw pain, confusion and something else pass over his features. 'Where did you come from?' He held her elbows and scanned her face.

'I arrived at Mary's about an hour ago. I came as soon as I could.'

'Bloody hell, it's so good to see you.' He pulled her against his chest and Eve wrapped her arms around his waist and breathed him in. His scent was fresh as mountain air and woody as a forest; beneath that was the aroma of dogs. It made her smile.

When he loosened his hold, she took a step back to see him better.

'Are you staying? I mean, for a while? Until after half-term?' His eyes were hungry as they roamed over her and she knew hers would appear the same to him.

'Yes.' She swallowed. 'Jack, we've things to discuss, but I have to know. Is... is Gabe all right?'

He frowned for a moment, then realization dawned on his face. 'Oh, yes. Yes, Gabe is fine.'

Eve released a sigh of relief. 'Thank goodness.'

'But we did lose a dog. A young male called Bailey.'

'Oh love,' Eve said, taking hold of his hands. 'What happened?'

He shrugged. 'Oliver wasn't sure, but he thinks it was heart failure. Sadly, it happens.'

Eve hugged him tight, offering the only comfort she could.

'Do you think I could see Gabe? I've missed him.'

'Yes, of course. He'll be thrilled to see you.'

Jack led her towards the stables. The dogs out in their pens barked and jumped and circled as they passed them. When they reached Gabe's kennel run, there he was; big, black and shiny. When he saw Eve, something flickered in his eyes, then he ran at the wire and jumped at it. He bounced up and down on his front paws, then circled again and again, his long tail curved upwards in a perfect semicircle.

'I said thrilled, but that was an understatement. He's elated!'

Jack undid the lock then opened the gate, and Gabe came rushing out. He leapt at Eve and his paws landed on her shoulders. She staggered with the impact but Jack supported her as Gabe proceeded to lick her chin, her cheeks and her forehead, giving her a thorough wash. 'Gabe! You're tickling me!' she laughed.

'Let's take him to the assessment room. We can sit with him while we talk.'

The three of them went to the end of the stable block and entered the small homely room.

Eve sat in the middle of one of the sofas and Gabe immediately jumped up next to her. He circled, then landed at the end where he'd sat before.

'He knows his place,' Jack said, grinning.

Gabe let out a long grunt of contentment and Eve giggled. 'I don't think I've ever heard a better noise than the greyhound grunt.'

'It's pretty cool, huh?'

Jack squashed onto the other end of the sofa then wriggled around to face Eve. 'So, about those messages you left me.'

Eve winced. 'I'm sorry.'

'Don't be. Unless you didn't mean what you said, of course.'

'Jack... don't take this the wrong way, but I was a bit drunk.'

He nodded. 'I guessed that. But don't they say that your true self emerges then, when you let your guard down?'

'I guess so.'

'Eve, the things you said. They got to me. Here.' He placed a hand over his heart. 'You know, after my wife left, I swore that I'd never take a risk again; that I'd never fall for another woman. I was doing really well... until you came along. I'm afraid to say the L word, yet I can't really describe how I feel without using it. This isn't some passing fancy or foolish crush. It's physical, I can't deny that, but it's also so much more. For me, anyway.'

'Oh God... did I say the L word?'

He laughed. 'Kind of... in a roundabout way. It was the things you told me about never feeling this way before and never feeling this way again that got to me. You said that you feared not seeing me again, that the idea of going back to your old life terrified you and that you wished you knew how I felt about you.'

The way he was gazing at her made Eve tingle all over.

'So... do you want to know how I feel?'

Eve reached out and ran her hand gently over Gabe's head, stroking him from ear to ear then back again. He smacked his lips and she smiled as his long tongue lolled out of the corner of his mouth.

'Yes, Jack, I want to know.'

'Before you came to Conwenna, I'd heard things about you from Mary and I was expecting a stuck-up, snooty, arrogant person. Not that Mary ever said a bad word about you, mind, but I read between the lines. I was already annoyed at you for the way you neglected your aunt when I'd spent most of my adulthood wishing for someone like Mary in my life.'

'I've apologized to Aunt Mary. How I treated her was wrong.'

'But she's so happy now, I think she's forgiven you everything. Not that she'd ever have held it against you.'

'I'm lucky.'

He smiled. 'When you arrived, I wanted to dislike you, but you made it so hard. With your cute haircut and your big green eyes; that air of innocence and vulnerability you try to hide but that emerges when you're unaware of it. Your beautiful smile, the way you treat animals, your kindness and your fabulous mind. I couldn't stay mad at you, Eve. Most of all, the thing about you that affected me was your heart. I love the way you care about others, the way you feel guilty over everything, because let's face it, not everything can possibly be your fault yet you're willing to accept responsibility for it. I love the way you feel in my arms and how your head feels pressed against my chest. I'm overwhelmed by you, Eve, and the thought of never seeing you again when you left Conwenna nearly broke me. I tried to forget you, to carry on with other things, but the hope that you'd return – as you said you would –

never left me. I couldn't let go of it because I would have gone mad.' He laughed. 'I'm serious.' He rubbed a hand through his hair then down over his face. 'Tell me I'm an idiot.'

Eve shook her head. 'I can't, because you're not. There's so much I love about you too, Jack.'

'But there's so much we don't know about each other. What if we're wrong?'

'Are you afraid of that?'

'Yes, I'm terrified, but the alternative, the thought of a future where I don't have you, is unbearable.'

'Same here,' she whispered. 'Which is why... I've handed in my notice. I'm not going back to Bristol.'

He closed his eyes for a moment and she watched his Adam's apple bob. When he finally spoke, his voice was clogged with emotion.

'Eve?'

'Yes?'

'I would kiss you, but there's a greyhound watching me.'

They started to giggle, and Eve felt happier than she had done in what felt like a lifetime.

'Jack, I want to adopt Gabe.'

'I'd be horrified if you didn't. Look at him. He clearly loves you; he hasn't taken his eyes off you.'

'But I don't have anywhere to live.'

Jack chewed his lip. 'How long are you planning on staying with Mary?'

'For a few weeks, but I'm going to look for somewhere in the village.'

'Well let's see how that goes, shall we?' he said, his eyes bright.

'Okay.' Eve suspected she knew what he meant but decided to leave it unexplored for now. *One thing at a time.*

–

Eve's stomach flipped as Jack let them into his cottage then locked the front door behind them. They'd spent an hour with Gabe, talking and laughing and trying to figure out how to deal with their feelings, but they'd both known what would happen when they went back to the cottage.

It was a fait accompli. There was no turning back now, and she wouldn't want to.

As Jack took her hand and led her up the narrow staircase, the tension seeped out of her body. He stood back to let her enter his bedroom first and she quickly absorbed all the details, capturing them in her heart and mind as if to store them there forever. The furniture was old and eclectic, from the large oak wardrobe to the mirror that hung from a hook above a tall pine chest of drawers. The window overlooked the back garden, which meant that his room was adjacent to hers, with only the internal wall separating them. All the nights she'd lain in bed there, Jack had been just here. Had he been thinking of her too?

He drew the curtains then turned to her. With the late-afternoon sun glowing through the thick material, the room was warm and cosy. Homely. Safe. And right now, filled with anticipation.

Eve took a deep breath, then released it slowly, determined to stay calm, even though this was all so new and so special. She'd been with other men before Darryl, yet this felt like her first time. Was it because she loved Jack? Was this how it felt when you made love to someone you really, truly loved?

'Eve?' Jack's voice was soft and low. 'I'm… nervous.'

She took his hands and gazed into his dark eyes. He cupped her face, sending shivers of delight through her entire body, and ran his thumbs over her cheeks.

'I'm nervous too. But this feels so right.'

'This *is* right. I want you, Eve.'

'And I want you, Jack.'

When he lowered his head and covered her mouth with his, Eve slid her hands around his neck to pull him even closer. She could feel his heart thudding against her chest and his burgeoning desire, which made her own passion even more intense.

When he gently released her, she knew why.

She stepped back and lifted her T-shirt over her head, then slipped out of her jeans. The hunger in Jack's gaze made her bold, so she helped him out of his clothes too. As she slowly revealed his body, love rushed through her. He was beautiful, from his muscular chest and arms to his toned stomach to his strong, shapely thighs. She lowered to her knees to help him step out of his jeans, then touched his scars and kissed every inch of damaged skin, needing him to know that she loved every part of him; to understand that she saw him as a warrior, a survivor and a whole man. They both had scars, inside and out, but those scars were what made them who they were and what made them perfect for each other.

When they were both finally naked, bared to each other, body, heart and mind, Jack scooped her up and carried her to the bed, laying her down on his cool white cotton sheets.

Then he lay down beside her and stroked her entire body, from the tips of her toes to the top of her head, following each caress with a kiss that sealed the bond between them. All of Eve's doubts and fears drifted away and she accepted that this was how it should be. Every one of her nerve endings stirred and tingled, as if being woken after a long time asleep, and the protective cage that had been around her heart for as long as she could remember finally opened and set her free.

Then Jack covered her body with his, and showed her how it felt to be loved.

–

The next day, Eve and Jack tried to act nonchalantly around each other as they helped Mary to make lunch. Edward ate with them, cracking jokes about the news and the weather and appearing oblivious to the change in the atmosphere.

Because something most certainly had changed, and Eve was amazed that her aunt and Edward didn't remark upon it. How could they not see it, feel it, know it? Or were they being too polite to mention the tension that crackled in the air and the intensity of the glances that passed between Eve and Jack.

She was struggling to fight the distraction that Jack represented. She spilled water everywhere when she tried to pour it into his glass. She dropped a spoon and it clattered on the tiled floor, making her jump. She tripped over one of the cats as it wound around her legs asking for some of the salmon she was dressing.

Her mind was not on her tasks. Her mind was elsewhere.

Her body still ached deliciously after their passionate night and her skin tingled where he'd kissed and caressed her. It was so hard not to take his hand, and to avoid kissing the back of his neck between his T-shirt and his hairline, where she knew he smelt of citrus and ginger. She wanted to dance around the kitchen, to sing as they did in Disney films, to fling her arms wide and proclaim her feelings for this man.

Now that her heart had been freed, she just wanted to be alone with him to continue to explore him and to be as close as they could be. She never wanted this feeling of elation to end.

She had sneaked back into Mary's around eleven the previous night. It was ridiculous really, but she wanted to keep things as normal as possible until she'd had time to adjust to their circumstances herself. Jack had agreed with her, although he'd also told her that he didn't want to spend another night away from her. Eve had reassured him that she was just the other side of the wall and that she would be thinking of him all night.

After lunch, Jack went up to the farm and Eve took the dogs for a walk along the beach, needing some time to clear her head. So much had happened in the space of a few weeks, yet she felt freer than she had done in months. Everything looked different now, clearer, sharper, more in focus, as if she'd been underwater or behind a screen, and now she was seeing it all properly for the first time.

After she'd walked the dogs up and down a few times, she went along the main street to pick up some groceries that Mary wanted for the next day. Eve was looking forward to attending the village fair with Jack; it would be their first official outing as a couple. She had agreed to help out with the dogs for some of the events, and to support Mary in the cake-off, although she had no idea what her aunt planned to make in the annual culinary competition. Still, it was all in the name of fun, and all proceeds would go to the dog sanctuary, so whatever the fair brought, Eve intended to enjoy it.

Chapter 25

The morning was bright and breezy, and although the weather forecast had predicted showers, the clouds were currently being swept along so quickly that Eve hoped the rain would hold off. It was typical that after weeks of fine weather, it seemed possible that it might change on the day of the Conwenna fair.

'I really hope it doesn't rain,' she said to Mary as they unloaded her car boot. It was full of cakes, ingredients, cake tins and mixing bowls, as well as other items including a picnic blanket and several pairs of wellies.

Mary raised her head and sniffed the air. 'It will stay fine… at least until after five.'

Eve took a deep breath, trying to work out what it was that her aunt could smell, but apart from salt, manure and the freshly cut grass of the field, she couldn't smell anything else.

'How'd you know that?' she asked Mary. 'What can you smell?'

'Oh nothing really, apart from cow poo, but the farmers' forecast on the radio said so this morning.'

Eve smiled. 'So that's your secret, eh?'

'Goodness me, how are we going to get all this across to the tents?' Mary asked as she eyed the pile behind the car.

'I'll do a few trips. You stay here and I'll go back and forth.'

'Okay, dear, but be careful not to drop anything.'

Eve picked up several bowls and a bag containing wooden spoons and a weighing scales, then set off towards the largest tent, which had a sign hanging from the opening that said *Convenna Cake-Off*. She ducked slightly to enter the tent and looked around. There were six long counters that reminded her of painting tables, each with a portable gas oven and a fridge at the end of it. The scene was not unlike that featured in several popular TV shows. She was glad that she herself wouldn't be under any pressure, and that her experienced aunt would be the one taking part in the baking competition.

After several trips between the car and the tent, Eve returned to find Mary chatting to some of the locals. She stood next to her aunt and smiled as they nodded at her in silent greeting. Mary was in full flow, telling them all about her wedding, and Eve's heart swelled with love and pride as her aunt spoke about the service they'd planned and about how they didn't want wedding gifts but instead were going to ask guests to make a donation to the dog sanctuary.

When Mary had finished and the villagers wandered off, Eve gestured at the boot. 'Do we need the wellies?'

Mary shook her head. 'I don't think so. Though the rain is meant to hold off, it can sometimes get boggy here, especially if the cows have been grazing in the field, but I think we'll be okay today.'

Eve nodded. 'It's starting to get busy.'

They looked around at the field cordoned off for parking and Mary smiled. 'Yes, our fairs are quite popular. There'll be visitors from surrounding towns and villages, as well as tourists. The dog show is a particular favourite, as is the cake-off.'

She adjusted the lavender silk scarf around her neck and buttoned her cardigan. 'It's a bit cooler than I'd have liked, and perhaps I should have worn shoes rather than sandals, but I do like to make an effort for these events.'

Eve glanced down at her aunt's footwear: a pair of strappy silver sandals with a thin heel. Perhaps not the best choice of shoe for walking across a field. Eve herself had walking sandals on with jeans and an emerald-green blouse with capped sleeves. Practical yet pretty, she hoped. *Pretty enough for Jack?* Heat flooded her as memories of the previous night rushed in. Since her return to Conwenna, they'd been virtually inseparable.

'Eve, are you blushing?' Mary asked.

'No... no!' Eve shook her head. 'I just felt a bit warm.'

'Best take your cardie, though, as it can get nippy when you're standing still.'

Eve grabbed her black cardigan from the driver's seat then locked the car.

'Come on, let's head on over to where they'll hold the dog show.'

They approached the area of the field where a square had been marked out with temporary fencing. The rails were decorated with ribbons and balloons in different colours that danced and waved in the breeze, and there was a speaker system set up on a trailer next to a table. People were already milling around the arena; some were getting their dogs accustomed to the route that they'd have to follow when they were shown, and a few children ran around excitedly, trailing balloons behind them as they played with new friends.

It looked to be a proper family day out and Eve's tummy fizzed with anticipation. She could be a part of this every year if she settled in Conwenna; it could be something that she looked forward to and that one day she'd bring her own family to. She shivered. Could she ever hope to achieve that? Did she deserve to feel that form of domestic contentment?

'Aargh!'

She turned to see her aunt flat on her face on the grass.

'Aunt Mary!' She dropped to her knees and placed a hand on the older woman's back. 'Are you all right?'

Mary lifted her head and spat out a tuft of grass. 'I think so. I don't know what happened. One minute I was walking next to you, then...' She gestured at the ground.

'Can you get up?' Eve asked. She helped her aunt to a sitting position then checked her over.

'I think I'm okay,' Mary said. 'Just a bit shaken.' She pushed her skirt over her knees, then winced. 'Ouch.'

'What is it?' Eve gently took her left hand.

'My wrist. Oooh!' Mary gasped as Eve carefully examined her.

'I don't think it's broken, but it could be sprained.'

'Oh no!' Mary rolled her eyes. 'What about the cake-off? Me and my damned vanity.'

'Aunt Mary, you're the least vain person I know.'

'It's these stupid sandals, though, isn't it? I just wanted a little bit more height today.' She blushed. 'You know, with the local news cameras coming to film the cake-off. But darn it! My heel got stuck in the mud and now look at me.' She gestured at herself and Eve realized that she was missing a shoe. She turned around and saw it held fast in the mud by its heel. 'I wouldn't have cared, but last year I could only just see over the counter and it was a bit of a disadvantage.'

Eve smiled. She also suspected that Mary was taking extra care with her appearance because of Edward. And why shouldn't she?

'We'd better get you to the first aid tent.'

Mary nodded and Eve helped her to stand, then held out her sandal so she could slide her foot into it. When they reached the small tent, they were welcomed by a balding first-aider wearing a name tag that read *Gary*.

'Hi, Mary, what have you done?' he asked as he helped Mary to a chair.

'Oh I'm sure it's nothing. Just a sprain.' Mary tutted at herself. 'Eve, while Gary has a look at my hand, why don't you go to the cake-off tent and let them know I can't take part.'

'But you always take part in the cake-off,' said Gary as he examined her wrist.

'I know.' Mary chewed her lip. 'If only I had a replacement. A wingwoman.'

Eve watched her aunt carefully. Was there something going on here?

'I don't suppose...' Mary raised her eyes to meet her niece's.

'Oh no! I can't. I just couldn't do that. I can barely make a lemon drizzle cake.'

'But that would be perfect, Eve! It doesn't matter if you don't win. It's just that it adds to the competition and excitement for everyone.'

Eve's pulse sped up and she felt perspiration rise on her top lip. She thought of all that her aunt had done for her since her arrival in Conwenna, of how she'd dropped everything to help her, of how she'd been so hurt in the past when Eve had been dismissive of her. She owed Mary, she really did.

'So I just have to make a cake?'

'Yes, dear.'

Gary kept his head down. It seemed to be taking him a long time to check Mary's wrist.

'Okay then. I'll do it.'

'Thank you, sweetheart.'

'I'll go and let them know.'

Eve headed out of the first aid tent and crossed the field. She had a feeling that she'd been set up, whether it had been planned or not. But what else could she do? Mary had been good to her, and she was family, and Eve knew now how important that was. When family needed you, you stepped up.

Inside the cake-off tent, she approached a group of women who were sitting around a table drinking from steaming polystyrene cups.

'Um… excuse me. I'm Mary Carpenter's niece. She's had a fall and won't be able to take part. So… if it's okay, I'll take her place.'

'Yes, of course,' one of the women replied. She had to be at least seventy, but her hair was the fabulous vibrant red of a fire engine. 'Fill this in and we'll get you set up.' She handed Eve a clipboard then returned to her group.

Eve quickly completed the form then handed the clipboard back. 'So I'll be back around eleven?'

'Yes, that's right. Don't be late!' The redhead waved a finger at her. The other women didn't even glance at her and Eve didn't know whether to be insulted or grateful. They were clearly engaged in their conversation and the last-minute replacement of a contestant was of no interest to them.

She decided to check on Aunt Mary then try to locate Jack. He'd said he'd arrive at around ten with the dogs, and Eve knew he was bringing Gabe. She couldn't wait to see the greyhound and hoped she'd be able to walk him around the show arena.

–

Jack led the four hounds he'd brought to the show across the field to the arena. There was quite a crowd there already and it lifted him. Every year that they'd shown dogs from the sanctuary, they'd managed to find potential owners for some of them. He hoped this year would be the same. Neil and Elena were bringing another four dogs, and even if they only homed one, that was one dog headed to its forever home. Of course they didn't just let the dogs go to anyone. It involved home checks and assessment of suitability of lifestyle and so on, but if people were genuine about rehoming, then they didn't mind being checked first.

He scanned the fields as he walked, looking for Eve. The thought of seeing her again, even though it had only been hours since they'd parted, made his stomach flip. He was in deep, and although it scared him, it also filled him with hope. He'd thought he might spend his life alone, not finding love, not finding someone who'd understand him, but Eve was different.

In spite of his joy, however, something was niggling at him. He sensed that she was still holding something back, that there might be something she hadn't told him. It was, of course, early days and he couldn't expect her to spill everything all at once. Trust took time and patience and he hoped he would win hers completely. The thought of

not being able to do so was something he couldn't entertain. His counsellor had worked through this with him,
coaxing him to explore why he'd shut himself down in
the past, encouraging him to admit why he was afraid, and
Jack thought he knew how to control this side of himself
now. He hoped he had the strength to remain open; he
needed to, because Eve was the woman he wanted as his
partner in life.

'Jack!'

He spotted her waving at him and smiled. Gabe pulled
at his lead and Jack laughed. 'Just as keen to see her as I
am, eh, boy?'

When he reached her, he glanced around quickly to
ensure that no one was watching, then leaned forward and
pecked her on the lips. She flushed immediately and Jack
was reminded of how she glowed after they made love.
He couldn't wait to be alone with her again.

'Everything okay?'

'Yes, fine. Actually, well, uh…'

His heart sank. Something *was* wrong. Had he upset
her by kissing her in public? Was it too much too soon?

'It's Aunt Mary. She had a bit of a fall, and I'm kind
of wondering if it was deliberate… I know that makes me
sound suspicious, but, well you know what she's like, and
see…'

Jack shook his head. 'Eve, slow down.' He was
concerned by the manic way her eyes were darting
around, as if she was searching for answers. 'Is Mary okay?'

'Yes.'

'And why do you think she would have planned this?'

'Well she asked me to take her place in the cake-off.'

'But why would she *plan* that?'

Eve worried her bottom lip and Jack had an urge to kiss her again. If he hadn't been holding four dog leads, he might have thrown caution to the wind and pulled her close.

'I'm not really sure, but I suspect it's something to do with trying to build my confidence.'

'By making you bake under pressure?' Jack clamped his lips together to stop himself from smiling. 'That would be some crafty plan.'

'I know. Maybe I'm wrong. It just all seemed a bit... convenient.' Eve crouched down and rubbed Gabe's ears, then let him lick her face.

'Hey! The dog's getting more of a greeting than I did.'

Eve smiled. 'I'll make it up to you later.'

'All right then, as long as you promise.' He winked.

'So what time are the dogs being shown?'

'Half an hour, I think. You okay to take Gabe?'

Eve nodded but her face fell.

'You know you don't have to lead him around.' He was thinking of her anxiety.

'I know. It's not that I'm nervous about being out there in front of people. More that I just don't want anyone else to want him.'

'Well just take him round and talk to a few people about what we do. He can wear one of the vests with "I don't need a home but my friends do" on it.'

'You have those?'

He nodded.

'Oh Jack, thank you.'

'Hey, no need to thank me. This gorgeous fella loves you too.'

Eve met his gaze and her lips parted slightly.

'Are you talking about you or Gabe?'

Jack threw back his head and laughed. 'I see what you did there.'

Eve moved onto her tiptoes and kissed him softly.

'I love the gorgeous fella too.'

Jack's heart pounded against his ribcage and he whispered, 'This has to be the best summer ever.'

—

Ten thirty came, and Eve waited with Gabe just outside the show arena. He leaned against her legs, his large, warm body comforting. Jack had given her the vest for Gabe to wear, to show that he was taken, and it had eased Eve's anxiety. Letting anyone else even entertain the thought of taking him would break her heart.

When Jack gestured at her to follow, she ran around the arena with the big dog at her side. He trotted along in stride with her and she was filled with pride. In many ways he reminded her of Jack: big, strong, powerful; yet gentle, affectionate and vulnerable. The three of them had such a connection and Eve cared about Jack and Gabe so much that the thought of not having them both in her future was unbearable.

They did three circuits, then returned to the gate.

'If you like, you can walk around with Gabe and speak to some of the people, then hand these out.' Jack gave her some leaflets featuring information about the sanctuary. 'If they just want to make a donation – however small – tell them they can do so at the desk there or via the website.'

'Will do. I have to be in the cake-off tent by eleven.'

'No problem.'

'Will you be there?'

'I'll try. If Neil's okay to take the dogs, that is.' Jack grinned at her.

Eve wandered around the outside of the show arena, handing out leaflets and talking to people, as well as stopping for them to pet Gabe and take photographs. When she next checked her watch, it was five past eleven. 'Oh no!' She hurried across to Jack and handed him Gabe's lead. 'I have to go. I'm already late.'

'Hey, don't worry. It's just a bit of fun.'

'I don't know, Jack. The women in there earlier looked pretty serious to me. I'll see you in a bit.'

She patted Gabe's head and he licked her hand, then she raced over to the cake-off tent, pausing by the entrance. Her heart thundered and her legs felt as if they might give way at any moment. Could she actually do this? Did she have the strength after everything else?

'Eve, dear?' A cool hand on her arm made her turn, and she found her aunt next to her. 'Are you all right?'

Eve swallowed her nerves. 'Yes. A bit late, but I'm ready.'

'You can do this, sweetheart.'

Aunt Mary's other arm was bandaged and resting in a sling.

'How's your wrist?'

'A little bruised but nothing to worry about.'

'Does Edward know?'

'Yes, dear, he's over there waiting for me.' Mary gestured at a row of seats and Eve saw her aunt's fiancé waving at them. 'Now keep a cool head and enjoy yourself.'

Eve nodded, then took a deep breath and walked over to the one empty counter, where an apron sat neatly folded on the spotless work surface. She washed her hands thoroughly in the small sink, then pulled the apron over her head. Her mouth was dry and her hands were trembling but she had to do this: for Mary, for Jack, for Gabe, for the sake of the village fair and for herself.

Chapter 26

Eve stared at the ingredients in front of her. Everything she needed to make a cake was right there. But her mind had gone completely blank.

What was she supposed to do first?

She looked around her at the other entrants, who appeared to be a mixture of male and female and different generations. They all seemed to be confidently creating masterpieces. Most impressively, they were all multi-tasking, something that Eve had yet to master in the kitchen.

There was only one thing for it.

She'd have to make lemon drizzle cake.

Or a Victoria sandwich?

Which one?

She took hold of the block of butter and a knife and weighed some of it out then dropped it into the mixing bowl. Then she grabbed a wooden spoon and began to beat it. As she did so, she watched the woman to her right melting chocolate over a saucepan whilst simultaneously whipping up egg whites. Was she making some sort of soufflé? That would be way beyond Eve's talents. In front of her, a teenage girl was flicking melted sugar back and forth with a spoon over a sheet of baking paper. Sweat broke out on Eve's forehead. She was way out of her depth. Her armpits tingled and she felt hot all over. This was too much. She didn't need to be under such pressure; pressure was her enemy.

Pressure makes me—

Get a grip! It's all fine, Eve!

She lowered her eyes and saw that the butter was soft and fluffy, so she stopped beating it and weighed out the sugar. *Good. Focus. This is all good.* She creamed the sugar into the butter and smiled. It was the right consistency. Now for the eggs and the flour.

She worked away diligently, blending in the rest of the ingredients, until the batter was prepared. All she had to do was mix in the lemon zest then pop the mixture into the oven.

But there were no lemons in the fruit bowl.

Or in the fridge.

Or on the work surface.

Why hadn't she thought to check?

She glanced around at the other contestants. They all had chocolate and sugar and strawberries and even mangoes. But no lemons.

Eve stared at her cake batter. Without lemons, it was just plain sponge cake.

'Eve!'

She looked to the doorway and there was Jack. Grinning. And juggling. He crossed the tent and dropped two lemons into her fruit bowl.

'Had a feeling you might need these.'

'But I wasn't even meant to be entered into this competition.' Eve frowned at him.

'I know, but when you told me about Mary, I suspected that you might make lemon drizzle cake. Luckily, they had lemons on the refreshments stand, so I pinched two. Just in case.'

'You are a life-saver!' Eve reached out and pulled him close. She planted a big kiss on his mouth and giggled when he blushed.

'Eve Carpenter! In public view too!'

She shrugged. 'Thank you.'

'Any time. I always want to be able to rescue you if you're a damsel in distress.'

'Oh Jack.' Eve gazed into his eyes for a moment, then realized where she was. Time to get the zest into the batter then get the cake into the oven.

'I'll let you get on. I'll be right over there.' Jack pointed to where Aunt Mary and Edward sat watching them both intently, beaming at what they'd just witnessed.

Eve nodded and got back to work.

When she'd finally placed the cake in the oven and squeezed the juice from the two lemons into a small bowl, she cleaned up and wiped a hand across her brow. All around her the other contestants were busy creating the most elaborate baked goods she'd ever seen in real life – of course she'd seen similar things on those TV shows – and they were extremely impressive. But they'd most likely been doing this kind of thing for years, whereas for Eve, baking a cake was a significant achievement.

Now all she had to do was sit back and wait for it to cook, then she could add the drizzle and it would be ready.

–

A hush fell over the cake-off tent as the judges sampled all the cakes. There was a chocolate marble tower decked with tiny chocolate stars, a lemon roulade served with a berry compote, a baked Alaska surrounded by a delicate glittering sugar cage and a chocolate and raspberry soufflé served with Cornish ice cream – probably from Foxglove Farm, Eve thought. Everything looked delicious.

Then there was Eve's lemon drizzle cake.

It had caught and browned slightly around the edges and she'd tried to disguise it by spreading the drizzle thicker there, but she knew that it paled in comparison to the other creations.

Even so, even though she knew she wouldn't win, she didn't care.

Because she had achieved something special: she'd baked a cake and it had turned out all right – certainly edible, if not as pretty as the others – *and* she had baked it under pressure.

And she hadn't crumbled.

She hadn't suffered an anxiety attack.

She hadn't thrown up or passed out.

She left the judges and the other contestants and went to find her aunt and Jack. They were standing near the doorway with Edward, sipping lemonade and talking quietly.

'Well?' Mary asked, nodding in the direction of the judges.

Eve shrugged. 'I was never going to win it, was I? I only learnt how to bake in the last few weeks and it'll take a while before I'm up to their standard.'

'I like the positivity there,' Jack said, sliding an arm around her waist and pulling her closer.

'Well I feel really positive. I do enjoy baking and I will get better, in time. But I know that this was about more than that.' She pointed at her aunt's arm, which was now out of its sling and seemed to be fully functional.

'Well, dear, I just wanted you to know that you've still got it.'

'It?' Eve chuckled. 'Yes, I guess I have.'

'Whether it's teaching, leading a school, making a dog happy or just being you, Eve, it doesn't matter. You're a lovely young woman with a lot to give and I wanted you to realize that you won't always crack under pressure. Your confidence has taken a battering of late but it will return, and although that might take time, it will come.'

Eve leaned forward and kissed her aunt's cheek. 'Thank you.'

'That's what family are for.'

Eve nodded, her throat too tight to reply. *Family*. Whether that was her aunt, Edward, Gabe or Jack... or all of them together. It didn't have to be as straightforward as a mother and father or sisters and brothers. It was about the people you spent time with and the people who had time for you. And even after everything that had happened, she was lucky enough to have people who wanted her around.

–

Later on, as the stars twinkled in the clear night sky and the moon cast a silvery light over the ocean, Eve and Jack lay on a picnic blanket spread on the deserted beach, gazing up at the sky. The wind had died down and the evening was calm and still. Eve wriggled over and rested her head on Jack's shoulder.

'You know... I feel like I've known you for years, not just weeks.'

'You're fed up of me already?' he asked, turning his head slightly to kiss her hair.

'No! Not like that. I meant that I'm so comfortable being with you, Jack. You make me feel safe and cared about. I can be myself with you and it's like you'll always be there. I don't doubt that you care or that you like me.'

'Of course I like you. How could I not like you?'

'I've spent my life wondering if people like me. My own parents weren't fussed, so why would anyone else be?'

Jack rolled onto his side to face her and stroked her cheek with his free hand. 'Your parents were fools if that's true, Eve.'

She shrugged. 'They're just people, and not all people should be parents.'

'I know that. But not us, eh?'

'What?' Eve gazed into his eyes and her heart filled with emotion. His eyes shone in the moonlight and she knew that she'd never seen anything more wonderful than his face.

'Well, Eve... if you do want me, then I see a wonderful future ahead for us.'

'You do?'

He nodded. 'I can't stand the thought of not being with you. I want you to stay here in Conwenna Cove forever.'

'I want that too.'

'And perhaps... one day, we can get married and have a family.'

'What?' Eve held up a hand.

'I was just thinking that when the time is right... Wouldn't you like that? A baby, or even babies?'

The sincerity in his eyes tore right through her, and when she tried to swallow, it was like she had broken glass lodged in her throat.

'Babies?' Her heart pounded furiously. 'What makes you say that, Jack?'

'You want children, don't you?' His expression was suddenly wary and Eve could see a vein throbbing in his neck. 'To have a family... with me?'

'Oh Jack.' Her voice cracked. She wanted to be with him but she hadn't thought beyond them as a couple; she hadn't thought of what might happen after that.

And now...

She sat up and looked around as panic seized her. 'I'm so sorry, Jack. I just can't do this. I have to go!'

She paused for a moment, then slid her feet into her shoes, jumped up and ran off along the beach. She didn't know if Jack was following her or if he tried to call her back, because she was running so fast that all she could hear was the wind rushing past her ears and the sound of her own sobbing.

Chapter 27

Eve ran and ran and ran, up the steep path, past the rocks and along the road towards the harbour. Her lungs threatened to explode and the muscles in her legs burned. Her chest heaved in and out as she tried to catch her breath. Her face was wet with tears and her throat was raw but she didn't know if it was from running or crying or both. She sank onto a bench in front of the dark windows of the harbour cafe and buried her head in her hands.

As her breathing slowed, she listened to the tide as it lapped against the harbour wall. Life was so fragile yet so tempestuous, just like the sea. One moment it seemed like she had it all; the next it had all been washed away.

She sat up and hugged her knees to her chest.

What would she do now?

She'd come so far, then when Jack had... What *had* he done? Proposed? Or not quite? She'd panicked and run away. But with good reason. She hadn't told him about the twins, about what a terrible mother she'd make. How could she? Where did you start with something so terrible? And yet look at the outcome. The man she adored had been left stranded on the beach, their beach, wondering what on earth he'd done wrong.

'Oh Jack!' She covered her mouth. How could she have done that to him? Run away with no explanation or reassurance? He would think he was to blame and she couldn't bear the thought of that. The idea of hurting him, such a good, kind, honest, caring man, was unbearable. She had to put it right.

She got to her feet, intending to head back down to the beach to try to find him. But as she turned, there he was just a few feet away, his arms full of things: the picnic blanket, her cardigan, his shoes, and the basket that he'd told her contained their celebratory supper — because she'd done so well at the fair that day.

Eve shook herself.

She loved this man. She owed him more than an act of cowardice. She was tired of running away and she certainly shouldn't be running from Jack.

So instead she ran towards him, and watched as he dropped the basket and the blanket and opened his arms. She leapt into them and wrapped herself around him, crying into his neck and telling him over and over that she was sorry.

'Eve.' He spoke softly, leaning back to look into her eyes. 'I don't understand. Have I got this wrong? One minute you're all over me, and the next it's like you're pushing me away. I'm up and down like a yo-yo. I can't do this, much as I… I love you. I just can't.'

She ran her hands over his broad shoulders and down his arms, then slipped out of his embrace. 'Let's sit down. I need to explain something to you.'

She took his hand and led him to the bench, where she sat sideways so she could face him.

'Jack, there's something you need to know about me, something bad… before you make any sort of commit-ment to me.'

'Go on.' His expression was so serious in the moonlight that her heart almost fractured. His eyes were deep black pools and his jaw was set, as if he was suppressing the emotion that bubbled inside him.

'I've fallen for you, Jack. I'm not deceiving you about that, I promise. But I haven't told you everything about my past, about why I had the… the breakdown, I guess you could call it. My job was everything to me, and I gave everything to it. I don't know if it was my way of trying to feel important, of proving to myself that I did matter, but it was a place in my life where I had control. I could achieve things, and I did. I was celebrated as a head teacher, I achieved an outstanding rating from the school inspection team. I was a good classroom teacher then a good manager of people.' She shook her head. 'But I failed at real life. Outside of work, I didn't really know what I was doing. I married Darryl, a good man, a kind man. But the wrong man. And I hurt him.'

'It happens, Eve.'

'Yes, but I should have slowed down, stopped for a bit, yet I just couldn't. Darryl wanted a family but I guess I didn't. We couldn't conceive naturally, so we paid for private treatment. It cost thousands but he said it would be worth it. Only I wasn't so sure. The money wasn't an issue, but having children was. I went into it half-heartedly. Then at sixteen weeks…' She gasped, the memories suddenly darting through her head with startling clarity. 'I started to bleed.'

'I'm sorry.'

She bit her lip. 'I could have done something about it. The doctors advised total bed rest, to take time off work and to just stop…'

'But you didn't?'

'No. I was stubborn. I refused. I guess I thought that whatever happened would happen whether I was resting

or not. So I went back to work, and three days later...'
She sighed and stared out across the harbour towards the
horizon. The sea was black but its surface glowed silver in
the moonlight.

'You know, Eve, people are as deep as the sea.' Jack
had almost read her exact thoughts. 'We all have hidden
depths, dark places we'd never want anyone else to know
about. Nothing in life is easy and everything comes with
a price. I've done things I regret. I blamed myself for a
long time for the deaths of some of my fellow marines.
If I'd been standing where they were or if I'd just spotted
that ambush in time... but life is full of these moments
and all we can do is learn from them and try to move
on. The alternative is to give up. Which some people do.'
He cleared his throat. 'But you're *not* a quitter. Losing the
babies was a tragedy, but I doubt you could have changed
it. Bed rest might have helped, but it might not. You'll
never know one hundred per cent and you can't spend a
lifetime blaming yourself.'

'But Jack, I lost them. I denied them the right to live.
I hurt them and I hurt Darryl. Don't you see that I'm not
fit to be a mother? I don't even deserve to be happy.'

'No! That's not true. It wasn't the right time. I know
people who've been through similar things; a buddy of
mine and his wife had IVF and lost their first two babies.
They finally conceived naturally and went on to have three
kids. Sometimes we just have to accept that what's meant
to be is meant to be.'

'You believe that?'

Jack shrugged. 'If we don't find some sort of acceptance
then we just go slowly mad. You're not a bad person; you
were driven by a need to succeed at work. That stemmed
from other things, things in your childhood. You married

323

the wrong man but look at how many other people do that. Look at me!' He patted his chest. 'But life is about learning, Eve. We don't always get it right first time. You weren't ready to be a mother when all that happened and maybe you never will be. But you don't know that yet. There's a whole life ahead of you to be experienced. Whether that's with me or not. But no pressure, right?'

She watched him carefully, amazed by his understanding and his bravery. After everything she'd just told him, he was still offering her comfort and freedom.

'Eve, I want you, I want to be with you, but if you don't want me, or if you want me but you don't want kids, then we can work around that. None of us knows what's around the corner, but right now, I do know that I'm bloody terrified of not waking up with you in the morning.'

'Oh Jack!'

He pulled her into his arms and she snuggled close to him as her heart expanded with love. He was right. The past was the past. It had happened and she couldn't change it; all she could do was learn from it. Whatever the future held, right now all she knew for certain, and all she needed to know, was that she wanted to be with him.

Because never before had she felt so warm, so loved or so complete.

Epilogue

Eve walked out of the school building and crossed the car park. The early summer morning was warm and she breathed deeply of the sweet scent of flowers. She'd had a good morning with the pupils and had been delighted, as she always was, by their interest and enthusiasm.

She stopped in front of the car. 'You're such a good boy, Gabe! They all loved you today, didn't they?'

Her large black dog wagged his tail then dipped into a greyhound bow. 'Yes, I know, you were the star of the show!' She opened the boot of the Range Rover and Gabe jumped up onto his quilt, then she made her way round to the passenger door. It opened before she touched the handle.

'Hello there, beautiful! How was your morning?' Jack leaned over and kissed her softly.

'Really good, thank you! Lots of questions and excitement and the head teacher asked if I'll come back in a few weeks' time to talk to the parents too. They're very keen to get involved in fund-raising as a school. I think it's partly because the head teacher has two greyhounds herself.'

'That's fantastic!'

'And how did your morning go?' She ran her eyes over his handsome face and her heart flipped, just as it did every single day when she looked at him.

'Well, I finished the illustrations for the fourth instalment of *Gabe's Greyhound Adventures*, then I put the changing table together for the nursery.'

'You didn't!' Eve grinned. 'I can't wait to see the table, and the illustrations. Oh Jack, the children loved the first book. I read them the whole thing and the teacher asked for an order form.'

Jack nodded. 'Couldn't have done it without your wonderful stories, Eve. I just drew some pictures to go with your cleverly crafted tales.'

She smiled at her husband. Together they'd had a successful year, creating a series about a greyhound named Gabe and his adventures in Conwenna Cove, as well as expanding the sanctuary up at the farm so that it now had a new and impressive website and Eve as its schools liaison. She went out into the local community and spoke to the children about greyhounds and the possibilities for adopting them, and spent time teaching them about animal welfare. The books were a way to continue that education whilst encouraging them to read and improve their literacy, which of course was one of her passions.

'Anyway, Jack, your son is telling me he's hungry, so how about you take us for some lunch?'

Jack leaned over and placed his strong hand on Eve's growing bump. She was twenty weeks along now and had filled out with her pregnancy. Most of the time she felt wonderful, though every so often she'd hit a wobbly moment when the pregnancy reminded her of the first one with her twins. But Jack was always there, holding her up, supporting her and helping her to accept that she couldn't change the past. He'd even persuaded her to return to the garden of remembrance at the cemetery in Bristol, where the twins' ashes were buried together in a small plot. She hadn't been before, terrified that she would completely crumple if she did. It had been incredibly painful and she had cried for days, but she had promised to return there every year on what would have been the twins' birthday. Acknowledging the fact that they had existed and would always be a part of her life had helped with her grief, and helped her to find that peace of mind that had eluded her for so long.

'So, little one, I need to take you and your mum for some food, do I?'

The baby wriggled in response and Jack kissed Eve's belly.

From the rear of the car came a high-pitched whine, and Jack turned in his seat. 'Don't worry, Gabe, we won't forget about you! Sausages, is it?'

He was rewarded with a bark and Eve's laughter.

As her husband started the engine and pulled out onto the road to Conwenna, Eve leaned back in her seat and smiled. It had been an eventful year since she'd first arrived in the pretty Cornish village and her life had changed beyond recognition.

She didn't know if it was magic, as Aunt Mary had suggested when she'd first arrived, but she had to agree that something very special had happened during her summer at Conwenna Cove.

Acknowledgements

My husband and children, for your tireless encouragement with my writing and for putting up with me during edits, as well as every time I suddenly need to write an idea down. I love you and you are my world. XXX

The fabulous team at Canelo, for showing faith in this story from the outset. Your enthusiasm and hard work are deeply appreciated. In particular, thanks to Iain Millar for your early emails regarding *Summer at Conwenna Cove*, and thanks to Louise Cullen, for all your hard work during the editorial process. *Summer at Conwenna Cove* is a much better book because of your efforts and expertise. Not forgetting, of course, thanks to Jane Selley for the rigorous copyedits.

The incredibly supportive authors I interact with daily. You make me laugh, offer valuable advice and are the best cheerleaders ever! In this case, special thanks to Trevor Williams for reading the rough draft of *Summer at Conwenna Cove* and offering me some great tips, to Holly Martin, Katie Graham, Andi Michael and Joanne Robinson, for your support behind the scenes, and to Ann Troup, for driving such a long way just to give me a hug when I needed it most.

To the blogging community, because, as ever, your support and friendship is incredible. I can't name you individually because I'd hate to miss someone out, but you are all amazing!

To my readers who come back for more. I love you guys! XXX

And special thanks go to Greyhound Rescue Wales, an amazing charity made up of fabulous people who work tirelessly to rescue and rehome greyhounds. Sandra Wynne, you matched us with Freya, and for that you have our deepest gratitude. Jonathan Baker, Emma Byrne and Kerry Baker, thank you for your stories about the real Gabe. Huge thanks to Kerry Sands, for your advice regarding the greyhound sanctuary and greyhound behaviour. Finally, thanks to all the members of the GRW Facebook group for your wonderful stories and photographs that make me smile – and sometimes cry – every day.